T0052091

THE
BAXTERS

A Prequel

Other Life-Changing Fiction™
by Karen Kingsbury

Baxter Family Stand-Alone Titles
Just Once (Coming Soon)
The Baxters: A Prequel
Forgiving Paris
Truly Madly Deeply
Someone Like You
Two Weeks
When We Were Young
To the Moon and Back
In This Moment
Love Story—The Baxters
A Baxter Family Christmas
Coming Home

The Baxters—1—Redemption Series
Redemption
Remember
Return
Rejoice
Reunion

The Baxters—2—Firstborn Series
Fame
Forgiven
Found
Family
Forever

The Baxters—3—Sunrise Series
Sunrise
Summer
Someday
Sunset

The Baxters—4—Above the Line Series
Take One
Take Two
Take Three
Take Four

The Baxters—5—Bailey Flanigan Series
Leaving
Learning
Longing
Loving

Other Stand-Alone Titles
A Distant Shore
Fifteen Minutes
The Chance
The Bridge
Oceans Apart
Between Sundays
When Joy Came to Stay
On Every Side
Divine
Like Dandelion Dust
Where Yesterday Lives
Shades of Blue
Unlocked

Angels Walking Series
Angels Walking
Chasing Sunsets
Brush of Wings

9/11 Series
One Tuesday Morning
Beyond Tuesday Morning
Remember Tuesday Morning

www.KarenKingsbury.com

KAREN KINGSBURY

THE
BAXTERS

A Prequel

ATRIA PAPERBACK

New York   London   Toronto   Sydney   New Delhi

ATRIA
PAPERBACK

An Imprint of Simon & Schuster, Inc.
1230 Avenue of the Americas
New York, NY 10020

This book is a work of fiction. Any references to historical events, real people, or real places are used fictitiously. Other names, characters, places, and events are products of the author's imagination, and any resemblance to actual events or places or persons, living or dead, is entirely coincidental.

Copyright © 2022 by Karen Kingsbury

Scripture quotations are from the Holy Bible, English Standard Version, copyright © 2001, 2007 by Crossway Bibles, a division of Good News Publishers. Used by permission. All rights reserved.

Published in association with the literary agency Alive Communications, Inc., 8585 Criterion Dr. Unit 63060, Colorado Springs, Colorado, 80920.

All rights reserved, including the right to reproduce this book or portions thereof in any form whatsoever. For information, address Howard Books Subsidiary Rights Department, 1230 Avenue of the Americas, New York, NY 10020.

First Atria Paperback edition October 2022

ATRIA PAPERBACK and colophon are trademarks of Simon & Schuster, Inc.

For information about special discounts for bulk purchases, please contact Simon & Schuster Special Sales at 1-866-506-1949 or business@simonandschuster.com.

The Simon & Schuster Speakers Bureau can bring authors to your live event. For more information or to book an event, contact the Simon & Schuster Speakers Bureau at 1-866-248-3049 or visit our website at www.simonspeakers.com.

Manufactured in the United States of America

1   3   5   7   9   10   8   6   4   2

Library of Congress Cataloging-in-Publication Data has been applied for.

ISBN 978-1-9821-0425-2
ISBN 978-1-9821-0426-9 (pbk)
ISBN 978-1-9821-0427-6 (ebook)

Dedicated to Donald, my husband of thirty-three years, my Prince Charming, the love of my life. And to our beautiful children and grandchildren. The journey of our days is breathtaking surrounded by you, and our moments together fly by like time borrowed from eternity. I love you with each breath, every heartbeat. And to God, Almighty, who has—for now—blessed me with these.

The Baxters: A Prequel will soon be a TV show.
Three seasons have been filmed and are ready to air.
When the show debuts, the following will be the theme song.
Every line applies to the Baxters . . . and to you.

"FAMILY"
Music and Lyrics

By
Tyler Russell

Theme Song for
The Baxters TV Show

If I ever lose myself
Don't know which way to go
I'll see the light that you left on
And know I'm not alone

I'll say a prayer
take a breath
turn around
lift my head
I'm gonna be okay

Cause life has a way
Of pulling us under
But we'll stick it out
If we've got each other
When it all feels too much
I know you'll come running
For me
Through the highs and lows
We'll find our way home
Family

Don't know where this road
    will go
Or who we're gonna be
As long as you are by my side
We can get through anything

So say a prayer
Take a breath
Turn around
Lift your head
It's gonna be okay

Cause life has a way
Of pulling us under
But we'll stick it out
If we've got each other
When it all feels too much
I know you'll come running
For me
Through the highs and lows
we'll find our way home.
Family
We're family
I know you'll come running
Family

I'll say a prayer
Take a breath
Turn around
Lift my head
I'm gonna be okay.
Cause life has a way of pulling
    us under
But we'll stick it out if we got
    each other
When it all feels too much
I know you'll come running
    for me
Through the highs and lows
    we'll find our way home
We're family
Oh, oh, oh Family

BAXTER
FAMILY

THE BOOK YOU are about to read is a prequel to my novel *Redemption*. Until now, *Redemption* was book one about the Baxter family. A quick look at the front of this book and you will see that I have written more than twenty novels about my beloved Baxters.

In recent years I have written stand-alone books with the Baxter family as minor characters—just so you could check in on them.

But always a piece of the story was missing.

Any time redemption comes into play, there is always a story that happens first. Life before redemption. The troubled times. Times of doubt and questioning and uncertainty. Moments when there is no way to see the good ahead or to understand the crazy turns life has taken or will take in years to come.

For that reason, in this book I will take you back in time to when the Baxter family was younger. A few years before *Redemption*. When life seemed to be going in all the wrong directions. It's the setup for the trials ahead.

If you are new to the Baxter family, this book is the perfect place to start. If you have been with the Baxters from the beginning, then this book will fill your heart with answers and understanding. I promise, you will finish this novel loving the Baxters more than ever.

Enjoy!

THE
BAXTERS

A Prequel

1

Outside Kari Baxter's French bedroom window, storm clouds gathered in the early morning sky over Bloomington, Indiana. Dark and tinged in green. Tornado clouds.

The kind that could destroy a person's life in a matter of seconds.

Kari's heart pounded and she sat up in bed. Something was happening today . . . She thought for a moment and then she gasped.

She was getting *married* today.

That's what was happening.

Her feet were instantly on the floor, her lungs grabbing at quick sharp breaths. Like she was running a race. Yes, she was getting married! How could she forget? It was Saturday, after all. Kari ran her fingers through her long dark hair and rushed to the window. At five this evening she would become Tim Jacobs's wife.

How could that not have been the first thing on her mind?

Even before she opened her eyes?

Kari exhaled. *Okay. Calm*, she told herself. *You didn't miss it. Everything is fine*. Her breathing slowed a little and she waited for that wonderful wedding-day peace and joy to replace her anxiety. Her heart raced and she kept waiting. And she waited some more. Then she dropped to the cushioned window seat at the base of the tall panes of glass.

Nothing.

Her eyes lifted to the stormy sky. Maybe that was it. What bride wouldn't feel stressed by such terrible darkness overhead? On her wedding day? Like it was some sort of sign.

This was crazy. The weather couldn't make or break her big moment. Even still, anxiety ran through her veins. Her breathing remained shaky. She closed her eyes and hugged her arms to her chest. *God, help me. Please.*

Across the room on the back of her door hung her wedding dress. Satin white with cap sleeves and a simple fitted bodice. Cascading tulle and a modest train. She and her mom and sisters had picked it out a week after Tim proposed. The girl at the shop called it a Cinderella dress.

A few times since then Kari had wondered if her decision had been a bit rushed. Impulsive because of the newness of her engagement. But in the last month she had talked herself into really liking the gown. A lot.

Yes, hers was going to be the perfect wedding.

Thunder rolled through the hills beyond Bloomington. The sound vibrated her window and even her soul. She was doing the right thing, marrying Tim. Right? Yes, she was. For sure. Tim was charming and intelligent and he made her laugh every time they were together. And he shared her faith.

That's how they met, after all. At a Bible study on campus.

They would share a beautiful life together. She would support his new position as professor of writing and when she accompanied Tim to his many university events and parties, she could see herself hanging on his every word.

Kari could hardly wait!

She drew a steady breath. There. That was better. Her heart wasn't racing as fast and she wasn't panting. She leaned her shoulder against the window and watched the wind move through the trees. What if a tornado hit today?

Would that be a sign?

No. Nothing was a sign. She closed her eyes and exhaled. God had led her to Tim Jacobs and today when she married him she would be the happiest girl in the world. She looked at the sky again. Greens and blacks, swirling low.

Enough of this. She stood and walked to her gown. Everything was going to be okay. She ran her fingers down the length of it. Such a pretty dress. Then it hit her. This strange morning of wild emotions wasn't because of the weather. There was a perfectly good reason. A troubling one.

His name was Ryan Taylor.

Kari walked back to her bed and lay down again. Her

mom had invited Ryan's mother to the wedding, which made sense. The two were neighbors. The Taylors had moved down the street when Kari was twelve. All through the seasons when Ryan had been the love of Kari's life.

Right up until two years ago.

Since then, their mothers had stayed close. Another perfectly acceptable detail. Because Kari was over Ryan Taylor.

But with his mother coming to the wedding, Ryan had to know about it. Which meant three doors down he was waking up in his childhood home knowing that later today Kari was going to marry someone else. Despite the fact that for most of his life he had thought *he* would marry her. They had both thought so.

And something about that made Kari sad.

Like she should run out back to the path behind her house. Run through his yard, knock on his door and give him one last hug.

Even though it was his fault things hadn't worked out.

She closed her eyes. This day was supposed to be a happy one. Didn't her groom deserve her best? *Be excited*, she told herself. *Don't think about Ryan.* The words had been her battle cry for the past twenty-four months.

Don't think about Ryan Taylor.

After all, he had cheated on her. Left her to find out about his actions in the middle of his gravest hours. When his life and future hung in the balance.

Another clap of thunder shook her window.

A few months after Ryan's betrayal, Tim entered her world. And all of life had been a whirlwind since. In the years when she was growing up and falling in love with Ryan, Kari had never imagined things would work out this way. With her marrying a different man.

Was her heart still unsure about this? Even now? On her wedding day?

She exhaled and a pit formed in her stomach. What an awful bride she was, questioning her commitment, doubting her intentions. *Definitely . . . I'm sure about this. Absolutely.* She was in love with Tim. She took a deep breath. *Tim. Wonderful, kind, considerate Tim. Intelligent, well-read Tim. The brilliant writer and witty conversationalist.*

Tim, the one she was marrying today.

Yes, her mind needed to be there. With her distinguished groom.

Images from the last few years came to life, and her recent past played out once more. After she met Tim at the campus Bible study, Kari came home and told her parents she had found a friend.

Only a friend.

He was in the last year of getting his PhD, teaching journalism students, and about to be hired full-time by Indiana University. But he was five years older, and Kari hadn't even finished her undergrad degree. She hadn't considered dating him. But they began meeting for coffee and then dinner. After all, professors and undergrads weren't allowed to date.

"Be careful," her mother had told her several times in those early days. "He's falling in love with you, Kari."

"No, Mom!" She didn't see it. "He likes talking to me. I make him laugh. That's all."

Once, over dinner, Tim asked her a question she wasn't expecting. "Tell me about him."

Kari had blinked a few times. "What? . . . Who?"

"Him. You know, your greatest heartbreak." He looked deep into her eyes. "I want to know everything about you, Kari. Even that."

The memory froze there. Again her heartbeat came louder, faster, and she could see him. Her greatest heartbreak. The handsome face of Ryan Taylor. Did she still love him?

Even now . . . on her wedding day?

She rolled onto her side and let the memories come, let them soothe her nervous heart one more time. Ryan was a senior at Indiana University, and Kari a sophomore, the year his ability as a running back took the national sports scene by surprise. Before his graduation, Ryan was drafted in the second round by the Cowboys, and everyone celebrated.

After he moved to Texas, though, Ryan didn't call as often. He seemed too busy for her. Kari tried to tell herself nothing had changed. After all, he still called, still told her he loved her whenever they talked. And that he missed her, and he would only ever love her.

One weekend during his first season with the Cowboys, Kari and a friend took a trip to Dallas to see him play. After the win, Ryan brought them to a team party. Kari had never seen so many beautiful girls—and all of them seemed to know Ryan. Discouragement whispered words of discontent on the flight home. He was bound to forget her. How could things work out?

They had entirely different lives, after all.

Despite her concerns, they didn't break up. Ryan talked about coming home once the season wrapped up. He told her he'd spend a few weeks in Bloomington before summer training. And once she graduated, he wanted to marry her. "I love you, Kari girl. I always have." He had said that every time they spoke.

She could still hear the sincerity in his voice. The warmth of his tone.

His injury was something none of them had seen coming. A single hit that ended his career. The Cowboys were playing the Bears at Soldier Field in Chicago that day. One minute Ryan was running like the wind, football tucked under his arm the way it had been all his life. Helping his team to a fourteen-point lead.

The next he was laid out on the field. Not moving.

Silence came over the stadium while trainers and coaches and medical personnel rushed to his side. In hushed tones the announcers talked about how Ryan Taylor's injury looked serious, and how they wished Ryan would move even his fingers or toes.

But Ryan didn't move at all.

He was driven off in an ambulance, and when the announcers revealed which hospital he was taken to,

Kari and her father packed their bags and set out for Chicago.

After an almost silent four-hour drive, they met Ryan's mother in the lobby of intensive care. Ryan was in surgery for a fractured vertebra in his spine and there was only the slightest chance he would walk again.

Kari remembered falling to her knees right there in the waiting room, begging God to heal the boy she loved. But even if Ryan were paralyzed, she had been sure she would never leave him. She would drop out of school and help him rehab. And whatever remained of Ryan Taylor, she would stay by him till the day she died.

That was her plan. Even when nothing was certain about the next few hours.

But in the morning everything changed. Ryan's nurse told Kari something more shocking, more devastating than the report of his broken neck. "You can go see him in a little while." The woman raised her eyebrows. "Right now his girlfriend is in the room with him."

His girlfriend.

Adrenaline pushed through Kari's veins and the floor beneath her feet turned liquid. Ryan's mother had said nothing about a girlfriend. How dare the woman welcome them after their long drive and not tell Kari the awful truth? Ryan was seeing someone else. One of the girls from those parties, no doubt.

And that was that.

Without waiting to see Ryan, Kari and her dad left

the hospital and drove home. From what his mother said, Ryan was still rehabbing, even now, years later. But he could walk and run. Last fall he'd even made another brief attempt at playing in the NFL.

Yes, God had granted Kari the miracle she had prayed for regarding Ryan's healing. But that's where her answered prayers ended.

A week after his injury, Ryan called. But Kari refused to talk to him, and so Ryan tried harder. Several calls a week in the beginning. A few times he even sent letters to her.

Her mother thought she was being coldhearted. "Talk to him, at least," she had told Kari more than once. "Hear his side of the story."

"His *side*?" The idea had seemed outlandish. "Mom, what side could there be? He's seeing another girl behind my back."

Her determination to avoid him never wavered. If Ryan could cheat on her after all they'd been through, then she was finished.

Kari glanced at her wedding dress again. She could still see Ryan sprawled out, motionless on the field. Playing football had been his life. Lying there on that cold Chicago grass, he had to have known that his playing days were over.

But since then Kari had often wondered who suffered more that day. Ryan had moved on, obviously. He was healthy, coaching in the NFL now, home for the summer. So maybe Kari had been the one truly paralyzed that day. Not her legs or her spine.

Her heart.

When Tim had asked her about Ryan that night at dinner, Kari had told him everything. How she had loved Ryan since she was in seventh grade, and how they had fallen in love his second year of college, after the sudden death of his father. And how his mom still lived three doors down. Kari even told Tim about that terrible morning at that Chicago hospital. When she found out Ryan was seeing someone else.

Tim listened and sympathized and his kindness warmed Kari's heart. She had wondered if maybe she was falling for the professor.

A few weeks later at Kari's graduation party, her mother found her in the kitchen. "I need to tell you something." She looked worried. "Ryan Taylor is coming by tonight. I just found out." Her mom hesitated. "Apparently he wants it to be a surprise."

Kari would have none of it. How dare Ryan come by her graduation party as if nothing had happened? An idea hit her. Tim was already at the party. She pulled him aside and asked him the craziest question. "Would you pretend to be my boyfriend? When Ryan comes by?"

"Why?" Tim had looked unsettled at first.

"Because . . . I don't want him to think I'm waiting around." The request was her desperate attempt to come against Ryan's surprise visit. As if he could come by her house like he'd done nothing wrong. She narrowed her eyes. "Ryan cheated on me. I want him to leave me alone. If . . . if he sees us together, he'll know I've moved on."

"Got it." Tim nodded slowly.

Then he stepped up to her, put his hands alongside her face and kissed her. A kiss that took her breath and made her jump back—not sure whether to laugh or yell at him. "What was that?" Her heart skipped a beat.

"That's yes." He grinned at her. "Just getting ready for my role."

They held hands the rest of the night, and when Ryan showed up, Kari introduced Tim as her boyfriend. Ryan looked like he'd been hit in the gut. He made polite small talk and after a brief stay, he left.

Only Tim never let go of her hand.

Sometime later, he admitted that his acting that night had been nothing of the sort. "I'm in love with you, Kari. I've been in love with you since the day I met you."

And just like that her mother was proved right. Like always.

At first Kari wasn't sure about Tim's declaration. She was leaving soon for a six-month catalog-modeling job in New York City. This wasn't the time to fall in love. But Tim had an answer for that.

"I'll wait." He took her hands in his. "However long it takes."

Which was exactly what he did. Kari was flattered and moved by Tim's determination and relentless pursuit. By the sound of his voice every time he called her during her months in New York.

Once he even flew to Manhattan so they could spend a day together.

They strolled through Central Park, and he impressed her with facts and bits of information about the city. When a thunderstorm hit, they ran for a cab and spent the rest of the day at Cooper Hewitt, Smithsonian Design Museum. He didn't fly back to Indiana until late that night, after dinner in Times Square and front-row seats at *The Lion King* musical.

Tim Jacobs had her head spinning, for sure.

In those months of modeling, Kari hadn't known if she felt the same way about Tim. But she knew one thing. Tim wasn't going anywhere, not unless she asked him to leave. And unlike Ryan Taylor, he would never cheat on her. Not in a million years. He loved her too much.

And that became more appealing to Kari with every passing day.

After her time in New York she returned to Bloomington to model for a local boutique. Tim called the day she got home and they picked up where they left off. By then Tim had gone from student teacher at Indiana University to full-fledged professor. The more time they spent together, the more she felt herself falling for him. He knew obscure details of every world war and political time period. Funny stories and little-known anecdotes about Charles Dickens and Ernest Hemingway and Mark Twain. Like a walking textbook, his knowledge seemed boundless. She could listen to him for hours without getting bored.

He talked about ancient philosophers and theology and his dreams of writing a novel someday. His faith was a priority through it all, and after spending time with her family, Tim stopped attending services at the campus chapel, and began going to church with her every Sunday.

"This is where I belong," he told her one Sunday. "Home is where you are, Kari. Every day I fall for you a little more."

Over the next few months she officially became his girlfriend, and things grew serious. Tim talked about marriage and raising a family and sharing forever together. Most of the time Kari felt the same way.

One Saturday evening Kari sat down with her parents. "Tim and I . . . it's getting serious."

Even now she could remember how her voice hadn't sounded perfectly excited or hopeful. That should've been her happiest conversation ever. Instead her tone was more matter-of-fact than awestruck.

Her mom had looked at her for a long while. "Are you asking us . . . or telling us?"

"Telling." Kari's answer had come quickly. But it wasn't exactly the truth. She exhaled and glanced at her dad. "Does it seem like I'm asking?"

Her dad nodded. "It sort of does, honey." He smiled at her. That look that always made her know everything was going to be all right. Her dad leaned closer. "How do *you* feel about him?"

"Well." They had been in the living room. Kari was seated next to her mother. "That's why I'm telling you." She forced a laugh. "I'm happy. Because we're getting more serious, of course."

"We've always told you"—her mother's voice was calm, full of peace—"whatever boy you give your heart to, we'll give our heart to him, too. We'll love who you love."

Something in her mother's tone caused the slightest discomfort for Kari. "But . . . ?" She looked straight at her mother. "I hear a *but* in there, Mom."

"Honey." Her mom turned to her. "My only hesitation . . . is whether *you* have one."

Kari rested her head on her mother's shoulder. "Tim's amazing." She stared across the room at her father. "He really is. And he loves me." Her voice fell a notch. "He absolutely does. Tim won't ever need anyone but me." She sat up straight again. "Which is something I could never say about Ryan Taylor."

They talked for the next half hour about all the ways Tim had delighted her and honored her and treated her like a princess. But the whole time she had felt like she was convincing herself.

Before she turned in that night, her parents each hugged her. Dad gently brushed her bangs off her forehead.

"Kari, it sounds like you love Tim very much." He held her gaze a long time. "We'll listen . . . if you need to talk again."

"We're both here for you." Her mom kissed her cheek.

A few times since then they'd talked about Tim. There was never a reason why Kari shouldn't love him. Why she should pull away from a guy who treated her so well. When he proposed to her over a candlelit dinner, her *yes* was out before he finished his question.

That had to mean something.

Since then she had worked hard to keep from thinking about Ryan, about how this season in her life was supposed to be about him and her. Most of the time Kari's heart had no trouble believing she was in love with Tim. He would make a wonderful husband.

But whenever she prayed about marrying Tim, the Lord's silence on the matter was deafening. She told herself that God didn't always respond with a clear answer. But it was one reason she had just the slightest doubt about moving forward.

A doubt she hadn't shared with anyone. One she tried to squash every time it reared its head. Tim was wonderful. Theirs would be a storybook life.

And later today, Tim would be her husband.

Kari sat up in bed again and smiled. Life would play out with love and beauty, with Tim caring for her and protecting her the rest of her life. Theirs would be a story marked by deep talks, and hours of laughter, and most of all a long happily ever after. She felt her heart gradually relax. Today would be perfect, whatever the storm held. With Tim she would never have to worry about where he was or who he was with. There would be no girlfriend on the side.

And always, at the end of the day he would come home to her.

Only her. For the rest of time.

2

Elizabeth Baxter stood on the front porch of her family's home and let the wind gust over her. Ominous wind. Dangerous. Foreboding. A shiver ran down her arms.

What was this terrible feeling?

Today was her second daughter Kari's wedding. The ceremony was being held at the chapel on Indiana University's campus. Dinner and dancing would take place in an adjacent hall. They'd be inside all day, whatever the weather.

No, Elizabeth wasn't worried about the storm outside. She feared the one in her heart, the one building between her grown kids. That one had a far better chance of tearing things apart.

Especially today.

Elizabeth turned back inside and walked to the kitchen. Along the way she studied the familiar walls and windows, the rooms that housed a million memories. This was the Baxter house. That's what they called the place. A white Victorian farmhouse with a wraparound porch and enough bedrooms for the five kids Elizabeth and her husband, Dr. John Baxter, had raised here.

They'd moved in when their youngest, Luke, was just six years old. Back when everyone they knew wanted to be like the Baxter family.

When Elizabeth and John's kids couldn't get enough of each other.

A dozen years had passed since then and in that time the house had seen more laughter, witnessed more love and life than most ever would. Elizabeth leaned against the kitchen counter and breathed deep. These days, her family just wasn't the same. Something had changed, and there was nothing she or John could do about it.

She stared at the cookies and chips on the kitchen table. After the reception, the family would return to the house for more celebrating. That was the plan. So what would these old walls hear today? Doubts about Kari's choice of a groom? Arguing between the middle kids? Scoffing at God from the oldest? If Elizabeth's bad feeling was right, this might be a day everyone would rather forget.

Even the house.

Stop, she told herself. Kari was getting married today. It was the happiest moment in her daughter's life. Of course Kari had chosen the right groom. *God, please, take this feeling of doom from me. I can't bear it. Not now.*

Thunder rumbled in the distance.

Daughter . . . I am with you. I go before you and behind you. I have loved you from the beginning.

The whisper caused Elizabeth to catch a quick breath. *Lord?* The wind screamed through the trees outside. Sometimes she was sure God was talking to her. He was with her. He loved her. But if this were one of those times, she still felt no peace.

No assurance.

The wedding was set to start at five o'clock. Ten hours from now. Kari's high school and college friends would be there along with Tim's colleagues from the university. Friends from church, several neighbors and their families. A hundred people in all. And of course Kari's four siblings.

Brooke, Ashley, Erin, and Luke.

Kids who used to play together and share secrets and believe that nothing would ever change. Back when everyone in the family agreed: Your best friends were the ones sitting around the dinner table each night.

Elizabeth pictured them, the way they were. Their happy young faces. What had happened since then? Where had those Baxter children gone? And what would they think if they knew their parents' gravest secret? That there weren't really five adult Baxter kids.

There were six.

The sound of a car came from the driveway. Elizabeth peered out the window as John pulled up near the garage. A smile tugged at her troubled heart. Everything was better when John was home. Maybe he would say something that might ease her increasing dread.

A creak of the heavy wooden front door and a sudden burst of wind howled through the house. The door slammed shut and Elizabeth turned to see John, a bag of groceries under each arm. "Big storm coming." A quick gaze out the window and John gave a low whistle. "Biggest storm in a while." He turned to her and a grin stretched across his face. "I found the streamers. The white ones you wanted."

Elizabeth watched him come closer, into the kitchen where he set the bags on the counter. A conversation about the tension between their kids could wait a few minutes. She closed the distance between them. Then she kissed his cheek and returned the smile. "You've always loved parties."

"True." A chuckle slipped from his lips. "Nothing better than celebrating our kids." He put his hand alongside her face. "And now Kari's wedding." His eyes held her. "Where did the years go, my love?"

She blinked and found two packs of streamers near the top of the first bag. "That's what I was thinking." She set the decorations on the counter. "Time never stops." Her voice trailed off as she emptied the first brown paper bag. A bottle of ketchup and two more packs of hamburger buns. Mayonnaise and extra potato chips and cookies. Halfway through the second bag she felt John looking at her.

Their gazes held, and John's blue eyes warmed the space between them. He was still so handsome. "Elizabeth . . . you're doing it again." He angled his head, clearly seeing her troubled heart. "I can see it."

Her focus fell to the groceries again. How did he always know? She sighed. "I'm worried. I can't help it. Every one of our kids is giving me a reason, John."

"Honey." He took hold of her hand. "Worry won't change a thing. You know that."

"Yes." She closed her eyes for a long moment. "I'll let it go. I will." Her gaze found his. "It's just . . . I have to help the girls get ready for the wedding in a few hours and I have . . . this feeling." She sounded weary as her voice dropped. "I'm afraid of something I can't see."

"Afraid?" Concern deepened the fine lines on his forehead. He put his other hand on her shoulder. "That bad?"

"Yes. Even for our *real* oldest. The one we don't know." She looked to the dark clouds outside the window. "He would be twenty-eight next week."

John drew her close. For a long moment he swayed with her. "His birthday and Cole's are on the same day."

"Yes." Elizabeth closed her eyes and rested her head against his chest. "I love that you remember."

"Our firstborn." John drew back and looked deep into her eyes again. "I still can't believe I never met him. The adoptive couple took him away too soon."

"I hate that." Tears stung at Elizabeth's eyes. "I . . . I had no choice. My parents . . ."

"I know." He kissed her forehead. "Shhh. We don't have to go over it again." He searched her eyes, her soul. "The social worker told you to move on, not to think about him." His hand framed her face. "But that would never be your heart, Elizabeth." He hesitated. "It's never been mine, either. I won't ever forget."

"Thank you." She leaned her forehead against his shoulder. It was enough to know John felt the same way, that he thought about their oldest son and remembered his birthday. Elizabeth looked at him once more. "It's still my prayer, John. That I find him. If it's the last thing I do."

"Mine, too." He held her a little longer. Then he stepped away and picked up one pack of the streamers. His tone lifted. "But for now, my dear, we have an after-party to decorate for! And a precious daughter who is about to have her dream wedding."

"True." Elizabeth basked in the way John made her feel. Like everything would be okay.

He raised one eyebrow. "And in the garage I have eight cases of pop that still need to be loaded into the van and taken to the reception hall." He stopped and listened. The wind was getting stronger. "Is Ashley here?"

"Not yet. In an hour or so. I have Cole's crib ready." A smile caught Elizabeth off guard. "He's the light of my days, that Cole. Such a happy little guy. He grins so big every time he sees us." She opened one pack of streamers and stretched out the white paper. "If only I could say the same about his mother." The words came before she could stop them.

John stepped back and leaned against the doorframe. He exhaled like this was a topic he didn't want to talk about. Not with Kari's wedding hours away. "Ashley tries." Patience softened his words. "She'll figure it out." Again he closed the distance between them. He ran his hand over her still-dark hair. "Our daughter needs time. The same way we did at her age."

He was right. Elizabeth put thoughts of their middle daughter from her mind. She held up the roll of streamers and remembered to smile. "A little tape and we'll make this a party."

Peace seemed to come over John as he helped her tack one end to the upper corner of the kitchen. Elizabeth felt him watch her as she twisted the thin white paper and stretched it to the opposite wall.

"You're quiet." John's eyes were still on her. "I didn't mean to shut you down."

There it was. Another reason Elizabeth needed him so. When her heart hurt, he felt the pain. Even now, on a day of celebration. When they were supposed to be happy. If something was wrong with her, John would get to the bottom of it.

He raised his brow. "Talk to me, my love. What are you thinking in that pretty head of yours?"

Elizabeth taped the streamer into place and ripped it from the roll. "How much time do you have?"

"Forever. For you . . . always forever." John wasn't only saying what she wanted to hear. He meant every word. His tone told her that much.

And so while they put up the next streamer, Elizabeth spilled every concern from her troubled heart. "The kids . . . they're so old now. Everything they're doing, the decisions they're making, the people they're dating . . . It all matters. A wrong choice could ruin their lives." She sighed. "I guess . . ." She taped another streamer to the high edge of the room. Then she turned and shrugged one shoulder. There was no hiding the sadness in her voice. "If I'm honest . . . this isn't how I pictured things going."

John took her hand. "Come outside. We have time."

She set the roll of streamers on the floor. Then she followed him to the spot where they'd laughed and cried and celebrated through the years. The swing on their front porch. Despite the wind, the air was warm. Typical for this time of year. It was the approaching cold front that made the sky unstable. They settled in, side by side, and looked at the familiar view.

"Do you remember the first time we sat here? The night we moved in?" He wove his fingers between hers and set the swing in gentle motion.

An easy laugh came from her. "The moving van got hung up. We slept on the living room floor."

"Yes." He turned to her. "And when the kids were asleep we came out here."

The distant storm was growing. A strong gust moved over them as the memories came to life. Elizabeth tilted her face to the sky and closed her eyes. "The kids were so young. Still in elementary school."

"Ashley hated it at first. She thought she'd never make a friend." John chuckled. "That girl has always taken the hard road."

For the longest, most precious moment Elizabeth remembered them again, her kids at that sweet young age, the summer they moved from Ann Arbor to Bloomington. Brooke was thirteen and Kari was eleven. At ten, Ashley was already sure she was going to be an artist. Erin was just eight and Luke was six. With everything in her, Elizabeth tried to hold on to their faces the way they looked back then. Their voices and laughter and innocence.

Their innocence most of all.

But gradually the images faded and Elizabeth opened her eyes. "Back then . . . we would just have a family meeting and everything would be okay."

"Ahh, the family meetings." John's smile held happy pieces of the past. "We'd pray and cry and talk it out." He shook his head. "After that there was always a whole lot of laughter." He put his arm around Elizabeth's shoulders and eased her closer. "By the time the kids trotted off to bed, they were giggling and making plans for the morning."

Elizabeth studied the familiar field in front of the house. The place where they'd held countless kickball games and Easter-egg hunts. She narrowed her eyes, seeing them again when they were little. "It doesn't work like that with adult kids."

"That's it, then?" John ran his fingers over her shoulder and down her arm. "The kids are at it again? Something new?"

The clouds of anxiety inside her grew darker than the ones headed their way. "Yes." She stood and walked to the porch railing. "Let's start with Brooke and Peter's broken faith . . . or Kari's obvious uncertainty about the man she's marrying. I could sense that even yesterday. And then there's Ashley's downward spiral." She leaned back against one of the pillars and faced John. "Even Erin and Luke. Nothing is how it should be. How I believed it would be."

"Their stories aren't ours to write." His tone was patient. No accusation rang in his voice. "When they're in trouble, we pray and make ourselves available. And when things go right, we cheer from the sidelines."

Why was he so sensible? Elizabeth looked straight at him. "You want the truth?" Thunder rumbled in the distance. Elizabeth looked over her shoulder and then back at John. "I'm afraid something terrible is going to happen today. A blowup like we've never seen before. Or maybe I'm afraid Kari is making . . . a mistake." There. She'd said it. On her daughter's wedding day.

Fear stood like a tangible force beside her. "What if he's not the right one, John?"

"Honey . . . Tim is the right man. Kari wants to marry him. I talked to her a couple nights ago." He paused. "Be specific. What's happening?" John was an optimist. He had been one from the first time Elizabeth met him at a University of Michigan dance. Most of the time his positive spin set her world right again. But here he seemed to know that wasn't what she needed. Instead he did exactly what she wanted in this moment.

He listened.

Elizabeth started with Brooke. Sure, she had married

Peter West, her college sweetheart, and now they were both doctors. A few months ago they had even started their own shared pediatric practice. Elizabeth felt a pang of sadness. "But every week Brooke grows farther from God."

John patted the spot beside him. Elizabeth joined him again and this time she leaned her head on his shoulder. She closed her eyes. "I took Brooke shopping last week. It was her rare day off and Peter called. Brooke didn't think I could hear her."

Elizabeth exhaled and the sound mixed with the wind. "I don't know what they were talking about. But Brooke told Peter that science was a lot more reliable than a God no one could prove." Elizabeth sat up straight and stared at John. "*Our* daughter actually said that."

For a while neither of them spoke. The heaviness was definitely there for both of them. Once more John took hold of her hand. "I've sensed that, too. With Brooke and Peter."

This time Elizabeth set the swing in motion. As if she could distance herself from the strangeness of the season. "And Kari . . . I'm telling you, she can frustrate me." Elizabeth shook her head. "What's she thinking? I mean . . . I will never understand why she walked away from Ryan Taylor. That boy loved her from the moment he first met her. A couple of kids right out there on that patch of grass." She paused. "He still loves her."

"Elizabeth . . . you know why." John ran his thumb over her hand. "And be careful Kari doesn't hear you. She's marrying Tim today. Not Ryan."

"Yes, because of his football injury. That other girl." Elizabeth waved her free hand around like she was swatting invisible flies. "What if that was all a big mistake?"

They were quiet for a few minutes. John drew a slow breath. "It was good between them, wasn't it?" He looked to the right, the direction where three houses down Ryan had grown up. "Neighbor kids who fell in love."

"They were more than that." Fresh tears blurred Elizabeth's eyes. "At the hospital after he got hurt, you were there. I've heard what happened." She blinked a few times. "He never got to explain himself."

"And now—"

"Right. Now she's head over heels for Tim Jacobs." Elizabeth made a face. "Something about the guy bugs me. I get a bad feeling, obviously." She let go a loud out breath. "I'm just not sure."

A pensive silence followed. Tim was a young professor at Indiana University and for the past year, since Kari's graduation, the two had been an item. But she seemed young to be dating a professor—even one just five years older.

"Does Ryan know she's getting married today?" John winced a little.

"His mother's coming to the wedding." Elizabeth laughed, but the sound held no humor. "Of course Ryan knows. Also, Ashley ran into him at the coffee shop a week ago and told him. I think Kari's still angry at Ashley for that."

John stood this time. He walked to the railing and faced the front of their ten-acre yard. "That's different now, too." He turned and caught her eye. "Kari and Ashley. They used to be best friends. They never stayed angry with each other."

Elizabeth rose to her feet once more and took the spot beside John. Always beside him. "You understand me, John. The deepest parts of me."

"It's all I've ever wanted." They stood shoulder to shoulder. He glanced at her. "And Ashley?"

"Yes." Elizabeth battled the onslaught of discouragement. "Ashley most of all." They often talked about their middle child, how the last three years had been more heartbreaking for her than anything they could have seen coming. "She was only ten when she met Landon Blake." Elizabeth glanced at him. "Do you remember that?"

"Her unlikely friend." John slipped his arm around her again. "Things changed on that class field trip. When they got lost at the zoo." John's smile was tinged with sadness. "I remember."

Three years ago it looked like Ashley and Landon would be together forever. But a series of tragedies had changed all that. Now she was a single mother, alone and without any interest in the young man.

"Landon will be at the wedding?" John raised his brow in her direction.

"He will." Elizabeth was glad she'd seen him at church last Sunday. "At least he said so."

"It can't be easy for him." John's voice held the same

heaviness weighing on her. "She's pushed him away so often."

"She's ashamed. Embarrassed about what happened in Paris." Elizabeth's heart broke for her middle daughter. "The accident changed Ashley. It's that simple . . . but she still loves Landon. I'll always believe that."

Elizabeth talked for a minute about Erin being lonely. "She's young, but boys don't chase after her the way they did the other girls. She feels like an outcast."

"That's hard." John thought for a moment. "I need to take her to lunch next weekend. I haven't done that in a while."

"Please, do." Elizabeth couldn't shake her mood. "And then there's Luke."

"Luke?" John's expression went blank. "What did Luke do?"

Elizabeth laughed. They'd had these talks since they first became parents, comparing notes and sharing insights about their kids. Praying for them. Cluing each other in on how things were really going.

This wasn't the first time John had sounded unaware. "That's just it." Elizabeth crossed her arms. "He did nothing. Luke didn't do anything wrong . . . and he knows it."

"Ahh." John nodded. "A little too smug for his own good. True."

"Smug?" Elizabeth put her hands on her hips. "He's downright arrogant, John. Luke criticizes everyone around him." She blew at a wisp of her hair. "I'm worried about who he's becoming. His attitude toward Ashley is ugly."

"I know." John kept his tone calm. "I'll talk to him."

Another clap of thunder rattled across the country-side. Closer this time. A shaky sigh came from Elizabeth. "I've been helping Kari plan this wedding for five months. I want it to be happy." She turned to him again. "For her. For all of us."

"I agree." He put his hand on her shoulder. "Then maybe today isn't the day to figure this out."

"Probably not. Except for Kari." She straightened. "She only has this morning to change her mind."

"I told you . . ." John smiled.

"She's excited. Tim's the one. I know, I know." Elizabeth felt tired. "I just hope she was telling you the truth." She allowed a weak chuckle. "I feel better talking about it . . . Even if it didn't actually accomplish anything."

John pulled her into a hug and they stayed that way for a long while. "It gave you a chance to remember. How it used to be."

"Yes." A rush of tears filled Elizabeth's eyes. Standing here on the porch always gave her time to remember. Especially today. When everything about her adult kids' lives felt so uncertain.

She wiped at her eyes and settled herself. *I trust You, God . . . with our kids. Even the one I had to place with another family. When it comes to our adult children please . . . help them follow Your voice.*

All of them.

No answer resonated through the shadowy halls of her heart. But Elizabeth reminded herself of one very real truth. God could make a miracle out of any mess. Her kids' worst choices and mistakes.

And her own.

It was why they were celebrating Kari's beautiful wedding today. Because after she lost Ryan, God had cared enough about Kari to bring her a second love of her life.

Tim Jacobs was living proof.

At least Elizabeth hoped so.

3

Rehabilitation was an ongoing process for Ryan Taylor. Probably would be for the rest of his life. His neck and spine were fused together in two areas, so mobility depended on a complex regular series of stretches and exercises. While he was home, twice a week he worked with a therapist who came by his mom's house.

Three doors down from the Baxters.

Ryan's family had lived in Bloomington as long as he could remember. His dad had been an administrator at the hospital before his death, and his mom was still a volunteer there. Ryan had an older sister who lived in California and only came home a few weeks each year.

"Bloomington doesn't do much for me," she had said more than once. "I don't miss it."

Ryan was different. He loved Bloomington for a hundred reasons. But maybe most of all because he could see Kari Baxter's house from his bedroom window. Where she still lived.

At least until five o'clock today.

Yes, whether he would've had a long career playing football or not, Ryan had always intended to return here

one day. He still did. So that when it came time to marry
and put down roots, he would get reconnected at his
family's church. Where his mother and the Baxter family
still attended. That had always been his plan.

It still was.

Ryan stretched his arms over his head, one way and
then the other. His therapist was Stan Guyer, a man in
his mid-forties. The guy practiced what he preached in
the gym because he didn't look a day over thirty. He had
helped Ryan set up a training area in the basement,
where they were now.

Pushing through the last ten minutes of a tough
workout.

"How you feeling?" Stan stepped back and studied
him. "You're slow today."

"Sorry." Ryan didn't know the guy well enough to tell
him what was really going on. How his pace that morning had nothing to do with his energy or his spine or the
way his body was responding to therapy.

It was his heart.

Ryan doubled his efforts. Two hundred pounds hung
on a bar resting on his shoulders, and under it he finished
a round of ten squats. The room was floored with thick
black rubber and outfitted with more than a dozen machines and exercise stations. He had spent a fortune on
the setup, a gift to himself. A reason to never miss a therapy session, and something else.

An incentive to come home and make things work
with Kari.

Two more. Ryan forced himself to move his legs, to finish. On the last squat, he slid easily out of the way and let the weights hit the floor. "I always wondered . . ." He was out of breath, and he could tell his face was red. "How putting a couple . . . hundred pounds on my neck . . . was good for me." Ryan laughed. "Given my history."

"I've told you." Stan chuckled. "The stronger the muscles around your neck and spine, Taylor, the more mobile you'll be. Even when you're old and gray."

"I know, I know." Ryan grinned and waved him off. He was still breathing hard. "You're the best. I get it."

Stan directed Ryan to the floor. Push-ups were next. Fifty of them. Stan was there not so much to count the reps, but to make sure Ryan's form was perfect. Anything less could hurt his back.

Working out was more painful now than it had been before his injury. But it was nothing to what he was about to live through when his watch hit five o'clock today. A part of him wanted to go by her house. See her one last time. Talk her out of it.

There was still a chance.

I can't do it, he told himself. *I have to let her go*.

"Seven, eight." Stan's voice rose. "Come on, Taylor. Really work it."

Sweat dripped down Ryan's face. "Yes, boss!"

The idea of seeing Kari, knowing she was about to wear a wedding dress and walk down the aisle toward some other guy, was more painful than anything Stan could ever put him through. Tim would probably be at the house before the wedding. So, no . . . he wasn't going to do it.

What would be the point? Just so Kari could look the other way and ignore him? Like she'd been doing since his injury?

Ryan could feel himself slipping into autopilot with Stan. The workouts were a part of his life. His muscles would respond even if his mind was years away. He closed his eyes and kept pushing.

"Eighteen, nineteen." Stan sounded happier. "That's the way, Taylor. There you go."

But Ryan could barely hear the guy. He was back on Soldier Field, two years ago, playing football like he was born to do it. Right there, carrying the ball in what would be his last minutes of owning the game.

Even then Kari had filled his mind.

Always Kari. Only Kari.

Ryan was on the field again. Running like the wind, carrying the ball toward the end zone when—

"Taylor? You with me?" Stan sounded frustrated.

"Yeah." Ryan stood. "Sorry." His knees felt weak and he needed water. "I'll be back."

"Five more minutes," Stan called after him. "You can do this."

Ryan grabbed a water bottle from the fridge in the next room and hesitated. The hit had been the single worst physical pain of his life. He closed his eyes and he could feel it again. The sickening smack of his helmet crashing into that of Russell Jones.

And then the searing heat, like someone had pressed a blowtorch to his neck. The explosion of hurt . . . Ryan took a swig of his water. It was a pain no words could define. Even now. And there he was on the ground, his face in the grass. He tried but he couldn't breathe. Couldn't draw a single breath. And that's when it occurred to him.

He was going to die. Right there in the middle of Soldier Field, and he would never see Kari Baxter again. Reporters and coaches had asked him since then what it was like, what he was thinking when he was laying there frozen on the field that day.

Surely his mind was ablaze with thoughts of football. That's what they all figured. After all, he had spent his whole life getting to this moment. Summers of Pop Warner and four autumns of high school games, then working to be the best in the NCAA. All so he could dominate in the NFL. The best the game had ever seen.

Ryan finished his water and headed back to Stan. They were all wrong. As the paramedics strapped him to a backboard and hurried him to an ambulance, he wasn't thinking about football at all.

He was thinking about Kari Baxter.

And late that night, when his mother came in his room and told Ryan that Kari had come, that she and her father were in the waiting room, Ryan didn't have to ask how his surgery had gone. It didn't matter.

He was going to be okay, because Kari was here. She had come for him.

Ryan dropped to the floor and resumed his push-ups.

"Find your position." Stan pointed to the floor. "You're slowing down. Twenty-two more, come on."

"Got it." Ryan began rattling them off. His form was better than perfect this time. Anger always did that to him. He clenched his jaw. Because when he woke up the next morning after the team's female trainer had been in to see him, his mother told him the news that still didn't make sense. Kari was gone. She and her father had left without saying a word.

Without an explanation.

Every day since then Ryan had waited for Kari to tell him what had happened, why she had turned her back at his lowest moment. But every chance she had, Kari avoided him. Didn't answer his calls or respond to his letters.

"Forty-nine, fifty!" Stan clapped a few times. "One of your best, Taylor. You must've really needed that water."

No, he wanted to say. *I really need Kari Baxter.*

Which was why he couldn't stop thinking about seeing her this morning. Even though the idea was crazy. He knew what would happen if he went to her house today. Kari wouldn't talk to him or give him her reasons or even the time of day. Ryan was never going to get the girl of his dreams.

He stood and stretched. Yes, he could walk. Thanks to God and the efforts of surgeons and therapists like Stan, Ryan Taylor was almost good as new. His body was healed.

But without Kari, his life was broken, and Ryan had no idea how to fix that.

"You sure you're okay?" Stan tossed him a towel. "You're a million miles away."

"Not quite a million." Ryan smiled. *Just a few hundred steps, actually.* But again he kept the truth to himself.

After a bit of small talk, Stan left, and when Ryan finished his shower he did something he hadn't done in years. He grabbed his senior yearbook from his bedroom shelf and took it to the oversize chair. "Where did things go wrong, Kari girl?" Ryan muttered the words to himself.

His mom was going to the wedding later today. Over the years she had told Ryan a number of times what he should do. "Go see her, Son. Talk to her. It's not too late."

If his mother knew what he was thinking, even now she would encourage him to go.

"She must be confused," his mother had told him at least twenty times since his injury. "I know Kari Baxter. I watched her grow up." His mom would shake her head. "Kari never would've walked out of that hospital without a reason." When Ryan would barely nod or not respond at all, his mother would try again. "Call her, Ryan. Work it out."

He had tried. Ryan opened the yearbook. If only it had been that easy.

His fingers found their way across the familiar glossy pages until he reached the football section. On one of the adjacent layouts was a spread for the cheerleaders. He didn't have to squint to find Kari in the mix of girls. She was the only one he could see. Then and now.

Long dark hair, bright blue eyes. The two of them met the summer just before Kari started seventh grade and Ryan, ninth. Their dads had worked together at the hospital. One Saturday in July his parents hosted a cookout and invited the Baxter family. Ryan had been outside playing football with a friend, shirt off, tan and sweaty, when his dad called him in to eat.

He was fourteen and she was twelve. It was the first moment he had ever seen Kari, and he hadn't been the same since. He remembered how it felt that day when their eyes met, how he was suddenly self-conscious. He slipped his shirt on. Kari was beautiful but she was young.

Too young to flirt with or tease or act interested in.

Even still they hit it off that night and hung out a number of times as July and August played out. That beautiful endless summer.

Ryan breathed deep and let his mind drift back to that first meeting. Their parents had been playing board games inside, and Ryan and Kari had taken a spot on the front porch to watch the stars. "I'm going to play football in the pros one day," he had told her.

"You'll be the best." Her eyes shone in the moonlight. "I'm going to be a cheerleader. And then a dancer. And maybe a writer." Her smile had set fire to his heart. "Wherever my dreams take me."

Ryan had loved that about her even then. Kari was a dreamer, a girl who saw the deeper side of life.

Their first rough patch happened that fall. She was

in seventh grade, and taller than her friends. Prettier. Their middle school included ninth grade, and anyone could've mistaken her for a freshman. And that's what happened when Kari came up to Ryan at his lunch table the first week of school.

His friends were instantly crazy about her.

Not sure what to do, Ryan played it cool. He told the guys to back off. She was a kid, just a seventh grader. Meanwhile, Kari took a spot with some girls a few tables away. Her expression told him she was hurt.

The guys did as Ryan asked. No one in ninth grade wanted to be caught flirting with a seventh-grade girl. But one of them, Buck Colter, pushed him, giving him a hard time. "What about you, Taylor?" His voice was too loud. "You got a thing for that seventh grader?" He pointed at Kari. "Go on, you can tell us."

"No!" Ryan had no choice but to respond. "She's a family friend, okay? That's it."

Ryan had only been trying to defend her. His buddies on the football team would never understand the truth, that his heart already belonged to Kari. Even if she was just a kid.

Kari didn't talk to him much the rest of the school year. But when June rolled around and their families took a camping trip, the two found their way back together. What they shared was nothing more than a friendship, really. No hand-holding, no talk of dating. They were both too young.

And when school started he was at Bloomington

High. They would wait two more years before she finally joined him, so summers were all they had. When she finally graced the halls of his high school, again Ryan kept his distance. Seniors didn't date sophomores. Kari was still too young.

Ryan looked at the yearbook page again.

Fall of his senior year had been the best, because she made the varsity cheerleading squad. Which meant she was there on the sidelines every Friday night. So that mid-game, a glimpse of Kari Baxter was as simple as shifting his gaze.

He leaned back in the chair and closed his eyes.

Their first date didn't come until her sixteenth birthday and that hadn't gone very well. Ryan had gotten permission from Dr. Baxter. Still, the awkwardness of that night had washed over him and filled his baffled heart. He could see her now, holding the roses he'd given her as he picked her up at her house.

At the end of the date, though, he told her the truth. He couldn't kiss her. Couldn't be her boyfriend no matter what he wanted. He was leaving for college. They needed to go their separate ways. At least for now.

Kari took the news hard, so as soon as Ryan got settled in his dorm he called her. He was sorry, he told her. He hadn't meant to end things. And so the friendship between them remained.

They didn't start truly dating until his father died just before Christmas break his sophomore year in college. Ryan survived the tragedy of that time only because of Kari Baxter. She had been there for him every minute of that sad season. Listening, leaning on his shoulder. Holding his hand.

Before he went back to school, he kissed her for the first time. After that there was no turning back. Ryan knew that he would love her till the day he died. He still felt that way.

Once more he looked at the yearbook. Whenever he tried to understand what had happened, how come she had walked away, he always landed on the same thing. She must not have wanted to date an NFL player. Which was weird, because she'd known that was his dream since they were kids.

But what else could explain it? She had come to the hospital to see him, come to make sure he was okay. And when she had her information, she and her dad had turned around and headed back to Bloomington.

Even now that story didn't add up. The Kari Baxter he had known would've at least talked to him, tried to explain herself. If she'd been afraid of his sport, or if she didn't want him going to player parties, she could've said so.

He closed the yearbook and slipped it back on his shelf. Then he walked to the window and focused on the house in the distance. The one he'd been to a thousand times. The Baxter house.

Surely Tim Jacobs wasn't in the picture back then? That was the only other scenario that made even the slightest sense. Maybe Kari had come to the hospital to make sure he pulled through . . . with the intention of telling him she'd fallen for Tim. Only once she got there she couldn't face him, couldn't tell him the news, because he was too badly injured, his situation too serious.

So she'd turned around and gone home.

Ryan considered the idea again and felt his frustration rising. That wasn't possible, either. If—while he and Kari were dating—she had fallen in love with Tim, then she would've been apologetic. Embarrassed or ashamed. And honest, that most of all.

Not angry.

And Kari was definitely angry. Hurt and upset and betrayed. That's how she'd looked each of the few times he had seen her. He stared at Kari's house. She hadn't even given him the courtesy of telling him she was getting married.

So why would he consider going to see her now?

"Not this time, Kari." He uttered the words and turned away. "Not on your wedding day."

At the sound of his own voice, a competitive spirit rushed through Ryan. Since when had he given up so easily? Wasn't he the one always ready for a challenge? He gritted his teeth. So what if it was her wedding day. He could go see her, try one more time.

People call off weddings all the time. Even the day of the ceremony.

He tried to picture how that would work, how it would feel to Kari and her family. No, he couldn't do that to her. Couldn't try to talk her out of it today. He was too late. She'd made up her mind. His chances were gone.

A panicked kind of anger took punches at him as he turned and pressed his hand against the window. As if by seeing her house he could reach out and touch her again. A deep breath and he turned his back to the view.

Maybe he would get in his truck and drive to Lake Monroe. As far away from the Baxter house as he could get. Whatever he did today, time was wasting. Because he had work to do. Sure, Ryan drew a paycheck coaching football in the NFL. But his most important job these days was something altogether different.

Putting Kari Baxter out of his mind for good.

4

The bridal room was set up in the downstairs den, and yesterday Elizabeth had helped John fit the space with two long folding tables, four chairs and four floor-length mirrors. They had talked about using the chapel, but Kari wanted to get ready at home.

In the house she grew up in.

Elizabeth tried to focus on that happy thought and not the feeling of dread still plaguing her. A soft rain fell against the window and a glance outside told her that the worst of the morning storm had passed. But a bigger one was building. Earlier, she had flipped on the radio news station to get an update. Apparently conditions were right for severe thunderstorms *and* a tornado outbreak.

Like something Indiana had never seen before.

Today. On Kari's wedding day.

Don't think about it, Elizabeth told herself. She carried a basket of makeup and hair tools into the den. *Stay positive. This is Kari's happy day.* The girls had planned to meet here at nine o'clock, but already Ashley had called to say she'd be late. Her little Cole hadn't slept much last night. The others would be here soon.

Better to give her attention to the matter at hand.

Elizabeth set her things down on the first long table. The mirrors were positioned horizontally on the tables, so each girl would have a spot. She plugged in the curling iron and blow-dryer.

After a lifetime of doing her girls' hair, Elizabeth was more than prepared for today. When Brooke and Peter married, they'd hired a few stylists from a downtown salon. Which was fine. But when Kari had asked her to be in charge of hair and makeup for her big day, Elizabeth was thrilled.

Now if she could only find it in herself to be thrilled about Kari's groom.

Elizabeth moved to the next chair and opened a new pallette of eye shadow along with new blushes and mascara. Kari had asked her sisters and a few close friends to be bridesmaids, but those girls were getting ready in their own homes. Elizabeth was glad. Maybe today would give her daughters a chance to feel close again. The way they used to be.

Footsteps sounded in the hallway outside the den and Brooke stepped in. She stopped and looked around. "Naturally." She rolled her eyes, set her bag down on the first table and hugged Elizabeth. "My sisters are late."

Here we go. Elizabeth smiled at her oldest daughter. "They'll be here soon. I told Kari to come down around nine-thirty."

"Mmm." Brooke checked her look in the mirror. "It's

awful outside. Not sure a style will do it." She grinned. "More of a makeover."

Elizabeth felt herself relax. At least Brooke was smiling. "You look beautiful, dear."

"And the dresses are here?" Brooke glanced over her shoulder and back at Elizabeth. "In the closet?"

"All three of them." Elizabeth walked over and opened the closet door. "They're so pretty. Pale pink. The perfect summer color."

"Not today." Brooke peered out the window. "Black might be better."

"Brooke!" Elizabeth's tone was sharper than she intended. So much for peace. "Watch your attitude. Please." She lowered her voice. "Kari might hear you."

"I'm okay with that." Sadness softened Brooke's eyes. "Mom . . . look at the weather. It's a sign, don't you think?"

"No." Her response was too quick. She searched her mind for a way to spin this. "Storms are beautiful."

"Yeah." Brooke took a seat in front of one of the mirrors. She muttered the next words under her breath. "Unless they kill you."

Elizabeth stared at her oldest daughter. "Try to be kind, would you? Kari deserves better."

Brooke reached into her bag and pulled out a hairbrush. She ran it through her hair and cast a quick glance at Elizabeth. "She deserves a better groom."

This was going nowhere. Elizabeth crossed her arms

and kept her voice low. "What exactly do you have against Tim?"

"Mother." Brooke shifted in her chair and looked straight at Elizabeth. "Don't kid yourself just because it's Kari's wedding day." She sighed and turned to the mirror again. "He's smug and . . . and overly intellectual." Brooke stroked the brush through her hair once more. "So he has his PhD, big deal. I'm a doctor and you don't see me acting better than everyone."

Panic breathed against Elizabeth's neck and made her heart skip a beat. "He's young. He'll outgrow that."

"What about the way he treats Kari?" Brooke set her brush down. "Like she's an imbecile." She waved her hand around. "An airhead. Just because she models for a living." Brooke paused. "You of all people should get it, Mom."

There was a sound at the door and they both turned. Erin was there, holding her makeup bag. She looked from Brooke to Elizabeth. "Am I interrupting?"

"No." Elizabeth reminded herself to smile. No doubt Erin had heard Brooke's last words about Tim. Either way Elizabeth wasn't going to touch the topic. She motioned to Erin. "Here. Come have a seat, honey. We were just getting started."

Erin was the youngest, and her shoulder-length blond hair, straight and clean, framed her pretty face. She took the chair next to Brooke and gave her a side hug. "Is Maddie ready?"

Maddie was Brooke and Peter's little girl. Elizabeth's precious granddaughter.

"She is." Brooke shot a quick look at Elizabeth, as if to say their earlier conversation could wait, but it was no less valid. She returned her attention to Erin again. "Peter's bringing her over in a few hours. She's had the flower-girl dress on since after breakfast."

Another reason to feel happy about the day. Maddie, not quite three years old, was Kari's flower girl. Peter would walk the child up the aisle while Maddie dropped fresh rose petals from Elizabeth's garden.

Another request from Kari. That her bouquet and Maddie's flower petals be from their own backyard.

Erin began brushing her hair, looking at herself in the mirror. "Kari said she's coming down in a little while." She glanced over at Brooke. "Where's Ashley?"

"Running late." Brooke's tone dripped with sarcasm. "Love her, but . . . you know."

Why was she doing this? Elizabeth shot her oldest a pleading look, and after that Brooke seemed to get the hint. Her haughty expression eased and she sorted through the makeup in her bag. "Thank you, Mother. For your help." She managed a partial smile. "No one curls my hair better than you. Even still."

"True." Erin seemed to sense that the tension in the room was letting up. She sounded more at ease. "I love when you do my hair, Mom."

And so Elizabeth took the curling iron and started

with her youngest daughter. Erin had offered to help watch Cole when Ashley got here, so she needed to be finished first.

When her hair was a cascade of gorgeous blond curls, and when her makeup was just right to accent her light blue eyes, Erin excused herself. "I heard a car in the driveway. Probably Ashley." She stood and kissed Elizabeth's cheek. Then she studied herself in the mirror. "Wow. I should have you do this every day. Maybe the guy in my comp class would finally notice me." She raised one shoulder and let it fall again. "Or maybe not."

Elizabeth watched her go. "Erin."

Her youngest daughter stopped and turned around. "Yes?"

"You're absolutely beautiful." Elizabeth hid her frustration. She hated that Erin was lonely much of the time, that she longed for a boyfriend. "The guy in your comp class just isn't—"

"The right one!" Erin and Brooke finished her sentence at the same time.

"Exactly." Elizabeth uttered a soft laugh. She moved to Brooke and checked the curling iron. "You ready?"

"As ready as I'll ever be." Brooke waved at Erin as she left the room, and then looked at Elizabeth in the mirror. "I'm right about Tim." She kept her words quieter this time.

"Please, Brooke. Let it go." Elizabeth couldn't bear to think of the truth. That she herself had doubts about

Kari's choice of husband. "She's in love with Tim. And Tim is . . . He's a very nice man."

There wasn't time for more conversation. Ashley walked in then and stopped short a few feet from the setup. "Why do I feel like I interrupted something important?"

"No, not at all." Elizabeth pointed to the chair next to Brooke. "We were just waiting for you."

"Sorry." Ashley set her things down on the table and hugged Elizabeth. "This looks great, Mom. Thanks for helping us."

Of all the kids, Elizabeth worried most about Ashley. But maybe today would be different. Ashley looked happy and relaxed, her usual defensiveness at bay. Elizabeth put her hand on Ashley's shoulder. "I'm happy to do it. Glad you're here."

"Me, too." Ashley leaned over and hugged Brooke. "You go next. Erin said she's good to watch Cole for as long as we need."

"Thanks." Brooke smiled at her sister. The two of them had a closer bond since Ashley's return from Paris. Which wasn't exactly a good thing.

Elizabeth set to work curling Brooke's hair. "Did Kari tell you girls when the limo will be here? To take us all to the chapel?"

"Yes." Brooke turned her head as Elizabeth finished a curl. "Three o'clock pickup. So the girls can get photos done before the wedding."

Ashley faced the two of them and wrinkled her

brow. "Please tell me they're not having a sermon. Pastor Mark should stick to saying nice things about Kari and Tim, and get straight to the vows."

"True." Brooke didn't hesitate. "No one needs an altar call at a wedding. That's a little manipulative if you ask me."

And just like that the tension returned with a vengeance. "Girls." Elizabeth started a new curl on Brooke's head. She worked to keep her tone controlled. "I'm almost positive Pastor Mark will talk about Kari and Tim's faith. Kari wants that and it's her decision." She glanced back at the door. "Kari will be down any minute. I'd hate for her to hear any of this."

Brooke shared a knowing look with Ashley. Then she turned to Elizabeth. "You need to get used to the fact that a few of us just don't believe the way you do." She put her hand on Ashley's shoulder. "It's normal that through academics or experience, young adults become enlightened to a bigger world, Mom. It's progressive."

Times like this Elizabeth wanted to shout at her oldest daughter, tell her to look around at the proof of God in every created thing. Including her little daughter, Maddie. But that wouldn't convince Brooke to believe again. And it wasn't Elizabeth's job to make Brooke and Ashley find their way back to faith.

Only God could do that.

Elizabeth drew a slow breath. "You and Ashley will never be forced to share your family's beliefs, Brooke." She finished the last curl and stepped back. Elizabeth's heart was breaking, but she worked hard to hide it. "Today, however, I'm asking you to respect whatever your sister wants at her wedding. Even if that means listening to the entire Gospel of John."

Ashley shot a look at Brooke and then turned to Elizabeth. "Brooke wasn't trying to start a fight, Mom."

"I know." Elizabeth exhaled. *Peace, God . . . give me peace. Please.* She took her time. "I'm sorry. I just . . . I don't want any problems today."

"There won't be." Brooke looked surprised. Like the idea was outlandish. "But we're allowed to have our opinions."

What could Elizabeth say to that? She worked her fingers through Brooke's hair. "How do you like it?"

"Pretty." Brooke smiled, as if none of the previous conversation had happened. "Now my eyes! I can never do them like you do."

For the next ten minutes while she worked on Brooke's eye makeup, Elizabeth fought another wave of heaviness in her heart. These two precious daughters, both rejecting the faith they'd been raised with? How was that even possible? Brooke had nearly died in childbirth with Maddie, but God had spared her. And now her daughter was the picture of health. Didn't that mean anything?

And Ashley? Home from Paris with Cole and a second chance at life? Welcomed back and loved by the family she left behind? How could the girls not see God at work? What about the countless times they'd seen

God rescue them and lead them and protect them? The million answered prayers over the years?

A crack of thunder shook the house.

Ashley peered out the window. "There's supposed to be a tornado later." She raised her eyebrows in Brooke's direction. "Probably just as they say 'I do.'"

Brooke shot her sister a side glance. "Mom thinks Tim is a very nice man." She sounded borderline mean. "So . . ."

"Girls!" Elizabeth cast a sharp look at Ashley and then Brooke. "Kari will be down any minute. I won't have that talk." She took a shaky breath. "Not another word."

"Sorry. We aren't trying to be rude." Ashley frowned. Sincerity replaced her tone. "I guess it doesn't matter. Too late to change things now, right?" Ashley hesitated. For a long moment she seemed to take in Elizabeth's expression, and maybe the hurt in her eyes. Ashley leaned her forearms on the folding table. "I really am sorry. You're right." She exhaled. "Kari is choosing him." She looked at Brooke and back at Elizabeth. "We'll stay positive."

"We will." Brooke must've known she'd crossed a line, too. "The past is the past at this point. We'll all learn to love Tim. In time."

"Exactly." Elizabeth couldn't tell them about her feelings of impending disaster or about the fact that deep in her heart she hoped Brooke was right. She felt the slightest bit of relief come against the storm inside her. "Thank you. Both of you."

Elizabeth finished Brooke's eye makeup and then she started on Ashley's hair. A change of subject. That's what her daughters needed. Elizabeth caught Ashley's glance in the mirror. "Landon's coming today. I told you, right?"

A myriad of conflicting emotions flashed in Ashley's eyes. "I know." She turned her head so Elizabeth could work better. "I might leave early."

"I thought you'd be happy." Elizabeth couldn't find solid ground here. No matter what they talked about. "You said it was okay to invite him. He's been your friend since—"

"Fifth grade. You always say that, Mom. Like I could ever forget." Ashley sat a little straighter. "I wish he wasn't coming." She blew a stray piece of her hair from her forehead. "Seeing him . . . it's too hard."

"You said you two were friends." Even Brooke looked confused.

"Me and Landon Blake?" Ashley's smile was tinged with a very deep sorrow. "We could never be just friends. And we could never be more." She shrugged one shoulder. "We've become very different people. Faith. The future. All of it. We've moved on." Her voice fell a notch. "If only I could get my heart to agree."

Elizabeth picked up on the deeper message in her daughter's expression. No matter what she told herself or how different she was now, one thing remained. Ashley still loved Landon Blake, just like she'd said earlier.

The proof shone in her eyes.

Again, Elizabeth changed the subject. Better to talk about the dresses and flowers and fancy dinner to be served tonight than to venture down long-ago back roads. They could talk about Landon later. She finished curling Ashley's hair and touched up her eyeliner. "So beautiful." Elizabeth stepped back and admired Brooke and Ashley. "You two look stunning."

"Thanks, Mom." Brooke stood and grabbed her bag just as Kari walked in.

Ashley was on her feet, too, and she and Brooke embraced their sister.

"It's here!" Ashley kissed her cheek. "You're getting married today!"

"I know." Something in Kari's eyes made her look more anxious than excited. She looked at her sisters one at a time. "Can you believe it?"

Brooke took hold of her hand. "We're here for you, Kari." She hugged her sister again. "If you're happy, we're happy." She hesitated. "We all love Tim. Really."

Elizabeth held her breath. *Thank You, God.* This was how she had hoped Brooke and Ashley would act around Kari. Keeping their deepest concerns to themselves.

"I'm glad." Kari laughed, but it sounded a little forced. "He loves all of you. And that means a lot. Thank you."

From the distance, they heard Cole start to cry. Ashley gathered her things. "Time to go." She looked at Elizabeth. "Thanks, Mom." She glanced in the mirror once more. "I can never get my hair to look like this."

Brooke thanked her mother again, and the two sisters left.

Now it was just Elizabeth and her second-oldest daughter, the bride. "Come here, sweetheart." Elizabeth held out her arms as Kari came to her. They hugged for a long moment. "It's your wedding day, my dear." Elizabeth pulled back and searched Kari's eyes. "What are you feeling?"

"So much." Kari exhaled hard. "Fear. Joy. Doubt. The whole mix." She set her things down on the table and turned back to Elizabeth. "I've never . . . done this." Her eyes met Elizabeth's. "How am I supposed to feel?"

Elizabeth wanted her answer to be easy and light-hearted, wanted to respond to her with the sweet assurance typical for a mother on her daughter's wedding day. But this felt different, somehow. She chose her words with care. "I think some of that is normal." Elizabeth hesitated. She would regret it the rest of her life if she didn't ask the question. She steadied herself. "When you say . . . doubt . . . do you mean like, you're not sure you want to marry Tim?"

Kari's answer should've been fast and sure. Of course she wanted to marry Tim. But instead she took her time. "I don't think so." Her eyes looked so young, the way they'd looked when she was a little girl trying to come clean about cheating on her history test. "I mean . . . it took a minute this morning to remember I was getting married today." She wrinkled her nose. "That can't be good."

Be careful, Elizabeth told herself. "Talk to me, Kari. What's in your heart?"

Her daughter lifted her chin and gave her reflection a serious look. "I love Tim. I know that." She nodded, as if she were convincing herself. "I want to marry him. I've asked myself a hundred times, and always that's my answer."

Elizabeth felt herself relax a bit. "Okay, then." She smiled at Kari. "I'd say you have your answer." Quiet fell between them for a minute while Elizabeth ran the curling iron through Kari's long dark hair. "Every bride feels a little nervous on her wedding day. The important thing is that God has made it clear. Tim is the man you want to spend the rest of your life with. That there's no question, he's your first choice."

Kari didn't respond. But after a few seconds, Elizabeth watched tears gather in her eyes. "First choice?"

"Yes." Elizabeth had worded it that way on purpose. No matter how much Kari had loved Ryan Taylor, he was her past. "That's how you feel, right?"

Kari sniffed and dabbed at the corners of her eyes. "My first choice didn't want me, Mother." She managed the saddest smile. "You know that." She drew a deep breath and her expression took on more life. "But yes . . . given that, Tim is my top choice." Her eyes found Elizabeth's. "I'm sure."

Nothing about that answer felt right to Elizabeth, but she didn't say so. There was no need to probe Kari about her hesitations. She was marrying Tim. Period.

Even though Elizabeth had hoped today would play out differently.

With Kari walking up the aisle toward one man and only one.

Ryan Taylor.

5

Ashley Baxter opened the door to her parents' room and peeked inside. Cole was asleep in the crib they'd set up before he was even born. Ashley could see her son's blond head through the slats in the bed. Without making a sound she shut the door and exhaled.

No one would ever understand why she was uncomfortable about Landon being at Kari's wedding today. They were two entirely different people now, it was that easy. No matter what her family wanted to believe about her. No matter what Landon wanted to believe.

The accident had changed her. She would never be the girl she'd been back then.

To think her mother would talk about elementary school again. As if Ashley could even remember the precocious innocent she'd been back then. Sure, Landon was the same. His character was woven into the fiber of his being. His soul would always be the same—loyal and compassionate, devoted to God and anyone else he met. Ashley might've been that way before, but that certainly wasn't her now.

Hardly.

Even still, her parents thought she'd eventually make her way back to Landon Blake. Somewhere down the road. But they were wrong. Ashley wasn't going to wind up with Landon any more than Kari was going to marry Ryan Taylor. Clearly.

Those days were behind them. In the past, where they would stay.

Ashley walked to the kitchen and sat at the familiar table near the boxed cookies. Why would Landon even want to come to the wedding today? He knew who Ashley was now, knew about her time in Paris and her pregnancy.

No one understood better than Landon how completely Ashley had changed. After the accident, she had told Landon she no longer felt connected to him or to her family. What did any of them know about the brokenness of the world? They had a blind trust in God and beyond that they were unaware. Sweetly ignorant.

Ashley could never be like that again. Not after the crash.

Hadn't she made herself clear to Landon? "You and my parents, you don't understand." She had told him from the hospital. "You're too safe, Landon. Too predictable. You won't even consider the idea that God is just a myth."

Landon could've given up on her. Instead, he had put his hand on her arm, his eyes never more kind. "You don't mean that."

"I do." Ashley's response had come sharp, ruder than she intended. Why wouldn't he walk away? Leave her alone?

Instead he never broke eye contact with her. "Ashley." He stepped back, his love for her as steady as his beautiful heart. "You're going through a phase . . . You'll believe again one day and everything will be okay . . . God will show Himself to you."

She lifted the lid off the nearest box of cookies and took one. Landon was wrong. God was finished with her—if there was a God. And nothing was going to be okay again. The cookie tasted stale. She stood and walked it to the kitchen trash can. Then she poured herself a cup of coffee and took it back to her seat.

Ashley was in charge of flowers for Kari's wedding. Something she loved. She had spent hours yesterday getting the arrangements just right. A mix of pink and white roses from the family garden, and accents of tiny baby's breath, which John bought from a local florist. Each vase had a burlap bow, which Ashley also had tied.

Today she needed only to fill a box with the bows and get them to the reception hall. One of the girls from the flower shop would add the bows to the arrangements and set them at each table. Working with flowers was like painting. Getting the colors just right, every shape and detail. For Kari's wedding, each finished centerpiece was a unique work of art.

Even after all that had changed in Ashley's life, her

love of art remained. Which was something else Landon Blake had believed about her. That she would find a way to make it as an artist.

Ashley leaned back in her chair and pictured him. The handsome guy who had turned her head since the first day they met.

Landon Blake.

She stared out the kitchen window and the years gathered like so many storm clouds. And there she was again, first day of fifth grade in Mr. Garrett's class. Ashley had accidentally dropped a bowl of ice cream on the teacher's head during the back-to-school social the day before.

Landon was one of the only kids in her class who saw the whole thing go down. He came up to her at lunch that first day of school and told her that she had handled the ice cream disaster quite well.

It took a month before Ashley realized Landon wasn't being a menace or making fun of her. And when they took their class trip to the zoo that fall, as the students moved on to the next exhibit, Landon stayed behind with her while she sketched the giraffe. Ashley smiled at the memory. They both got lost that day, and finally in the dark, dank reptile encounter, a zoo worker had spotted them.

"Hey! You two!" The guy ran toward them. "Stop!"

Instead, Landon had grabbed her hand and the two of them had run through the zoo in search of their class. Trying to avoid zoo jail. A couple of explorers, they had called themselves. Ashley smiled. She could feel Landon's young fingers against hers.

That was also the year when some kid named Elliot accidentally blew a giant gum wad into Ashley's hair, and after her mother had taken her to the salon to have the sticky mess cut out, it was Landon who helped her survive.

The other boys were picking on her because of her short hair. But Landon told them to quit it. "Ashley is a gymnast," he told them. "Short hair is better for her sport." Then he'd smiled at her and nodded. "I like it."

And soon the whole class felt that way about her new look.

Yes, Landon had her heart from the beginning. Cutest boy she'd ever seen. Then, and still. With Landon, there hadn't been any doubt that the two of them would end up together. Back then, Ashley would dream about the years and decades ahead and always she saw Landon.

Ashley closed her eyes and it was her sophomore year again, the time Landon came to her house and knocked at the door. Before that they'd studied together at his house or hers, but he'd never just come by un-announced.

Her mom answered the door that day. Ashley was up in her room drawing, but when she heard his voice her heart skipped a beat. Why had he come over? She had hurried down the stairs. And there he was, that swoop of brown hair hanging just above his amber-colored eyes.

"Ash . . . I wanna show you something." He looked

like he had just won a gold medal. They stepped outside and Ashley saw the reason. Not a gold medal. But an older Chevy Camaro. Golden brown. "I passed my driver's test!" He grinned.

"You did?" She squealed at the news.

"Ninety-five percent!" He raised both fists and jumped around a few times. "My dad bought me this for an early birthday gift."

They walked to the car and Ashley ran her fingers along the shiny door. "I love it." She grinned at him. "It's weird that we're old enough to drive."

"Well." He gave her a teasing look, the one he'd been giving her since fifth grade. "*I'm* old enough. You still have a few months."

She gave a light kick at the toe of his tennis shoe. "I'll catch up. And I'll be a better driver. Hundred percent. That's my goal."

Landon's laughter faded and he took her hand, something he hadn't done since they got lost at the zoo. But that day, with his car a few feet away, there had been something very different about the feelings between them.

He looked into her eyes. "Actually . . . I don't want to be in separate cars, Ashley." He took a step closer. "I want to date you. Be my girlfriend. Then you can sit in my passenger seat. For now." His smile had etched itself in her heart, where it remained even now. His voice fell to a whisper. "Maybe forever."

A shyness had come over them. Something Ashley

had never felt with Landon Blake. Her heart fluttered and she put her arms around his neck and hugged him. "I'd like that." She leaned back and laughed. "And maybe sometimes you can be in the passenger seat." The car caught her attention again. "Because that Camaro is the sweetest."

"No, it isn't." Landon never broke eye contact. "The Camaro is just a car." He touched her cheek. "You're the sweetest. And the spunkiest." He grinned. "I've always loved that about you."

It was true. Landon had called her spunky from the first week in Mr. Garrett's class. And after that day at her parents' house with the Camaro, Ashley never dreamed of dating anyone else.

Marriage wasn't something they discussed. They were too young. But neither of them ever thought about breaking up. And to hear her parents lately, clearly they had also thought Landon was going to be in her life forever.

She opened her eyes and stared out the window once more. The two of them dated right up until their senior year. Their families attended the same church and on Wednesdays during youth group, Ashley and Landon always sat together. Their conversations were deep—about God and creation and miracles. About the gifts and talents He had given them. And about the future ahead of them.

Landon wanted to be a teacher or a basketball coach, like his dad. And Ashley, well, Ashley had always known

what she wanted to do. She would go to Paris and become a famous artist.

But in the months before graduation, they went to
dinner one night and the mood felt heavy. Landon
pushed his fork around in his spaghetti. "I've been thinking." He looked up and their eyes held. "You really want
to go to Paris?"

"Of course." Her answer was out before she could
stop it. "It's been my dream as long as I can remember."

He took his time before responding. "What about . . .
being an artist here? In Bloomington?"

And in that moment, Ashley understood. Landon
was looking ahead at the one thing they had never talked
about. The coming goodbye. She stared at her salad
plate. "I mean . . . I won't live in Paris forever." Her eyes
found his again. "Are you staying here?"

He had applied to a few different schools. Last time
they talked about it, Landon was torn between Indiana
University down the street and Baylor in Texas, his dad's
alma mater.

That night at the restaurant, Landon shrugged. "I'd
stay here if . . . if you did."

Then, for the first time since she met Landon Blake,
Ashley felt the walls closing in. "You mean . . . like stay
here and go to school? And just . . . never leave?" The
idea made Ashley feel trapped, the way she had felt once
when she got stuck in the mall elevator.

The conversation died there. Landon was too young

to make promises, too green to want to talk about marriage. The two of them had kept their physical relationship at bay. "Nothing good came from kissing a boy too soon," her mother used to tell her.

In those simple early days, Ashley had taken the advice to heart, and Landon never pushed. He was a good boy, that's what Ashley's dad always called him.

Landon Blake, the good boy.

They didn't share their first kiss until senior prom a month later. Ashley found the palest blue dress, one with shirred shoulders and a swishy skirt that hit just above her shoes. Landon wore a dark gray tux and when he came to the door to pick her up, Ashley could barely breathe.

He was tall and tanned, his shoulders filled out from spring football practice. That night Ashley was sure hers was the most handsome prom date any girl had ever had. She couldn't remember anything about the other kids at the dance. There was nothing in her memory about what guys her friends went to the prom with or who was crowned king and queen.

When she looked back on that night all she could see was Landon. All she could feel was his hand on her waist. His cheek against hers.

When the dance was over he took her to get ice cream, and as they drove home, he turned onto a hilly street and stopped at a place where they could see the lights from downtown Bloomington. He cut the engine and turned to her. "Tonight was . . ." He stared at her, his eyes shining. "Perfect."

"I felt like a princess." Ashley still wore her wrist corsage. She looked at Landon in the moonlight. "I don't want it to end."

Landon took her hand and slid his fingers between hers. The radio was on and Simple Minds was singing "Don't You Forget About Me." Neither of them said a word at first. They just looked at each other. Ashley blinked back tears. "Weren't we just in Mr. Garrett's class?"

"And you were coming through the door covered in mud." His laugh was soft. "Remember that day?"

"I fell in a puddle getting out of my mom's van." She laughed. "Things like that always seemed to happen to me. And you wouldn't let me forget." She angled her head, memorizing the sight of him. A silence fell over the moment. It was as good a time as any to tell him her news. A surprise she had saved for that very moment. "So . . . guess what?"

He looked dizzy in love with her. "What?"

Ashley grinned. "I got accepted to Baylor."

Landon looked like he might jump out of his seat, or maybe out of the car altogether. "You what?" He shook his head. "Are you serious? You never . . . you never told me you applied."

"Artists are a tricky bunch." Even as she said the words, she hadn't been completely sure about her decision. But she didn't have money for Paris, and school wasn't a bad idea. The walls weren't closing in anymore. As long as she got out of Bloomington for a few years, it didn't matter if it was Paris or Baylor. And Baylor had something Paris would never have.

Landon Blake.

And so Ashley had decided Paris could wait.

A hundred questions seemed to flash in his eyes that night. But instead of asking a single one of them, Landon leaned close and framed her face with his hands. "Can I . . . kiss you, Ashley?" He didn't blink, didn't look away even for a second. "I've wanted to since I held your hand at the zoo."

Ashley laughed. "You were only eleven." She put her other hand over his, their faces closer than before.

"Didn't matter." Landon was laughing now, too. "I was smitten. I still am."

"Well, then . . ." She moved in toward him. "I'd say . . . the answer is yes."

"Really?" Landon seemed surprised. "I can kiss you? Now?"

"Yes." Rivers of emotion deeper than anything she'd ever known welled up in Ashley's heart. "Please, Landon." Her words became a whisper. "Please, kiss me."

Even now, years later, Ashley could remember that kiss. How her heart soared that night. The way Landon's body felt warm near hers. The taste of his lips, the smell of his cologne.

Ashley could've remained lost in that moment for an hour. Forever. But they left after that single kiss. Landon knew better, even when Ashley wanted to stay. She remembered thinking that Landon had been looking out for her since Mr. Garrett's zoo trip.

He wasn't going to let anything happen to her now.

As they drove home that night, Ashley kept stealing glances at Landon. His jawline and shoulders, his strong hands on the wheel. She couldn't stop looking. There would never be anyone else for her, she was sure of it back then.

And as the days took them toward graduation, they made their decisions known to their parents. They were both going to Baylor. They would leave mid-August and have rooms in dorm buildings near each other. Landon would study teaching and Ashley would dive into the school's art program.

Ashley still planned to visit Paris someday, but that year all she wanted was to be with Landon. Their families shared Fourth of July together at nearby Lake Monroe, and Ashley and Landon played Frisbee on the shore. All of life was just ahead of them, the fringe of tomorrow within their grasp. And nothing could tear them apart.

Nothing.

But on that hot summer day at the lake, laughing and playing and teasing each other, neither of them could've imagined the turn life would take. The events that would happen just twenty-four hours later. They couldn't have known about the heartache around the corner or the way their lives would be torn apart. And most of all as that summer night played out, they didn't dream of the disaster headed straight for Ashley.

Or the drunk driver who would change both their lives forever.

6

Bloomington High School was Landon Blake's favorite place to jog during the summer. Something about being home from Baylor University made him long for days gone by, the years when he and Ashley were teenagers.

Especially on a stormy day like this.

Landon tightened the laces in his shoes and set out. He was about to start his senior year and he'd made a decision. He wasn't going to be a teacher. Ashley had pointed out a number of times in the last three years that Landon was too safe. Too predictable. Too much like her parents. Too much like his.

In some ways she was right. Nothing was going to change Landon's faith in God. Not even his love for Ashley Baxter. But she had a point about his predictability. His father was a respected teacher, and for that reason he would admire teachers as long as he lived. Maybe one day when he was older, Landon would follow in his father's footsteps and get his teaching credentials.

But for now he was going to take his friend Jalen's lead. When Landon graduated next May he was going to come home to Bloomington and do something he never dreamed of doing until recently. Something he hadn't told Ashley or her parents. Only his mom and dad and Jalen knew the truth.

Landon was going to fight fires in Bloomington. The bigger the better.

Being a firefighter was an admirable profession, of course. But it wasn't safe. Nothing predictable about waiting for the next local disaster. Running into a burning building when everyone else was running out . . . that was the epitome of danger.

Which was exactly what Landon wanted now. He picked up his pace. Not just because the girl he loved had accused him of being too safe. But because it seemed like the right thing to do. Helping people. Risking his life so that someone else might live.

Up until now, the only risky thing Landon had ever done was fall in love with Ashley Baxter.

Faster, he told himself. The competition to become a firefighter was intense. Next year at this time he would have to be in the shape of his life if he wanted to get hired. Fire departments loved applicants with a college degree. He knew that much.

But that was only the starting point.

He hit the one-mile mark and looked at his stopwatch. Seven minutes, fifteen seconds. Down from twelve minutes a year ago. All those seasons of football had done nothing to make him faster. But working out with Jalen had changed his fitness level entirely. This summer he was in the best shape of his life—and still he had to improve.

Landon jogged the next lap. Being a fireman meant he'd need to run up flights of stairs carrying a seventy-five-pound sandbag while wearing a weighted vest. He'd have to pull a heavy hose more than two hundred feet and kick down a locked door.

Something he hadn't been able to do with Ashley, by the way.

He let loose a sad, quiet chuckle.

Focus, Blake. Make it count. Spending the past few semesters getting ready for the host of physical and mental tests ahead had been good for Landon. It took his mind off the girl back home. The one he was going to see in a couple of hours. He kept jogging. Another four laps and he'd wrap up the workout. He was staying with his parents this summer, the way he had since he started at Baylor. They supported his new dream of fighting fires for Bloomington.

But they weren't fans of his feelings for Ashley.

More times than Landon could remember, his mother or father—sometimes both—had sat him down to talk about Ashley. "How many times does that girl have to break your heart, Son?" His mother would shake her head, concern in her eyes.

Just a few weeks ago when he came home from school, his dad said something similar over breakfast. "You need to let her go, Landon." His dad looked genuinely worried. "Tell us about the new girl. Hope."

The new girl.

Landon lifted his face to the stormy sky and slowed

his pace. Hope Hale was a rising senior, just like him. Jalen's twin sister. The three of them met their freshman year and they'd spent most of their free time together ever since. Just a group of friends making their way through college.

Until a year ago. When his feelings for Hope grew.

He was back at the starting line. Time to cool down. Landon walked to the nearby grassy field and ran through a series of stretches. Being limber was also very important for a firefighter.

But today he didn't want to think about rushing into flaming buildings. He didn't want to think about going back to Baylor or Hope or his adult life just ahead.

Today, after too many months, he was going to see Ashley Baxter.

He breathed in deep and moved into the next stretch. As he did, the months and years peeled away and he was eighteen again. Sitting next to Ashley in his brown Camaro, taking her home from their senior prom.

The night of their first kiss.

He would've done anything for Ashley, lived anywhere, promised her the moon and found a way to get it. From the moment he saw her in Mr. Garrett's fifth-grade class, Landon had told himself this much: He would marry her someday. It was a commitment he planned to keep. And that night after senior prom, Landon was sure he was going to make good on it.

Three years had passed since that kiss, and every time summer came around he and Ashley were farther apart. More like strangers. No matter how Landon tried to help her find her way back, nothing worked.

And he could trace every mile of that distance to the accident.

Landon took a deep breath, bent at the waist and eased his hands to the ground. He could still see it all.

One day they were playing at Lake Monroe, tossing a Frisbee, toes in the sand, while their families grilled burgers nearby. Life was good and sweet and the future was perfectly planned. And the next day, Ashley was doing the most mundane task. Driving to the store for milk and eggs.

Just to get out of the house.

Her brother, Luke, had a friend over that day, and the kid asked Ashley to give him a ride home. Just down the country road and a few blocks from Main Street. Not far from the grocery store. But before she could make the turn, a truck crossed the centerline and headed straight for them.

The kid in the passenger seat leaned over and jerked the wheel, forcing a sharp left turn and taking Ashley out of the direct hit. That's what the reports showed. A witness had seen it all. And so the truck missed Ashley and slammed into the kid instead. Jefferson Bennett. A sixteen-year-old sophomore wrestler at Bloomington High.

The drunk driver died at the scene, and Ashley and Jefferson were airlifted to Bloomington Hospital, where

Ashley's dad worked as a doctor. For three days Ashley and the kid fought to survive on life support.

Landon barely left the hospital.

He took turns sitting beside her bed or waiting in the hall. He visited Jefferson, too. The kid was in a coma, but Landon liked to believe Jefferson knew when a friend stopped by.

All during that terrible time, her medical team believed the worst: Ashley had a brain injury. Her brain had swollen upon impact and it still wasn't back to its right size. They drilled a hole in the back of her head to relieve the pressure, but there were no certainties.

No guarantees.

One afternoon Ashley's dad, Dr. John Baxter, pulled Landon aside. "You understand the situation, right, son?"

Landon wasn't sure what the man meant. "She's . . . very sick. I know that."

"More than sick." Tears welled up in the man's eyes. "She might never be the same. Her brain . . . We don't know how damaged it is."

If John Baxter had been trying to give him a pass, a reason to leave the hospital, it didn't work. Landon straightened himself. "She'll be okay." His words rang with conviction. Nothing would make him leave Ashley's side. Strength filled his voice. "She'll wake up and she'll walk out of here. I know she will."

"Landon." Dr. Baxter put his hand on Landon's shoulder. "It means the world to me . . . to our entire family . . . that you're here. That you won't leave." His voice cracked. "But she might never get out of that bed. Never be the same. You have to know."

After that Landon was at the hospital more often, not less.

He sat by her bed and prayed and when he couldn't stay there, he held vigil in the waiting room. He tried to imagine Ashley in a vegetative state. The spunk and spark in her eyes, forever gone. Better she stay in a coma asleep than wake up as someone none of them recognized, he would tell himself.

But even then Landon didn't waver.

He remembered one particularly bad day, an afternoon when Ashley's lungs had filled with fluid and she was battling a fever. John Baxter found Landon in the waiting room and sat beside him. "It doesn't look good, son." The man's eyes were red. "She has pneumonia. It'll be a miracle if she makes it through the night."

"So . . . we pray for a miracle." Landon hadn't cared about the tears that spilled onto his cheeks that day. "Ashley is a fighter. She'll pull through."

The two of them had joined the rest of the Baxters and formed a prayer circle. Right there in the waiting room. And by some miracle of God, the next day Ashley opened her eyes. Landon was in the room when it happened and from the moment their gazes met he knew.

She was the same Ashley. Something in her eyes told him that. Her brain might've been through a lot, but the accident hadn't taken her memory or depth or all the things that made her Ashley Baxter.

Landon sat beside her in the hours that followed, long after her mother and siblings came and went home, and even as Dr. Baxter was making rounds to see other patients. While Ashley slept, Landon sat there not moving a muscle, afraid to say or do anything that might cause her to struggle.

Anything that would get him kicked out of her room.

When she woke up again, her medical team surrounded her. They checked her vitals and asked her basic questions. Her parents spent time with her, too, while Landon waited in the other room. When it was finally his turn to see her, he walked in and their eyes locked. He took his familiar seat beside her and after several seconds, his first question came. "Hey, Ash . . . are you okay?"

All of time stood still as he watched her, waiting for her response. With slow determination she nodded. No one else might've recognized the movement, but Landon knew her. She was nodding.

"I love you, Ashley. Do you know that?"

The corners of her mouth lifted a fraction of an inch. Just enough to tell him that somewhere beneath the bandages and wires, far beyond the machines working to keep her alive, she was back.

Just like he had known she would be.

Landon was there the morning Ashley said her first word since the accident. "Home." That was all. She had looked into her mother's eyes and said the word *home*. As if there was no place she wanted more to be.

An hour later down the hall, Jefferson Bennett suffered a stroke. He died before sundown.

Of course, Ashley had no idea about any of that. No one on her medical team thought it right to tell her. They agreed it would be days before she could talk about details of the accident.

But outside the hospital, the town grieved.

There were no words for the loss of Jefferson, no way to explain why he'd jerked the wheel, and whether he had known he was putting himself in danger. Improving Ashley's odds. Saving her life.

Landon attended the memorial along with most of Bloomington High's student body. Before the service got underway, Landon found Luke Baxter. The two hugged, and Landon spoke straight to Ashley's brother. "I'm sorry, Luke. Your friend . . . he gave his life for Ashley's."

Luke nodded. "Jefferson always had a crush on her." Luke wiped at an errant tear. "People say they aren't sure if he jerked the wheel so he'd take the impact." Luke nodded, as his lip quivered. "I know my friend. He did it on purpose. Of course he did."

Luke stared at the casket near the front of the church. "Jefferson loved Jesus. And he loved people." He turned and looked at Landon once more. "I'll see him again. I know it."

When the memorial was over, when all the tears for that day had been cried and all the honoring words and memories had been spoken, the crowd dispersed and Landon made his way back to his Camaro. There was just one place he wanted to be.

At the hospital, next to Ashley.

Landon remembered how his own tears fell as he made the drive to see her that afternoon. What would she feel when she found out what happened? Would she think the accident was her fault?

The answers wouldn't come quickly or easily, Landon knew that.

Ashley had been asleep when he got there. He took the chair by her bed and waited, watching her, studying her. As horrific as the crash had been, she didn't have a scratch on her beautiful face. All the damage had been internal. Her organs and hip bones. Her bruised brain and cracked sternum.

After a while he left her room and grabbed a sandwich in the cafeteria. When he returned, Ashley was awake, sitting up in bed. Landon took his familiar chair, but this time Ashley didn't stay quiet. She didn't seem as drugged or sleepy. Her expression was dark.

He took her hand. "Hey."

"Hey." She didn't smile. Her eyes locked onto his and held. "What happened, Landon? Tell me . . . about the accident."

Landon's mind raced, thinking of the right thing to say. But in the end he didn't have to find an answer. Just at that moment her parents entered the room. John Baxter looked at him. "Landon . . . if you don't mind." He nodded to the door. "We need a few minutes alone with her. Please."

"Yes, sir." Landon didn't learn the details of their conversation until later that afternoon. Her dad found him in the cafeteria and explained.

"She needed to know. It was time." Her dad pressed his lips together. "We told her . . . about the accident, how serious it was." He paused. "And about Jefferson."

A sinking feeling came over Landon. As strong as Ashley was, the news could actually cripple her. Landon had feared that from the beginning. "How . . . did she take it?"

"She's in shock." Dr. Baxter looked concerned. "She took my hand and squeezed it. Same with her mother." He shook his head. "But she didn't say a word."

Before Dr. Baxter got up to leave he warned Landon. "Don't try to talk to her right away. Give her time." He stood. "But in time . . . if she's going to open up to anyone, it'll be you."

Landon nodded. Ashley's mother joined in then, and the three of them hugged. "Go to her, Landon." Her mother took his hand. "She needs you. Whether she knows it or not."

Those words stayed with Landon as he went to see her. *Whether she knows it or not. Strange thing to say*, he had thought. Of course Ashley knew it. The two of them were in love. They were about to spend four years together at Baylor University. Ashley would never doubt that she needed him.

Especially now.

But when he walked through the door of her room, she was staring at the opposite wall. He took his time crossing the floor and taking his chair. "Hi."

She didn't answer. Didn't look at him. And for the first time since Ashley Baxter had walked into his life, Landon felt something he'd never felt before.

Fear.

He waited like her father had said. Waited while ten minutes became twenty, and twenty became an hour. Only then did she turn and look at him. "Why?" There was a coolness in her eyes that Landon had never seen before.

He didn't have to ask what she meant. He already knew. Why did it happen? Why Jefferson? Why not her? Landon had no answers. Finally he said the only thing that came to mind. "Luke thinks . . . Jefferson turned the wheel on purpose. To save you."

Anger flickered in her eyes, but her voice was almost too soft to hear. "That makes it okay? For God to take his life and I'm still here?"

The air in the room suddenly felt thick. Landon worked to take his next breath. She had never talked to him like this. "Ashley . . . God knows the number of our days. He didn't . . . 'take' Jefferson." Landon studied her and a silent prayer formed in his heart. *Please, God . . . don't let her turn against You.* He searched her eyes. "God didn't cause the accident." He reached for her hand. "You know that, Ash."

"No." She pulled her fingers from his and looked at the wall again. "I don't know anything. Not anymore."

The sadness in the air hung heavy and real and paralyzing.

After another hour, Landon didn't know what else to do. He touched her shoulder. "I need to go." He was desperate for a way to connect with her. "Can . . . I pray for you?"

She turned and looked at him. "No, Landon. Please don't." Her eyes softened just the slightest bit. "I'm sorry." Tears filled her eyes. "This isn't your fault. I know that."

He wanted to take her in his arms, hold her and soothe his hand over her still-bandaged head until everything was okay. But something in her tone told him it wouldn't matter. Whatever he did.

And that single fact terrified him. What if she had changed for good? What if nothing was ever the same again?

Her father's words came back to him. *Give her time.* If she was going to open up to anyone, it would be him. Landon stood and touched her arm. "I'm not going anywhere, Ashley. We'll get through this."

"No." She shook her head. "Don't . . . don't come see me tomorrow." The anger in her voice was gone. But her expression told him her resolve was rock-solid.

Landon had no choice but to respect her wishes.

Though it about killed him, he gave her space. Waited for her to want him again. Every morning he would call the hospital and ask her nurse if he could come by. And every morning the answer was the same. No. She needed time. She wanted to be alone.

Two weeks later Ashley was discharged from the hospital. Her parents invited Landon over for a small welcome home dinner where he could see that Ashley could walk and talk and think and eat. But as with Landon's greatest fears, Ashley wasn't the same. Her heart kept beating, but the best part of her seemed to have died after the accident.

Landon kept his promise. He was still there. Still available for her, even now. But she wasn't interested. Not in him or his offer of friendship. Not in her family and their way of faith and life. Especially not in God.

And there wasn't a thing Landon could do about it.

He had spent enough time in the past. He stood and brushed the grass off his legs. The terrifying feeling of almost losing Ashley in that accident was something he would remember forever. But he'd never considered for a minute that after her surviving the ordeal, he would lose her anyway.

Not in a million years.

Landon finished his workout and headed home, only a few miles away. He found his parents in the kitchen working on breakfast, but he didn't linger. Instead he gave them a quick smile and headed for the shower. He didn't have the heart to tell them he was going to Kari

Baxter's wedding. Or that he was putting himself out there for Ashley one more time.

But that's what he was about to do. It was good practice for the life ahead of him. Rushing into a burning building.

Even when anyone in his right mind would be running out.

7

Between the storm and her conflicted heart, Kari had almost forgotten something. Today was her last day to call the Baxter house her home. After today she would wake up with Tim Jacobs. First in Alaska, and then in the house where he lived not far from the university.

Most of her things were already moved in. But some of the precious memories of her childhood and teenage years would remain. Here where they belonged. On the walls and in the closet of the bedroom she grew up in.

Now with her hair and makeup done, and with a few hours before she needed to get into her wedding dress, Kari made her way back to her room. She stepped inside and remembered what it felt like to see it for the first time. The day her family moved here from Michigan.

When they were younger, Kari and Ashley had shared the space and they had thought this bedroom fit for a pair of princesses. Tall ceilings and a picture window that spanned most of the far wall. Beneath it was a built-in padded bench. The place where Ashley and Kari had sat and laughed and cried and prayed over the years.

Kari glanced at the wedding dress still hanging on the door. But her hasty heart didn't linger there. Instead she walked to the closet and found a box of letters and photos that hadn't made the move to her new home. Precious memories she couldn't quite part with. She held the box and lowered herself to the floor.

Here, alone in her closet, time seemed to stand still. As if this wasn't the biggest day of her life, and she wasn't expected to show up at the wedding chapel later today. She opened the box and slid her hand toward the bottom. The feel of the envelope was something she knew by heart.

She'd read the letter that many times.

Ryan had scribbled her name across the front. *Kari girl*. Not Kari. Since the first week they met, Ryan had called her Kari girl. The name had taken hold, and once in a while her dad called her that, too. But the nickname would always belong to Ryan.

The edge of the envelope was worn, so she was careful opening it. As soon as the piece of paper was in her hands, she felt her heart jerk into a strange rhythm. *What am I doing?* She lowered the letter and shut her eyes tight. *Why are you doing this?*

Kari opened her eyes and unfolded the single sheet. Because she wanted to, that's why. This was her last day in her bedroom, and this letter was part of what she was leaving behind.

She held it up and let her eyes run over his familiar handwriting. *Ryan, why couldn't you tell me? If you had someone else, I would've been okay with it.* In time, anyway.

Instead he had sent her this letter.

Dozens of times she'd read his words, and each time they hit her the same way. She started at the beginning.

Dear Kari,

I've been home for a while, working every day to recover. The injury nearly paralyzed me, but then, I guess you know that. God gave me a miracle with the surgery, Kari. I have feeling in my feet and legs, and I'll be able to walk and run like before. The doctors say if I work hard enough I might even play again.

But you know what? None of that matters compared to getting through to you.

Every time I call, you don't answer. And no matter how hard I try, you won't talk to me. I drive by your house and see your car and all I want to do is stop. Talk to you. Have you explain to me what happened.

I seriously don't get it, Kari. I'm there in Chicago playing one of my best games ever and next thing I know I'm on the ground. I can't move. And you, Kari girl . . . you and your dad come to the hospital to see me.

That's where things get crazy. Because that night you were there, and in the morn-

*ing you were gone. Just like that. With no
conversation or explanation. And I'm left here
doing rehab ten hours a day trying to figure
it all out.*

So what happened? Why did you leave?

*The details keep running through my mind
but they never add up. All I know is you're
there, and I'm here. Stuck in Dallas trying
to get better and trying to understand why
we're not together.*

*Please, call me. Write to me. Tell me what I
did wrong. Whatever it is, I'm sorry. I can't
stop thinking about you. Honestly, I miss you
with every breath, Kari girl.*

*Love you always,
Ryan*

Tears slid onto her cheeks before Kari could stop
them. She dabbed at them with the bottom of her
T-shirt. Now she'd have to fix her makeup before she got
dressed. She sniffed and blinked her eyes. *Do not cry over
Ryan, Kari. Not today. Please, God, help me get a grip.*

She stared at the page and gradually her eyes dried. It
was one thing for Ryan to cheat on her, to have another
girl in his hospital room. But this letter? The whole page
of lies? As long as she lived Kari would never understand
why Ryan had done that.

Things were dead between them. Why try to breathe

life into it with these delusions? Of course she wouldn't talk to him. Did he really think she didn't know about the other girl? Wouldn't it have occurred to him when he realized that not one—but two—girlfriends had showed up at the hospital?

Kari guessed things hadn't worked out with the other girl. Otherwise Ryan would've given up long ago. And he wouldn't have said the things he did in the letter. He couldn't stop thinking about her? He missed her with every breath? And how dare he call her *Kari girl* now, when they both knew about his cheating.

Her eyes stung again, but she was done crying about Ryan Taylor. Since the day they met, Kari had known him to be honest. But clearly the NFL had changed him. Maybe he thought having a girl on the side was just a way of life. The old Ryan never would've felt like that. But this new Ryan, maybe he believed he could still be close to Kari and tell her he loved her and call her *Kari girl*.

All while he had other girls in the wings. Girls he didn't really care for.

Kari had heard of professional athletes who lived that way. She folded the letter and stuck it back in the envelope. Then she slid it again to the bottom of the box. If Ryan Taylor assumed Kari was okay with that sort of lifestyle, then he was gravely mistaken.

And he had changed even more than she thought.

She stood and put the box back on the shelf. Then she crossed her room and sat on the edge of her bed. Her eyes fell on her wedding dress again. It was so pretty. The gown practically screamed at her to put the past behind her. Today was about Tim. Her forever with the man she loved.

Which was maybe why it was so important to read Ryan's letter. So she could remind herself that those days were over. She could never leave Tim for someone who lied to her. Someone who had so completely betrayed her.

Kari looked around the room again. The fashion calendar on the wall near the closet—the one where she was both February and July. And the four framed photos on either side. Her three sisters and her at the lake, Kari and her parents at her high school graduation. And a couple pictures of all five kids when they were little.

Strange. No pictures of Tim and me. She let the thought go. After today there would be plenty. In her new home with her husband, and here, at this house. Her parents would find a perfect spot for their wedding photo. Somewhere near the one of Brooke and Peter, no doubt.

Yes, of course that would happen. As soon as they returned from their honeymoon.

Thunder cracked outside and the wind picked up. Kari stood and walked to the corkboard on the opposite wall. Mementos from college were still pinned there. Her report card from her freshman year at Indiana University. The handout someone had given her inviting her to the campus Bible study.

The place where she first met Tim.

Kari smiled. There it was. Proof that she loved Tim. Otherwise she wouldn't still have that slip of paper on her wall. She walked to the window. Was there really going to be a tornado today?

Please, no, Lord. Clear the weather. She thought for a moment. *Clear my heart first.* Again there was no response, no reassurance. This was ridiculous. She was making herself sick sitting up here, waffling between thoughts of Tim and Ryan. If she didn't stop, she'd talk herself out of getting married.

All because she was letting her mind get away from her.

Fresh air, that's what she needed. Never mind the storm outside—suddenly that was the only place she wanted to be. Where she could talk to God and clear her head. She hurried out of her room and skipped down the stairs toward the back of the house.

Brooke and Ashley were in the living room together and they both saw her at the same time. "Hey." Ashley spoke first. "Where are you going? You need to get ready."

"Outside. I'll get dressed later." Kari didn't stop to talk. She couldn't. Not until she had a firm grasp on the events of the day. Not until she was so excited there was no room to think about anything but Tim. She glanced over her shoulder. "I just need a minute to think."

Out of the corner of her eye Kari saw her sisters exchange a worried look. She didn't blame them. A little time outside and everything would be okay. "Go get ready! I'll be back in a bit."

She knew exactly where she was headed. The back porch swing, the one where she always went when she needed to be alone. She sat down and slid as far back as she could. A bolt of lightning lit up the distant sky. Her hair would be a mess after this wind. Her makeup, too. But it was worth it. Her mom could touch her up later. Right now she needed this.

For the first time since she woke up that morning, Kari drew a full breath. She set the swing in motion and looked at the clouds overhead. All day she'd been seeing the storm as a sign, proof that she was making the wrong decision. But now that she was here, with the humid summer air filling her lungs, she saw things differently.

Kari loved the Indiana storms. She always had.

No, she didn't want a tornado. But thunderstorms always made her feel closer to God. As if His majesty was so clearly on display she could do nothing but look to Him. Talk to Him. Lean into Him.

Yes, that's what this storm was all about. God's way of drawing her close on this, her special day. *Thank You, Lord. If the storm is a sign, I'll take it.* She settled back into the swing and thought about her groom.

Then without warning another memory took shape.

The time she and Tim had made choices they both regretted.

Anxiety ran through Kari's blood as that night played in her mind. She'd been back from New York City for two months, and she and Tim had been seriously dating for most of that time. That evening they had dinner in downtown Bloomington at Perry's Pizza.

Tim teased her that she could lighten up on her eating and have a few slices—since her modeling stint was over.

"Sure." She laughed. "For a week. The next one starts Monday."

She settled for a salad and after dinner they had planned to get coffee. Instead Tim talked her into watching a movie at his place. The house that would soon be her home.

She shouldn't have gone. They both knew better. In the early days of their relationship they had talked about never being at his house alone together. But that day Tim was extra flirty and Kari had felt impulsive. An hour into the movie they started kissing.

By the time they stopped, Kari was horrified at herself. More herself than Tim. They hadn't gone all the way, but they'd come close. "How did that . . . how did it happen?" She was still breathless as she turned to Tim.

"I'm sorry." He slid back, as if he wanted to distance himself from her. "It's my fault."

"No." Kari shook her head. "It was me, too." But there was truth to what Tim had said. Even if Kari didn't want to assign blame.

With Ryan, Kari had felt tempted more times than she could remember. But always Ryan found a way to keep them safe. He put up boundaries so they wouldn't do something they'd both regret.

That night at Tim's house, Kari felt a fear she'd never known with Ryan. A vulnerability. Like anything could happen, and if she wasn't careful she could become a single mother. Like Ashley.

When Tim realized how upset she was, he led her to the dining room, where he sat at the table across from her. He reached over and held her hands. "Kari, this won't happen again. I promise you."

"You have to mean it." Kari didn't trust Tim. Not in this area. After all, he was the one who had talked her into the movie. At his house. Alone.

That's when Tim said something that stayed with her, the reason this memory surfaced here and now. He looked intently at her. "After what we just did . . . it's a good thing I'm going to marry you someday."

At first Kari didn't track with him. "How is that good?"

"I mean . . . we're going to get married, anyway." Tim smiled at her, as if his logic gave them both a pass. "You wouldn't have let it go so far if you didn't want to marry me."

"Tim!" Kari wasn't sure whether to laugh or yell at him. "You're saying tonight was my fault? That's ridiculous."

"No." He was on his feet and around the table to her side in a matter of seconds. "Baby, no. Not at all. It was my fault." He took the seat beside her and cradled her face in his hands. "All I'm saying is . . . you love me more than you've ever loved anyone else. That's why things got out of hand."

Kari stared at the table. "I don't know."

And then Tim asked her something. "You . . . you've never done that before." He hesitated. "Right, Kari?"

"No." Kari was still mid-struggle. Still thinking about how they had let things go too far. Even if they hadn't lost control completely. And there Tim was, in a round-about way asking her about *Ryan?* She shook her head. "We . . . we never did more than kiss."

The weird thing was, Tim never said Ryan's name. She understood now, after being engaged to him. Talking about the specifics of Kari's past wasn't Tim's style.

Sure, when he first realized that Kari's longtime childhood love was Dallas Cowboys running back Ryan Taylor, Tim freaked out a little. He admitted he'd actually been a fan of Ryan's at one point.

And then he pretended to walk away, teasing her that it had been nice knowing her.

But that reaction had happened just one time.

After that he never brought Ryan up again. Never talked about Ryan's performance with the Cowboys, never asked Kari if she thought about him. Sure, Tim would refer to Kari's "past love" or her "younger days." But Tim avoided saying Ryan's name. As if he were too good to mention it.

Too good to be jealous over Ryan Taylor.

Kari took another deep breath. The memory made her feel dirty.

At the time, they were nowhere near being engaged. Tim's talking about marriage in light of what had happened between them had been manipulative. Whatever he had been thinking, if Kari found peace in his reasoning, it was short-lived. She could barely sleep for the next week.

A chill ran down her bare arms. Shock surged through her and made her feel sick. That wasn't why she was marrying Tim, right? Because they'd gone farther than they planned one night?

She shuddered at the thought. Absolutely not. She was marrying Tim for a hundred other reasons. Mostly because she loved him. Because he made her head spin with his lofty ideas and eloquent speech. And because he was loyal to her the way Ryan never had been.

As if on cue, at the thought of him, Kari heard Ryan's voice.

She put her feet on the porch floor and the swing stopped. Great. Now she was imagining things. She should've known. Spend enough time on her wedding day letting Ryan's name drift through her soul and she was bound to start hearing voices.

But then she heard it again. Not in her head, but coming from the front of the house. She had to remember to exhale. This couldn't be happening. For all the ways Ryan had torn her heart in two, he wouldn't dream of coming by her house on her wedding day.

Would he?

Kari turned in the swing and listened. As she did her heartbeat pounded in her throat. It was him. Ryan Taylor was here. She would know his tone anywhere. Not because they talked anymore, but because the sound of his voice was woven into her very being.

Dear God, what am I supposed to do? She held her breath and closed her eyes. Thunder shook the ground and she blinked. What was happening? Why was Ryan here? If anything could stir the doubts plaguing her today, it was the guy she had loved most of her life. Seeing him would put her over the edge. Because it would force her to do the one thing she never planned to do again.

Look into the gorgeous eyes of Ryan Taylor.

8

Ryan had to see her.

That's how the argument with himself had ended. Even if he wanted to stop himself, he couldn't keep from driving to Kari's and talking to her, seeing her one more time before she got married. Not that he could change her mind or convince her of his feelings for her. The feelings he still had. But because of something Ryan hadn't thought about before. By tonight she would no longer be Kari Baxter.

She would be Kari Jacobs.

And when Ryan let that reality hit him, he had no choice. He had to see her. The moment would be brief. He would congratulate her on her wedding day and tell her he wished only the best for her. He would be polite and friendly, keep things on the surface. But at least he could look into her eyes one more time.

His Kari girl.

At first he thought he'd take the path behind their houses and come through her backyard. But then . . . what if Tim were there? If things went poorly he would need a speedy exit. The last thing he wanted was to upset her.

Plus the rain was coming now, hard and steady.

He parked as close to the front of her house as he could and with his heart pounding in his throat he hurried through the pouring rain to the door. After a second knock, Kari's mother opened it and then for the longest few seconds she just stood there. Staring at him.

By then rain had soaked Ryan's T-shirt and jeans. It was dripping off his hair and face. For a moment, he wasn't sure if Mrs. Baxter was going to faint or let him in, but all at once she seemed to collect herself.

Her familiar smile found its place. "Ryan! You're drenched!" She ran her hand over her hair and opened the door wider. "I . . . we weren't expecting you."

"No." A quiet chuckle came from Ryan. "This didn't . . . I wasn't planning to come by." He hesitated. "Probably bad timing." He let their eyes hold and then he shrugged. Like a man out of options. "I had to see her, Mrs. Baxter. One more time."

Kari's mother stared at him for a few seconds. Then she nodded. "Okay." Her eyes glistened and she blinked. "Come in, Ryan. Please." She studied him. "I'll get you a towel."

"Thanks." A few steps inside and Ryan stopped. He touched Mrs. Baxter's arm. "Tim isn't . . . he isn't here, is he?"

"No. He's at the chapel with Kari's dad. The others . . . they're upstairs." She shook her head. Was that relief in her eyes? "Kari's out back. On the porch."

In all the years Ryan had known Kari's mother, the

woman had never looked like this. Shocked, maybe. Like she wasn't sure if he was actually standing there.

She sized him up again. "Wait here." She hurried off and returned with a worn blue bath sheet. By then Ryan was starting to take off his tennis shoes, but she shook her head. "Don't worry about the rain. These old wood floors have seen worse."

"All right." He took the familiar-looking towel and thanked her. How many times had he and Kari come in from the rain only to have Mrs. Baxter help them like this? Ryan ran the cloth over his face and body and handed it back to her. "Is it okay? Can I . . ."

"Yes, Ryan." She crossed her arms, as if she were suddenly cold. "Go to her."

The Baxter house was as familiar as his own. He made his way through the foyer, into the living room. Good that the others weren't around. This moment had the potential to be more than awkward.

He took the few steps through the kitchen and out back.

Water dripped down his face as he stepped onto the porch and shut the door behind him. And then—like a thousand times before—he turned and saw her. She was in sweats and a thin white shirt, but she looked stunning. Her hair and makeup ready for the big event. Sitting on the porch swing. The place where they had talked and laughed and looked at stars all those summer nights.

"Ryan? You're soaking wet." She was on her feet, fear clouding her pretty blue eyes. "What . . . why are you here?"

He came to her slowly. No way he wanted to frighten her, not now. The minutes were too precious. When he was a few feet away, she sat back down. As if the idea of a hug was out of the question.

For an instant he thought about taking the seat beside her. But that wouldn't do. Not based on her expression. He leaned against the porch railing and faced her. Never mind the rain still hitting the back of his neck. At the same moment, thunder clapped overhead and the downpour grew loud against the porch roof.

He glanced over his shoulder and then back at her. "Nice weather." He raised his eyebrows and gave her a goofy grin. One that had always made her smile.

Kari clearly wanted to stay serious, angry even. She had a right. He hadn't even asked permission to be here. But something in his tone or his silly expression must've caught her off guard because her laughter came and like that the air between them was easy again.

The way it had always been—right up until his injury.

"Okay." She exhaled. "You're crazy, Ryan Taylor, you know that?"

"I've been told." He laughed, too. And if only for these precious seconds they were the same as before. Kari and Ryan. Together again.

"Here." She patted the spot beside her. "Sit down. Out of the rain."

Ryan held his breath as he sat beside her. So close he could smell her shampoo, feel her arm against his. He slid over some, giving her room. "I'm sorry."

"Yeah." She turned so she could see him. "You should be. It's my wedding day." With one hand she gave an exaggerated wave at the sky. "And clearly the weather is on my side."

They both laughed again and the familiarity of it felt better than Ryan had ever dreamed. But he didn't have long. He had something to say and now was the time. "I shouldn't be here. I know that." He allowed himself to get serious again. The rain let up just enough so he didn't have to raise his voice. "Today . . . it's the last day you'll be Kari Baxter."

Tears filled her eyes and she nodded. "Yes."

"And I guess . . ." His wet shirt stuck to his skin and he brushed a few raindrops from his eyelashes. "I couldn't miss the chance to say goodbye."

Kari closed her eyes and tears slid down her cheeks. When she opened them she let out a sound that was more cry than laugh. "My makeup doesn't stand a chance around you."

And there it was, just like that. Kari might not have meant to tell him, but she had. Her feelings for him were still there. Otherwise she wouldn't be crying. Ryan reached out and with the gentlest touch he caught her next few tears. "What a bad friend." His voice was soft, for her alone. "Making you cry on your wedding day."

"Ryan . . ." She searched his eyes. "I can't do this." His fingers were still on her face, and she removed them, easing his hand back down to his side.

Without thinking he caught her hand in his. In a

move as familiar as his own heartbeat, he eased his fingers between hers. She didn't pull away. As long as he
lived he would remember that single fact.

On Kari's wedding day when he took hold of her
hand . . . she let him.

The feel of her skin against his took his breath.
Ryan worked to press on, to say what he'd come to tell
her. He ran his thumb over her hand, his eyes never
leaving hers. "I don't know what happened between us."
He searched her pretty face. "After all this time, I still
don't know."

The fear was back in her face, but even so she didn't
let go of his hand. "It's too late. This isn't the time, Ryan."

"It's all the time I have." He slid closer. Lightning
split the sky over the rolling hills, but he barely noticed.
He could think of only her. "I'm not trying to . . . change
your mind or make today more difficult."

Her expression eased. "I know." She cast a quick look
at the door and then back at him. "Tim's coming by. He
could be here any minute."

"Mmm." Ryan wanted to scream. Couldn't she see
the way they both still felt for each other? Why was she
marrying some other guy when she was holding *his*
hand? Instead he nodded. "I'll make it quick."

"Please." She blinked back fresh tears. "I can't believe
this is happening."

"Bad timing." He worked to get hold of her eyes
again. "My fault."

"You think?" Now the sound that came from her was

more of a laugh. "Ryan! This is the last thing I should be doing."

Get to the point, he told himself. *Hurry.* "What I'm trying to say is, I'm sorry." He shifted so he was looking straight at her. Then as easily as he drew his next breath he took hold of her other hand. "Whatever happened, I'm sorry."

"I know." Kari hung her head. Her laughter faded, as if the weight of all this was really too much. She seemed to stare at the place where their hands were joined. "I read your letter." She sniffed again. "Too many times."

"You did?" *Too many times?* Ryan felt his heart rate double. "Then why . . . why didn't you call me?"

"Because . . ." She lifted her eyes to his again. "It doesn't matter now, Ryan. What you did, what happened. It's too late."

"Okay . . ." What did she mean? Of course it mattered! That's why he was here. Either way she didn't seem like she was going to explain herself. Ryan grabbed a quick breath. "Then I have a question for you." His words came faster. He knew she had to go, had to get into her wedding dress. He looked all the way through her, to her heart. "Do you love him? Are you in love with him?"

For the briefest seconds, Kari hesitated. A hesitation that screamed louder than anything she might say in response. Then she seemed to catch herself. She nodded, even as tears slid down her cheeks. "I am. Of course." She squinted through her tears. "I want to marry him, Ryan. Yes."

Nothing had ever hurt more than hearing those words. Ryan straightened. "Okay, then." He smiled at her, for all that they had once been. "That's what I needed to hear."

There was a sound at the back door and they both turned to see him.

Tim Jacobs. Kari's groom.

Anger flashed on Tim's face, and just as quickly it was gone. "Ryan Taylor. I believe your visit with my bride has gone on long enough, don't you think?"

He was out of time. Ryan stared into Kari's eyes once more and then before he could stop himself he lifted her hand to his lips and kissed it. Tim was coming for them now, but Ryan didn't care. He gave Kari's hands three squeezes, their longtime signal. A way to say *I love you.*

Then with his voice barely more than a whisper he said it. The only words that mattered. "I love you, Kari girl." He felt tears in his own eyes. "I love you."

With all the effort he'd ever needed, Ryan did the one thing he didn't want to do. He released Kari's hands and stood. He gave her the slightest grin and his familiar wink as he turned away. Then he forced a smile at her groom. "Hello, Tim." He stuck out his hand. "I'll be leaving now."

"Good thing." Tim shook it. His voice dropped, but it was deep with thinly veiled rage. "Stay away from my bride."

"Yeah." Ryan was almost to the door. He looked back. "Speaking of which . . . I thought it was bad luck to see the bride before the wedding?"

His eyes caught Kari's once more and then he walked inside. Again the house looked empty. Something he would remain forever thankful for. No one else had to know about this encounter.

On his way to the front door Mrs. Baxter came toward him. "Ryan? Is everything . . . is she okay?"

"She is. She's with Tim." Ryan could feel his tears building. He stopped as Kari's mother reached for him, and he took hold of her hand. "Thank you. For this."

"Tim found you?" A mild panic crossed her face. "Oh, dear. Is . . . ?"

"The wedding?" Ryan could only guess that was what Mrs. Baxter was talking about. "It's on." He gave her a quick hug. "Thanks again." He nodded. "Goodbye."

"Goodbye, Ryan." She stood at the door and watched him leave.

Rain was falling harder as he made his way to his truck. And in the distance the coming clouds were darker than earlier that morning. Ryan gave the sky a long look and then slid behind the wheel.

Only now—as he started the engine—he wasn't leaving Kari behind for the last time. He was fourteen and seeing her for the *first* time. He was sweaty and tanned, a football tucked under his arm, and she was the prettiest twelve-year-old he'd ever seen and he was promising himself that someday . . . someday when she grew up he'd take her on a date. And she was sixteen and he was carrying a dozen red roses up her front steps and making good on his promise.

Ryan backed out of her driveway, his breaths coming fast and hard. Tears clouded his vision but that didn't stop him from remembering clearly. They were sitting side by side under the summer stars in the bed of his father's truck . . . and he was feeling his fingers brush against hers. "You're my best friend, Kari girl, you know that?"

And she was giggling and looking over at him, the moon shining in her eyes. "And you're mine, Ryan."

And she was beside him and he was taking her to his senior football banquet, the one that kicked off the season. And she was in her cheerleading uniform on the sidelines and he was running across the goal line and while all his team was shouting and celebrating, he was looking at her.

Always and only at her.

And she was smiling at him as the band played on.

Then he was signing a contract while a hundred lights flashed in his face and his heart was racing because, Dallas? That far away from Kari? But they were talking and laughing and he was telling himself everything would be okay. It had to be okay. She would graduate and he would marry her and they would never spend a day apart again.

Then the hit and he was lying on the ground and all he wanted, all he would ever want, was to look into her eyes again. One more time. And he was in an ambulance, his mother at his side, and everyone was talking at the same time.

Oxygen. Vital signs. Start the IV. *Move your toes, Ryan. Come on, move your toes.* And he couldn't. No matter how hard he tried he couldn't but somehow he knew if she were here, if she were the one asking him, then just maybe . . .

And he was in the hospital trapped in metal and bars and ropes and his mother was giving him the only news that mattered. *Kari's here. Her father brought her.*

Peace overcame him. He could figure out the rest, but if Kari was here then everything was going to be okay. And he was smiling and praying and believing. This was a road bump, but it wasn't going to stop the two of them. He would walk again and he would hold Kari again and all of life would be just like he'd always dreamed.

Like the two of them planned.

And then it was morning and he was awake and the expression on his mother's face was the saddest of all. *She's gone, Ryan. I . . . I'm sorry, she didn't say goodbye.*

Then suddenly the room was spinning and nothing made sense. Ryan tried to sit up, tried to swing his legs onto the floor so he could run after her, but he couldn't move. They'd operated on him and he was in some sort of contraption that wouldn't let him do anything but call her name. "Kari!" The sound was frail and then it grew louder. "Kari girl! Where are you?"

And suddenly the reel of memories came to a stop.

Tears spilled and mixed with the rain on his face as he put the truck in gear and pulled onto the road. As he drove away he glanced back at her house once more. The Baxter house. His words came in a broken whisper. "Bye, Kari girl."

No matter how things ended later today, one thing would always be sure. He didn't believe her. The idea that she loved Tim and wanted to marry him. How could Ryan believe her?

The two of them were still holding hands when Tim walked up, after all.

Either way, there was no changing the ending. What they shared had been over for a long time. Years, really. But after today there was no looking back. He hadn't set out to change her mind, but deep down he had hoped that maybe . . . like some Hollywood-movie ending . . . she might've explained what happened.

The feelings between them would be good again and she would hug his neck and he would kiss her. And if Tim walked in on them, so be it. Because Kari had found the one she really loved. And that would be him—Ryan Taylor—forevermore.

But it hadn't worked out like that. This was real life, and Ryan hadn't gotten the girl. He'd lost her for all time, and he still didn't know why. But at least he'd done the thing he'd set out to do. Before it was too late. Before she changed her name.

He'd shared one last moment with Kari Baxter.

9

Elizabeth's heart beat in double time as she shut the door and hurried to the back porch. What had just happened? What was Ryan thinking, coming here, talking to Kari on her wedding day?

And now Tim was with her.

The weather was growing worse by the minute, and Elizabeth's bad feelings about the day were coming true. She stepped out onto the porch and saw them, Tim standing in front of Kari, and Kari sitting on the swing.

The tension was thicker than the humid air around them.

"Hello." Elizabeth wasn't sure they saw her.

They both turned her way and nodded. Kari spoke first. "Everything's fine, Mom."

"It's great, actually." Tim grinned and gave a single clap of his hands. "Where's Dr. Baxter?"

"At the chapel. With the other guys." Elizabeth worked to keep from showing her confusion. "I thought you were meeting them there."

"I am." He turned to Kari. "I wanted to stop by here first. Give my bride a kiss and make sure the weather didn't have her too upset. Apparently it's a good thing I did."

Elizabeth winced. Every word Tim said felt like it was dripping in disapproval. She watched him bend down and kiss Kari on the lips. "Maybe stand. So you can hug me."

Kari scrambled to her feet. "I'm sorry." She glanced at her mother, as if all of this was beyond embarrassing. Her words were a stifled cry. "You have to believe me. I didn't know he was coming!"

None of this seemed real. Elizabeth wasn't sure if she should go back inside or stick it out here on the porch. The whole scene was a nightmare.

"Don't worry about it, Kari." Tim initiated the hug and as he drew back he smiled at her. "Everything's fine. Go get ready." He kissed her again. "Oh . . . and stay away from that Ryan Taylor." Tim shot Elizabeth a look and then turned to Kari again. "Somehow . . . I don't think he has your best interest in mind."

With that, Tim backed up. "See you at the church." He nodded to Kari and then to Elizabeth as he passed by. "I'll let myself out."

When he was gone, Elizabeth and Kari stayed in their places, as if they were too afraid to move. Too shocked to say a single word.

Elizabeth breathed out. She needed to make things right here. If that were even possible. "Kari." She walked over and took her daughter in her arms. "I should've sent him away. I'm sorry."

They sat down on the swing and Kari stared at her hands. They were trembling. "I heard his voice before he came out here." She turned and looked at Elizabeth.

"I wasn't sure what to do." Elizabeth put her hand on Kari's slim shoulder. "He wanted to see you so badly."

"I know. It's not your fault." Kari's cheeks had tearstains on them and her eye makeup was smudged. Clearly she was still stunned by what had just happened. "I can't believe it. That he would come here." She hesitated. "Today."

Elizabeth wasn't sure if she should ask, but she had to know. Earlier Kari had said she had no doubts about marrying Tim. But after seeing Ryan . . . had things changed? Was her heart torn? Elizabeth had to find out now. Before she ran out of time. "What did he say?"

Kari took a slow breath just as thunder cracked around them. "Look at this weather." She shook her head and then stared at her engagement ring. "Don't worry. He didn't try to change my mind. That's not why he came."

"Okay." Elizabeth didn't want to rush her. Whatever had gone on, Kari would tell her. The two of them had always been close.

"He asked me about that day. At the hospital. He wanted to know what happened. Like he still didn't get it." Confusion came over her expression. "How could he ask that?"

"Maybe he really doesn't know. Maybe you—" Elizabeth stopped herself. They'd had this conversation before. No reason to go over it again now. When she was hours from walking down the aisle.

"He knows." Kari stood and walked to the porch rail. She looked out, her face to the clouds. "Is this a sign, Mom?" She turned and stared at Elizabeth. "This terrible weather?" She slumped back down on the swing. "I mean, tornadoes are in the forecast right about the same time as I'm supposed to say 'I do.'"

Elizabeth steadied herself. Enough of the doom and gloom. "The weather isn't anything to worry about, Kari. If God has been giving you signs all along, then that could be something." She looked intently at her daughter. "He wouldn't wait till your wedding day to give you colossal proof that Tim's the wrong guy."

Again Kari stared at her diamond solitaire ring. "True." She lifted her eyes to Elizabeth. "I love Tim. I really do." She shook her head. "Ryan can't expect me to act like nothing happened that day at the hospital. He knows about the other girl. Obviously. And by now he must've figured out that I know, too."

"Yes." Elizabeth nodded. "You're right." But she still wondered if there hadn't been some kind of mistake, a mix-up that could be explained if only Kari would confront him directly about the other girl. "Did you . . . ask him? About her?"

"Mother!" Kari slid to the far edge of the swing and crossed her arms. "Of course not! What would it matter now? I'm getting married today."

That was it then. Elizabeth drew a slow breath. "So

you're still sure? About marrying Tim?" She paused. "Ryan didn't change that?"

Kari ran her fingertips over her face. "My makeup's a mess. I can feel it. My hair, too."

"I'll help you fix it." Elizabeth waited. "Sweetheart . . . are you going to answer me?"

A loud breath came from Kari. "I love Ryan Taylor, Mom. I always will." Her voice cracked. "But he's all wrong for me. There." She waited a few seconds. "Is that what you wanted to hear?"

"Honey." She took Kari's hand again. "I'm not trying to upset you. But it's a question you have to answer. Now." She kept her tone gentle. "Before you go slip into that dress."

"I already told you." Kari seemed to force herself to be calm. "I love Tim."

Elizabeth wanted to be clear. "I didn't ask if you love him." She angled her head. She cared so much for Kari. *Lord, let her hear me. So she doesn't make a mistake today.* She sighed. "I asked if you were still sure about marrying him."

"Yes." Kari leaned over and kissed Elizabeth's cheek. Then she stood and took a deep breath. "Rain or tornadoes, I'm getting married today, Mother. I'm going to have you fix my hair and makeup. Then I'll take that gorgeous gown to the bridal room and you and the girls can help me get dressed." She smiled. "I'm marrying Tim Jacobs today. I'm sure."

With all her being, Elizabeth wished she could believe her daughter's seemingly forced enthusiasm. Because at this point she had no other choice. "Okay." Elizabeth stood and hugged Kari again. "I'll come help you in a minute."

"You have to get ready, too." Kari seemed to work up a bigger smile. "The limo will be here in a few hours."

Kari walked inside and Elizabeth sat down again and breathed. Just breathed. She didn't want to push her daughter, didn't want to probe and pick, looking for a different answer. The problem was obvious. Kari's eyes had looked entirely different when she talked to Ryan than they had when Tim showed up.

Wasn't it worth a longer conversation between Kari and Ryan? Elizabeth had been hoping for that—praying for it—since the incident at the hospital. But Kari was too hurt to ask questions. *What was the point?* Her daughter always said Ryan's actions had done all the speaking.

And now . . . well, if Kari was convinced she was supposed to marry Tim, then that was that. *I just wish I believed her, Lord.* Elizabeth stood and exhaled. Then without waiting another minute she headed back into the house.

Kari was right. Elizabeth needed to get ready.

She was about to be mother of the bride.

•   •   •

JOHN HAD BEEN at the university wedding chapel since before lunch. After his conversation with Elizabeth, he had taken a quick shower and he and Luke had grabbed their tuxes and set out.

"Don't worry," he had called out to Elizabeth before he left. "Everything's going to be okay. The storm will pass."

The wind picked up outside and rattled the window of the small room where John and Luke were finally getting ready. He glanced at the sky. Famous last words. Then he turned to the wide mirror on the opposite wall. He and Luke were dressed except for their jackets and bow ties.

John stood next to his son as they both worked to get their looks just right. "It's whipping out there." He shook his head. "At least there aren't any tornado sirens."

"Not yet, anyway." Luke rolled his eyes. "I imagine those will come during the vows."

The air in the room was tense, something rare for the two of them. John let Luke's attitude slide. Instead he ran through his personal checklist for the day. What else had to be done? So far he had directed the rental company where to set up tables and chairs and he'd talked to the caterers about the best spots for the various food and drink stations. Salad and side dishes. Prime rib and chicken.

And of course the cake table.

John thought hard about the things Elizabeth had asked him to handle. He had it all written down in the pocket of his rain jacket. Better to go by the list. He found the piece of paper and looked it over. Yes, he'd paid the florists and pianist and band. He still needed to connect with Pastor Mark about final logistics for the ceremony.

"How's this?" Luke turned to him. His tall blond son looked striking in the dark gray tux. "Is the bow tie right?"

"Bow ties were never my expertise." John set the list down and went to Luke. "I'd say it looks perfect." His was still hanging around his neck. "Maybe you can help me with mine."

Luke smiled. "You're just trying to make me feel good." He checked his own tie in the mirror. "I think mine's a little crooked."

They worked together until they were both happy with their outfits. John glanced at his watch. "Tim should be here any minute."

"Yeah." Luke took one of the chairs. "He's half an hour late from what he said yesterday at the rehearsal."

"Wedding days can be like that."

"True." Luke nodded. "Tim's a good guy. He'll be here."

At least Luke was in favor of Kari marrying Tim. The guy needed a few allies in the family.

"I will say." Luke raised one eyebrow. "I think Kari's getting married too soon. I'd never get married so young."

Here we go. John forced himself to smile. "She's out of college, Son. Not like she's nineteen."

"Still . . . you won't find me marrying this young."

Luke looked at the mirror again. "I have dreams to chase, places to see." He held up his hands. "No one's going to tie me down for a long time."

That was it, the end of the conversation. Another monologue proving Luke's obsession with himself. John didn't want to defend young weddings. Tim would walk through the door any minute. No point talking about this now.

John took the nearest chair and remembered something else. "Hey, so Cole's first birthday is next weekend. After Kari and Tim get back from their honeymoon. Sunday afternoon." He paused. "Just wanted to make sure you have it on your calendar."

At first Luke only sighed and didn't say a word. The look in his eyes told John this new topic was even more frustrating than the last.

"You are going, right?" John folded his hands and leaned over his knees. "We'll all be there."

This time there wasn't a trace of humor in Luke's laugh. "Really, Dad? Cole won't know we're throwing him a party. He's just a baby."

"He's your nephew." John didn't mind the sharpness in his voice. Luke hadn't treated Ashley the same since last spring when she came home from Paris pregnant. "And she's your sister. I'd like you to at least make an effort, Luke."

"Come on, Dad, the party is for Ashley. Not Cole." He was on his feet again. "And why would we throw a party for her? She's . . ." He seemed to realize how loud he was talking. His voice fell a few levels. "She's a terrible mother, Dad. She leaves Cole at your house all the time and stays out late with friends."

"Luke, that's—"

"No . . . please, let me finish." He turned toward the window and for a long minute the two of them watched lightning split the sky. When Luke looked back at him, his eyes held more pain than accusation. "Don't you see, Dad? She made a mockery of our family. She goes to Paris and gets pregnant? By a married man?" Disgust colored Luke's words. "And now we're supposed to gather round and throw her a party?"

John felt like he'd been kicked in the leg. "Ashley made a mistake. She knows it. We all know it." He stood and crossed the room. "We don't judge each other in this family. We forgive and move on. We show the grace of God to people like Ashley." He hesitated. "The grace God showed each of us."

"Yeah, Dad, I know all about grace." Luke crossed his arms. "You think Ashley's learned her lesson? She stays out all night with people we don't know. Half the days she leaves Cole with you. So she can *paint.*"

Luke rose and paced to the window. "She doesn't go to church with us, and for all you know she doesn't even believe in God." He turned and looked at John. "And don't blame the accident." His tone was loud again and there was a catch in his voice. "My best friend died in that accident. For what? So Ashley could waste her life and leave her kid with you and Mom every day?"

"Son." John took a seat at a small table in the corner of the room. "Sit down. We need to talk." John had always suspected Luke's distance toward Ashley was motivated by the accident. Because he lost his friend Jefferson that day.

"I'm just saying." Luke did as he was asked. When he was seated he looked straight at John. "She should be living the best life anyone ever tried to live. Because Jefferson traded his existence for hers. If he could see her now I'm not sure he would've jerked the wheel."

The reality of Luke's pronouncement hung in the room. "Son . . ." John ached for Luke. But what he was implying was wrong. "You'd rather have *her* dead than him? That's what you're saying."

Luke groaned. "No. I don't want that." He leaned back in his seat. "Of course not." He stared at the ground for a while. Finally he lifted his eyes to John's again. "I just mean . . . there's Landon Blake. One of the best guys on the planet, Dad. I mean, really. And the poor guy never gives up on her. It'll be Ashley for Landon till the day he dies."

John understood Luke's frustration on this point. "She's very stubborn."

"Yeah." Luke took a few breaths. Probably to calm himself. "Landon doesn't care what Ashley's done or who she's become. He'll be here today, same look on his face." He shrugged. "It's just . . . you'd think my sister might notice that. Landon Blake is the best thing that ever happened to her. And one of these days, if she doesn't figure it out, he'll be gone."

Luke had barely finished speaking when the door opened. Tim stepped in wearing a black tuxedo, and with him were four guys dressed in the same gray tuxes John and Luke wore. "Here you two are! We were looking for you." Tim couldn't have smiled any bigger if he tried. He walked up to John. "Big day, huh! It's finally here."

"Yes." John was on his feet. Luke, too. "Big day!"

"Congratulations." Luke was trying. None of the guys would've guessed his foul mood from just a minute ago.

The three of them shook hands and then Tim motioned for the other groomsmen to join them in the small room. When they were all gathered, Tim introduced his friends.

"Surprised to see Tim so bright-eyed today." One of the guys slapped Tim on the back. "Last night was a late one."

Last night? John felt his heart drop to his knees. "After the rehearsal?" He and Luke hadn't been told about any bachelor party.

The look on Tim's face made it clear he hadn't planned to talk about whatever had kept him and the guys out so late. Tim gave his buddy a light shove. "Joe's the wild one. Not me."

"Yeah, but you—"

"Thanks, Joe." Tim chuckled and gave the guy a rougher shove this time. "What're you trying to do? Get the wedding called off?"

The guys all laughed and a few of them gave Tim hearty slaps on his shoulders and back. Tim was still

smiling. "Go on now, get out of here. Do your groomsmen thing, whatever that is."

Joe led the way out of the room talking about pop
cans and finding Tim's car. Luke seemed unsure what to
do, but then Tim motioned to the door. "Luke . . . go
hang with them. They want to get to know you."

John knew what Tim meant. He wanted a few minutes with John. Alone time to undo the damage done in
the previous conversation. When the others were gone,
Tim gave him a quick look. "Joe's a clown. He didn't
mean it."

A lecture wasn't something John intended to give his
future son-in-law. Not today. But the insinuation hung
like so many knives in the room. John cleared his throat.
"Is it true? You all went out last night? After the rehearsal?"

"We did." Tim gave a single laugh, but the sound was
much weaker now. "It was Joe's idea." Tim raised an invisible glass. "You know . . . one last night of freedom.
That sort of thing."

"Actually . . . I don't know." John remained standing.
He didn't want this talk to last much longer. "When I
married Elizabeth, she was all I could think about. I
didn't need any . . . last night of freedom."

Something in John's tone must've gotten Tim's
attention. Because he straightened up and his smile
faded. "Nothing happened, if that's what you're asking. It
was just the guys hanging out. Nothing else."

Nothing happened? John felt his heart skip a beat.

Why did Tim even feel the need to say that? The whole thing felt sketchy now. He narrowed his eyes at the young professor. "You love my daughter, Tim?"

"I do." He sounded breathless now, like he was in trouble and he knew it. "I love her with my whole life. I'll make her the happiest girl in the world, Dr. Baxter. I promise."

Tim's words seemed to come from a clearly apologetic heart. When John didn't say anything, Tim continued. "I've asked God to help me be the man Kari needs. And my goal is to put her first in everything I do. Always."

John nodded. "It's okay, Tim." He studied the man. "Save that for the vows. Right now I have to get going." He pointed out the window where a long black limo had pulled up. "Luke and I are going with the driver to get the girls."

Tim shook his hand again. "Sounds good." His palm was sweaty and he wiped it on his black tux pants. "I meant what I said."

"I hope so." John's eyes found Tim's again and held. "Kari deserves your best."

"She does." Tim walked with him to the door of the chapel and handed John an umbrella. "The rain's still coming down."

Not until John and Luke were in the limo and halfway back to his house was he able to sort through his array of feelings. Whatever Joe the groomsman had been referring to, John didn't like it. And he didn't like the way Tim had talked about a last night of freedom. Or the way he defended his love for Kari. In quick bursts and rushed sentences.

Like he was guilty of something.

Which John hoped was not true.

But it wasn't only Tim's strange behavior. There was something else scraping against John's heart. He peered out the limo window as they pulled up to the Baxter house.

He was about to escort his daughter Kari to the chapel, about to walk her down the aisle toward Tim Jacobs, and place her precious hand in his. About to watch her change her name.

And all he could think about was the baby girl he'd held in his arms that day at the hospital, the day she was born. His Kari. He could see her riding her pink tricycle with the streamers and heading off for her first day of kindergarten. Back then, when they were raising their family, he and Elizabeth talked weekly about how quickly time passed.

How the little kids at the table looked less little all the time. Especially his four daughters. "I'll never make it through their weddings," he used to tell Elizabeth.

He still wasn't sure he would. The limo pulled up to the house and John sighed. He'd done this before, of course. With Brooke a few years ago. But no matter how many times he was father of the bride, one thing was sure.

Giving his daughters away wasn't only something he'd spent a lifetime dreading.

It was the hardest thing he'd ever do.

10

Ashley zipped up Brooke's dress in the makeshift bridal room and next to them Kari was helping Erin. It was almost time to head to the chapel. Outside a steady rain still fell, but the storm was between sets. For the first time all day they could work without the sound of thunder.

Erin looked over her shoulder at Kari. "These are such pretty dresses." Her smile was the sweetest ever. "You picked the perfect shade of pink."

"Thanks." Kari stepped back and looked at the three of them. "I don't think it's the dresses, though. It's my beautiful sisters wearing them."

The mood was lighter than before, and Ashley was glad. There was nothing any of them could do to change things now. Kari was going to marry Tim, for better or worse. "It's your turn." Ashley grinned at Kari. "Let's get that wedding gown on you."

"Yes." Kari's eyes were shining. A vast improvement from how she'd looked when she joined them half an hour ago. Her makeup had been redone and Mom had helped her fix her hair.

Whatever had made Kari cry, Ashley wasn't sure. She'd find out later. It didn't really matter, as long as Kari was happy now.

"Hello, everyone!" The photographer, Daisy, found them and immediately she threw her arms in the air. "Okay, beautiful bridesmaids!" She did a little scream and set her camera bag down. "These are going to be the best photos!"

Daisy directed them through a series of poses. The girls fussing over each other's dresses, and then the three of them helping Kari into her gown.

"Nice and slow!" Daisy's energy could fuel a fleet of cars. "We don't want makeup on that bright white lace."

Ashley and her sisters buttoned up the back of Kari's bodice. And when she turned around, Ashley's breath caught in her throat. "Kari!" She touched the pretty skirt. "You look . . . stunning."

A few more photos of the sisters preening and prepping around Kari and then Daisy waved them off. "Someone get your parents. I need pictures of them with Kari before we can move on."

Just as Ashley was about to find her mother, she heard her baby crying. Then her mother's voice coming from the living room. "Ashley? Cole needs a bottle, honey. I have to finish getting ready."

"Sorry." Ashley checked the time on the kitchen clock as she hurried past. Actually Cole had needed a bottle an hour ago. But she'd been busy, so this would have to do. She grabbed the can of formula and in ten seconds she had a warm bottle, ready to go.

Nursing had never been Ashley's thing. Her body didn't adjust to it. Six weeks was all she could handle, and then she moved on. Since she was out a lot, painting or with friends, the powdered formula had been super convenient.

Ashley carried the bottle to the living room and took Cole and his blanket from her mother. "Shh, baby, it's okay. Mommy's here."

"Ashley . . . can I talk to you?" Her mother had looked worried all day. Whatever was on her mind, it clearly wasn't good.

"Sure." Ashley bounced a little as she put Cole on her hip. "Everything okay?"

Her mother sighed. "I don't know. I hope so." She bit her lip. "Your father says Luke's in one of his moods. I'm just asking if you can please . . . be nice to him today. So nothing happens."

Ashley felt her heart begin to pound. "Me? You want *me* to be nice?" Cole started to cry again. "Shh, Cole. It's okay." Ashley kissed the side of her baby's face and glared at her mom. "I'm not the problem here, Mother. Luke is the problem."

"I know . . . I'm just asking if—"

"Ask Luke." Heat built up in Ashley's cheeks. How could the situation with her brother be her fault? "He's the one who barely talks to me, the one ashamed of me ever since I came home. And what about Cole?" She worked to keep her tone even. So her baby wouldn't get more upset. "Luke hasn't held Cole once. Did you know that?"

Her mother froze. "Ashley . . . you've never told me that."

"Why bother?" She ran her hand along the back of Cole's head. "He's the golden boy. I'm the black sheep. Why should he even care about Cole?"

"That's enough." Her mother took a step back. "You and Luke need to work this out. Your father and I won't have the two of you acting this way toward each other."

As her mother started to leave, Cole cried louder and held his arms out to her. Not to Ashley. As if he wanted her mother—not her—to feed him his bottle. Her mother didn't seem to notice as she headed upstairs to finish getting ready.

"Well, little Cole, sorry to tell you." Ashley sat in the glider and gave her son the bottle. She positioned the blanket over her dress so it would catch any drips. "Looks like you're stuck with me."

Ashley set the glider in motion. Her little boy's eyes met hers and Ashley felt a twinge of guilt. "Mommy's just kidding." She kissed his velvety soft forehead. "I know you love me."

Cole never blinked, never looked away. As if he were telling her not to leave him so much, not to pass on the job of raising him the way she did too often. Or maybe he was only confused. They were here at the Baxter house, so why was Ashley here, too?

Whatever it was, Ashley felt herself relax. Moments like this she loved being a mom. She might even be good at it someday, the way her mother had always been. She nuzzled her cheek against his. "I love you, Cole. I'm try-ing to be a good mommy," she whispered near his face, brushing his nose with hers while he drank. "Do you know that, baby? I really do love you?"

Cole gradually closed his eyes and his sucking slowed. What had she done to deserve such a precious little boy? If God was real, then He should've struck her dead long before Cole was even conceived. That's what she deserved.

He never should've let her survive the accident.

Ashley closed her eyes and the memories returned.

Not long after the accident, Ashley had suddenly known what she was going to do with some of her settle-ment money.

She was going to move to Paris.

It had been her dream since she was in fourth grade, and now she would have the finances to make it a reality. If Jefferson were alive, that's what he would tell her to do. Why be some second-rate painter in a community college art class when she could take her talent to Paris and become a legitimate artist?

Jefferson had lost his chance to pursue his dreams. But Ashley's were just beginning.

The next week she had talked to her art professor about the idea. The woman was thrilled with the possi-bility. "I have an artist friend with a flat in Paris. She has a bedroom she rents cheap to art students. I'll call her to-night and check her availability."

When the class met again, the teacher had good

news. Her friend could take Ashley, in January, middle of what would've been her sophomore year. Not only that, but the friend would arrange for Ashley to work at a local art gallery.

The news was more than Ashley could wrap her mind around. She had stared at her teacher and grinned. "Please." Ashley had been breathless, her head spinning. "Tell your friend I accept. I'll be there in January."

And just like that Ashley's dream became a reality. She told her parents her decision that night. Told them . . .didn't ask them. "I'm moving to Paris. I already have a room lined up."

Her mother's face went pale. "Ashley . . .what will you do in Paris?" Her voice was more concerned than kind. "What about school?"

"I don't need school to learn how to paint, Mother." Ashley could feel the defiance in her eyes. "I'll be working at an art gallery." She lifted her head. "I'll learn from the best."

That night and dozens that followed, her parents tried to talk sense into her. Finally, they had a family meeting and they asked Ashley to tell her siblings what she was about to do. Ashley had kept the conversation brief. "I'm for sure going. I won't change my mind . . .Mom and Dad thought you should know."

There had been silence around the room for a minute or so. Then Erin spoke in a quiet voice. "I wish you'd stay." She blinked a few times. "I'll miss you."

Luke was sixteen and not a fan of Ashley's move

from that very first moment. "You're just trying to hurt us." He muttered the words.

"Luke." Her dad had caught Luke's tone. "Ashley is figuring out her life. She isn't trying to hurt anyone."

That's when her brother's voice got louder. "Yes, she is. Ever since the accident!" He glared at Ashley. "We didn't do anything to you, Ashley. Why are you acting so different?"

At that, Ashley had stormed out of the room. Kari had found her a little while later. "I'm happy for you."

She'd sat on the edge of Ashley's bed. "If this is what you want." She had reached for Ashley's hand. "You always dreamed about seeing the Eiffel Tower."

"Yes." Ashley had never been more thankful for Kari. "You're right."

Only one thing remained before Ashley could leave her old life behind. She needed to tell Landon Blake. It was a conversation she couldn't have over the phone, so she waited until he came home for Christmas break.

This time the phone call came from her. She asked if she could come over to talk. Landon agreed before she finished the question, and the look on his face when she arrived at his house told her one thing.

He had expected this to be a reunion. Not a coda on their breakup.

There in his parents' front room she made her intentions clear one last time. "I care about you, Landon." She looked into his eyes. "But it's really over between us. This isn't . . . a phase." She stepped back, putting more space between them. "I won't ever be the girl you loved . . . before the accident." She had to get the words out before she changed her mind. "I'm different. Everyone says so."

"You're not." He tried to reach for her, but she pulled away.

"I am." She steeled herself against her emotions. "The two of us . . . it could never work now. Not ever." Her pause was heavy in the room. "I'm leaving for Paris. And I'm not coming home again."

In no time, she was having a going-away party and then her last night at home before her flight to France. Landon tried both nights to get her to stay, but she wouldn't change her mind. And finally she was in a window seat flying to Paris, money in hand and four paintings in a suitcase in the belly of the plane.

Saying goodbye to Landon Blake had almost killed her, but she'd done it. She had convinced him that the two of them no longer had the important things in common.

Specifically, their faith. Which was still true.

And finally on that flight to Paris, Landon was the last thing on her mind. She was free, she told herself. No longer did she have to live by her family's expectations. No one could force her to believe in God or follow someone else's dream. She was following her own path, and nothing could stop her.

She kept that attitude and leaned in toward the adventure ahead as she set herself up in the flat her teacher had arranged for her. She met Celia the day she moved in, an American girl her age with a love for writing. The two grabbed coffee together a few times in those early weeks in Paris. Celia didn't believe in God, either. They talked about concepts Ashley had barely thought about before.

Atheism and evolution. Enlightenment and freedom of choice.

"You need more self-love, Ashley," Celia had told her. "This life is about finding peace and acceptance. However that feels right to you."

Ashley wasn't sure about the girl's ideology. But in Paris, she took it to heart. She was ready to make her mark on the city, display her artwork in the gallery where she would be working and make her start as a serious artist.

But all those dreams fell flat Ashley's first day on the job. Turned out the gallery owner wanted her for one reason—she could speak English. Period.

The next day she brought her paintings in, still hoping for her big break as an artist. Instead the owner took one look at her work and wrinkled her nose. Like a skunk had walked into the shop. "This is trash, Ashley." Her accent made the statement almost impossible to understand.

But there was no mistaking her expression.

Ashley's work wasn't allowed back in the gallery and for a week she wondered if she'd made a terrible decision coming to Paris. Celia urged her to find another gallery, see if someone else in Paris was better at appreciating her paintings. In the end, though, it wasn't the encouragement from Celia that made Ashley glad she didn't take the next plane back to Indiana.

Rather, what kept her in Paris was a famous artist whose work was featured in a show at the gallery that weekend. A married man who swept her off her feet from the first time they spoke. What happened after that was too disgusting for Ashley to think about.

Never mind the fact that Celia was happy for her. The memory made Ashley sick. She didn't have to be a Christian to know that what she had done those next few months was wrong. By every possible standard it was wrong.

The man had no intention of leaving his wife or keeping Ashley around. He didn't care about her. She was nothing more than a pretty dalliance. A bit of American entertainment, good for a little while. Until he tired of her.

By then she was pregnant. Another detail that hadn't mattered to the artist. He gave her an envelope of cash—not quite a hundred dollars—along with the address of a clinic and told her never to talk to him again. And so on her darkest day, the cash clutched in her trembling hands, Ashley waited in a dirty lobby for her name to be called.

For some unethical doctor to tear into her and remove her baby. Before the tiny child ever had a chance to open his eyes.

Tears slid down Ashley's cheeks as she looked at

Cole. How could she have gotten that low, that detached from her own heart, from what mattered? "Baby Cole," she whispered his name. He was asleep now, his bottle empty. His soft cheek snuggled against her chest. "How could I have thought for a minute that . . ."

Ashley couldn't finish her thought.

She could still see herself sitting in that lobby, talking to one of the workers and realizing what was about to happen. All she could think about was her family, and everything she'd ever been taught. And how if she went through with the abortion there would be no going back, no second-guessing that decision. When they called her name, Ashley stood and ran out of the clinic.

As fast as she could.

In the season that followed, Ashley worked at a bakery before finally calling home. And while her parents had welcomed her back to Bloomington, Luke accused Ashley to her face of trashing the Baxter family name and behaving in a way that was hardly Christian.

"I'm *not* a Christian," she had shouted at him a number of times.

But he would only sneer at her. "Yes you are, Ash. You're just a bad one."

A bad Christian? Ashley breathed in sharp through her nose and ran her thumb over Cole's little arm. How could Luke say such a thing? Not that it mattered, because she had told her brother the truth. She didn't believe in God the way her family did anymore.

She wasn't a bad Christian as Luke had so often

pointed out. But she was a bad daughter and sister and mother. She was bad. Period.

Which was something Landon Blake didn't fully understand about her. Sure, he knew she had a baby and he could clearly see there was no father in the picture. She hadn't waited until marriage the way she'd planned and she wasn't following her family's faith. He didn't seem to care. He still pursued Ashley, determined they were meant to be together.

But Landon had no idea that Cole's dad was a married man, or that Ashley had been a willing party to the whole sordid affair. That it had practically been her idea.

If Landon ever knew that, he would stop trying. Stop coming around and looking for ways to convince her they might still have a chance. Maybe that's what she needed to do, tell him the truth. The entire truth. So he would realize she was right about being different now. So he'd finally move on. Because somewhere out there was a girl who was innocent and pure and true, like Landon.

He needed to wait for her.

Not Ashley.

She kissed her baby's cheek again. "Cole, what's your mommy going to do tonight?"

They would all get in the limo any minute now.

For a moment, she tried to picture it. There would be music and dancing and she would be dressed like Cinderella at the ball. And in the midst of all that Landon would walk into the room. Handsome and tall, he would take her breath. And then he'd ask her to dance.

And all she'd want was to feel his arms around her one more time. Which could never happen. No, if Landon asked her to dance tonight Ashley would have just one choice. She would look for the quickest way out. Even if it was nowhere near midnight.

11

The limo was in the driveway of the Baxter house, and Kari's sisters were ready on the covered front porch. The spot where they would take a few last pictures before heading to the chapel. Upstairs, her mom was putting the final touches on her makeup and her dad was getting things ready in the kitchen for later.

Which left Kari alone in the bridal room.

Her parents would come for her any minute, ready to escort her to the car. The way they'd planned. She looked at herself in the full-length mirror, the one set up near the window.

Every line and drop, every bit of lace and tulle was just how she had pictured it. When she imagined her wedding day the way girls sometimes do, she'd always pictured looking just like this. Exactly.

Kari smoothed her hand over the bodice and stared at her reflection. Once a few years ago, she had spent three days modeling wedding dresses for a catalog shoot in Indianapolis. At the time she'd still been in college, still in love with Ryan.

Between sets, Kari had taken a moment alone in

what had been her favorite dress of the job. Turning one way and then the other, for a few seconds she had seen herself not as a model doing a job. But as a girl standing at the front of a church facing the only guy she had ever planned on marrying.

Even then she had known something that thrilled her. Despite the stunning dress and her professionally done hair and makeup, when her actual wedding day came she would feel even more beautiful. Because she wouldn't be a model showing off a gown.

She'd be the bride.

And here she was. Kari spun so she could see all angles of the dress, the way she looked in it, the way Tim would see her in a few hours. All of it was perfect except one slight problem, something she had tried to forget for the last few hours.

Not the fact that Ryan Taylor had come by today or the way she'd felt being near him again. The way his fingers felt intertwined with hers. Those things could be understood and excused. They didn't mean she was having doubts or marrying the wrong guy. Ryan shouldn't have come. Her mother shouldn't have let him in.

None of that was Kari's fault.

No, the issue was something so much smaller, and yet bigger than her tears or anything else today. Something someone else might've missed. The one thing she couldn't stop thinking about.

Her hesitation.

That was it. When she replayed the minutes with a

drenched Ryan Taylor sitting next to her on the back porch swing on her wedding day, breathing hard, his eyes locked on hers. When she pictured the way his rain-soaked T-shirt clung to his arms and chest and the feel of his eyes on hers, the thing that made her most alarmed was that single slight pause.

Ryan's question played again in her mind, the way it had twenty times since he asked it. *Do you love him? Are you in love with him?*

She swished the hem of her dress over the tops of her shoes. What sort of bride was she, anyway? Her reply to Ryan should've come as easily as her name. Quicker than her next breath. Sooner than her next heartbeat. If she had it to do over again she would've jumped at her answer.

Of course she loved Tim. She was definitely in love with him. How could Ryan even ask such a question? She loved Tim more than anything she'd ever felt for Ryan Taylor.

That's what should've spilled out of her mouth.

But it didn't.

Instead she had paused. Just the slightest hesitation, as if her heart knew better than to run ahead with such an answer. Especially when the question came from Ryan. Looking into his gaze she simply couldn't bring herself to form the words. Which could only mean one thing.

She wasn't sure.

Even here less than two hours before walking down the aisle, she was having doubts. There was no other word for how she was feeling. A sigh came from the recesses of her heart. Maybe it wasn't doubt. Maybe she was only afraid. Cold feet. That's what they called it, right? Those nervous moments before saying "I do."

Kari walked to the window and stared over the open fields to the Taylors' house.

If only she'd gotten a few more minutes with Ryan. If she would've finally heard him out. Once and for all. Clearly he'd come with something on his heart. Only he didn't get to finish.

Because Tim showed up.

The rain was heavier again and Kari felt her gaze blur, and again images from a thousand yesterdays ago filled her heart and mind and soul.

Before Ryan had left for Dallas, the two of them had taken a day trip to Lake Monroe. At the beginning there had been no clouds, only a clear blue sky. But they were hiking halfway around the lake when a storm came up.

"Did you hear that?" Kari had stopped and looked up at Ryan. "In the distance."

That part of the trail was cloaked in trees and shrubs. The view of the lake was completely obscured by the various shades of green that surrounded them. The sound came again.

"I heard it that time." Ryan had never been good at hiding his feelings from her. Not since they were kids. And there on that path the sudden concern in his eyes was easy to read. "Let's get up ahead a ways so we can see the lake."

She had followed him another hundred yards or so until their view opened up. Only then did they both realize the trouble they were in. The distant sky was an eerie dark greenish color and a wall of ominous clouds was headed straight for them.

Before either of them could speak, the tornado sirens went off.

"Ryan!" Kari could remember how her heart picked up speed, how panic came over her as quickly as the storm. "We need to get back!"

A deep calm eased Ryan's expression as he turned to her. He took both her hands and stared straight at her. "We don't have time." He studied her. "I've got this, Kari. You have to believe me." That familiar steely determination rang in his voice. "I won't let anything happen to you."

The sirens were still blaring from the other side of the lake. Kari glanced at the choppy water and then again at Ryan. "But . . . the storm." She wanted to run as fast as she could back to the parking lot. Anything so they could get home before they were trapped. "Ryan, look at the trees around us. Even if a tornado doesn't get us, the wind will."

"I know." Ryan had put his hands on either side of her face. "You have to trust me. I absolutely will not let anything happen to you. I promise."

This time something in his tone made her relax. Even now she could remember feeling a sense of surreal calm come over her. Ryan would take care of her. He had promised.

Lightning had split the sky just over the far shore of the lake. Ryan took her hand and hurried her back to the path. "Come on."

Together they ran for a few minutes—all while the tornado sirens continued to wail through the humid summer air. The first drops of rain began to fall and then without warning Ryan stopped. He turned onto an over-grown path, one that led up a hilly embankment. "Hurry, Kari girl."

She didn't have to be asked twice. The climb was steep but she kept up with him until they reached a pla-teau. And there built into the side of the hill was a rock cave Kari had never seen before.

Ryan still had hold of her hand. "In here. We'll be safe till the storm passes."

The cave had a wide-open mouth and wasn't too deep. Nothing about it seemed scary or dank. No bats hung from the ceiling—at least not as far as she could see. They sat side by side on a large rock ten feet back from the cave's opening. Kari had waited till she could feel the warmth of his body next to hers. "How . . . how did you know about this?"

He grinned at her. "I found it when I used to come here a long time ago."

"How long?" Kari was no longer afraid. "You never told me about it."

"A guy has to have some secrets." He gave her a play-ful nudge with his elbow. Then he slipped his arm around her shoulders. "I don't know, maybe the first year we moved here. My dad and I were fishing and we tried to find a shortcut back to the parking lot." He looked around the cave. "Instead we found this."

Not only was the place safe from falling trees and lightning and tornadoes, but from where they sat they had an incredible view of the lake and the approaching storm. "This is amazing." Her voice had dropped to a whisper. She sat there safe against Ryan, aware of his arm around her. After a minute she spoke again. "I hate that you're leaving in a week."

At first Ryan didn't say anything. But then a long sigh came from deep inside him. "I wish you were finished with college. You could move to Dallas. Get a place with some roommates. Find a modeling job or whatever."

Kari remembered how it had felt to hear him say that, how her heart had soared at the fact that he wanted her with him. Even if it wasn't possible just yet. She leaned her head on his shoulder. "A year feels like a long time."

"It does." He ran his fingers along her arm. She wore shorts and a T-shirt because it had been eighty-five degrees when they set out. But the temperature had crashed with the coming storm, and as the wind picked up it actually felt cool.

He shifted so he could see her, his hand on her shoulder now. "Things might get a little crazy, Kari. Pro football camp takes every minute of the day. That's what my agent says."

She nodded. How was she supposed to respond? She

had no choice but to understand. More than that, she was happy for him. Her smile came from deep in her heart. "This is your dream year, Ryan. What you've been hoping and praying for as long as I've known you." Her smile remained. "If I don't hear from you as often, I'll understand."

"Thanks." His hand was on her face now, and he brushed his thumb across her cheek. "I'll be thinking of you every day. No matter what."

"Me, too." A crack of thunder had caught their attention and for a while they watched the storm. The wind picked up, and tree branches crashed down around the cave's entrance.

Kari slid closer to him. "So intense."

"It is." He took her hand in his, pressing his fingers between hers. "But I sorta like it. Safe in here where the storm can't get us." He faced her again. "Sharing this with you."

And then in a way that was inevitable, the electricity between them was suddenly greater than the raging storm outside. Protected in the shelter of the cave, Ryan moved his other hand alongside her face and into her hair. Without any more talking, they came together, his lips warm on hers.

Against the backdrop of pouring rain and pounding thunder, Kari remembered her heartbeat most of all. Racing, pounding as the kiss became another and another. A desperation had filled their hearts and bodies, the realization that time was running short. Their chemistry had never been stronger.

Just when Kari was about to pull away, about to tell him she needed a break, Ryan eased back and studied her. His eyes burned with passion for her, but his next kiss was more controlled. Gentle and tender. Same as his voice. "I'll never love anyone the way I love you, Kari girl."

And with that he helped her to her feet and they walked to the mouth of the cave. He slipped his arm around her shoulders and held her close as they watched the storm wane.

Yes, the kiss was one Kari still remembered. One she had known even in that moment she would never forget. When the danger passed, Ryan looked long at her. Tanned and handsome, the guy she had thought she'd be with forever.

His smile had lit up his eyes. "I'll remember this day as long as I live."

Of course he would, she had thought. They would both remember it. Who gets to live through a moment like that? Safe in a cave, sharing a breathless kiss while a storm pounded across the lake?

The memory lifted and Kari blinked. What was she doing? How could she be remembering that stormy afternoon now? Here in the bridal room? She felt ashamed of herself. She was not marrying Ryan Taylor today.

Nor did she want to marry him. Absolutely not.

So why was she standing here at the window staring at Ryan's house and remembering that summer day? Ryan had cheated on her. He wasn't honest or loyal. Period.

Tim was everything she had ever wanted.

Kari exhaled and turned back to the mirror. Then for the first time that day she noticed something on the end of the folding table. A framed photo of herself with Tim. Who had put it there? Her mother—or maybe one of her sisters—must have set it up. Part of turning the den into the bridal room, no doubt.

It was a shot of the two of them against a backdrop of hearts. Last February at the Valentine's banquet at church. Kari crossed the room and picked it up. For a long time she stared at it, at the way Tim grinned at her, laughing about something she'd said. She turned her gaze to herself, and she smiled. The way her eyes sparkled, the way her hand fit so well into his. She exhaled.

And for the first time all day she felt her heart relax.

The photograph was exactly what she needed to see in this moment before leaving her childhood home for the chapel. Never mind her hesitation earlier. She did love Tim Jacobs. She loved how he looked at her and how he lit up her face from the inside out.

Tim was smart and clever. He challenged her and protected her. And something else, something the picture made utterly clear. The one thing Kari needed to be reminded of right now. Tim Jacobs adored her.

She smiled at the picture for another few seconds.

Ever since Kari had invited him to Clear Creek Community Church, he'd gone with her. A few Sundays ago they were leaving the service when Tim grinned at her. "This is home for me, Kari."

"Home?" She hadn't been exactly sure what he meant. "Bloomington?"

"No." He stopped and looked deep into her eyes. "Clear Creek. It isn't your church anymore. Not to me." A smile tugged at his lips. "This is *our* church. Where I want to come every week and bring our babies someday. Our home church."

The memory stirred an even greater sense of peace, one that swelled in Kari's soul. This was helping. Remembering the good times with Tim. She put down the photo and looked at the mirror again. More good Tim memories. That's what she needed.

And in that same instant another one filled her mind. The first Saturday of February Tim had come to her house in the afternoon and knocked at the door. She wasn't expecting him, so the moment was happy. Impulsive. "Come on," he told her. "I've got a surprise for you."

Even now Kari remembered how her heart had lit up. She grabbed her coat and walked with Tim to his car. "A surprise date?" She shivered as he opened the door for her. Snow covered the ground and the temperature was barely above zero.

Tim only smiled and winked at her as he slipped behind the wheel. "You deserve it."

Ten minutes later they pulled into a parking lot and Tim laughed. "Here we are. Western Skateland."

Kari had laughed. "Roller-skating?" She turned so she could see Tim. "I haven't been here since I was in middle school."

"Exactly." Tim parked the car and looked at her. "I didn't know you then. So I thought we'd take a trip back in time." He leaned over and kissed her. "That way you have at least one memory of us roller-skating together."

Her smile stayed while they laced up their skates and as they spent an hour on the floor, holding hands and moving to the music. Disco lights splashed prisms of color everywhere and Kari could feel herself falling for him.

Taking time like that, surprising her, Kari had known how hard that must have been for Tim. His students were in midterms and that week Tim had often been busy grading students' assignments from home, working late into the night.

But Tim cared for her. He treasured her.

He would love her that way all the days of his life.

She could see them again as that evening wore on, making their way around the curved end of the roller rink. Halfway through Kool and the Gang's "Celebration" Kari lost her balance. She giggled again now, picturing the way she must've looked, one skate sliding forward and the other straight back.

If Tim hadn't caught her she would've done the splits right there on the rink.

But he was there for her, catching her, helping her keep her balance. Making her feel special. The way he had done when he threw her a surprise birthday party in her parents' backyard. Tim had set the picnic table so it looked like something out of a magazine, then he'd hung twinkling lights above it.

The result was the most unforgettable night with family and friends.

And Tim was still making life wonderful for her. Even today when Ryan came by, there was Tim. Keeping her on her feet. Always by her side . . .

Kari drew a deep breath and straightened her shoulders. This was her wedding day, no matter what the weather was doing. She would marry Tim and they would begin their happily ever after.

If only they had a cave where they could hide for the next few hours. A place where she and Tim could stay safe inside. Watching from the quiet while the storm passed.

A place where her hesitation from earlier couldn't hurt them.

12

Time was slipping away, and Elizabeth didn't want to be late. Especially with the weather. She gave her face a final bit of powder and hurried downstairs to the bridal room.

As soon as she stepped inside and saw the vision that was her second-oldest daughter, Elizabeth felt it.

Something had changed. The look in Kari's eyes was completely different than it had been when they were all gathered here earlier. Elizabeth walked slowly up to her daughter, taking in the sight of her.

"You look . . . stunning, Kari." She stopped a few feet away and studied her, the way her dress swished around her satin white pumps, the sheer elegance of her hair and face. But none of that had caught Elizabeth's attention nearly as much as her eyes had. She found Kari's gaze. "You look . . . different. Better."

"Yes." Kari's smile was more sincere than at any time that day. "God helped me remember." She reached for the framed photo of Tim and her. "He reminded me of all the good times with Tim. The way he's been thoughtful and honest and loyal." Her eyes sparkled. "I'm in love with Tim, Mom. I'm making the right decision, marrying him."

Elizabeth exhaled. "I prayed. That God would show you . . . that you wouldn't have doubts. Especially after . . ."

"After Ryan had the nerve to stop by?" A laugh came from Kari, but it wasn't funny. "He was wrong to do that. But maybe it was a good thing."

It was hard to imagine how Ryan coming here today was a good thing. Elizabeth waited.

"That probably sounds ridiculous." Kari's expression relaxed again. "The thing is, Ryan did me a favor, Mom. He forced me to remember him all over again. Every season and year and special moment."

"Oh, dear." Elizabeth brought her fingers to her lips. "My poor girl."

"No." Kari shook her head. Her poise was undeniable. "I remembered it all, and then I saw this photo." She smiled at the picture for a long moment. "And God let me think again about all the good times with Tim." She set the frame back on the table. "More than that, He reminded me of Tim's loyalty."

"Yes." Elizabeth still wondered about the whole story with Ryan, the situation at the hospital the day of his injury. But clearly Kari had moved beyond that. No point bringing it up now, not when Kari had worked through her conflicted feelings.

The time for Ryan had gone. He would forevermore be always and only in Kari's past.

"Mom." Her daughter's smile took up her whole face. "I'm ready. I want to marry Tim and spend the rest of my life with him." Another laugh came from her, this one filled with joy and light. "In fact . . . I can't wait."

John popped into the room just then, and stopped at the sight of Kari. Again Elizabeth took a minute before she could speak. "Hi, John." Their eyes met and then they both turned to Kari.

"My beautiful Kari." John walked up to her. "There are no words to describe how beautiful you are today."

"Thanks, Daddy." Kari's eyes shone, the tears from earlier long gone.

Elizabeth grinned. She felt better now, happier knowing how sure Kari was about the wedding. This was their daughter's shining moment. Elizabeth came up alongside John and hooked her arm through his. "Is everyone ready?"

"They are. Luke and the girls are gathered on the porch. Peter's at the church with Maddie." John turned once more to Kari. Tears filled his eyes and he shook his head. As if his words couldn't get past his emotions. "Kari, sweetheart. My breathtaking little girl." He took both her hands in his. "Are you ready?"

That's all he said, all he had to say. John had been close to each of their children, but he and Kari had shared a special bond. She had stayed the course, stuck with their family's faith and values.

Kari was easy to love. Always.

Elizabeth watched as Kari leaned forward and kissed

John on the cheek. "I am, Daddy." She must've been overflowing with happiness because she was truly glowing. "I'm ready."

"Okay, then . . . let's do this." John released her hands and held out his elbows. "I'd like to escort my two beauties to the porch." He winked at Elizabeth. "For another round of photos."

They all laughed. John wasn't a fan of long photo sessions, but Elizabeth wasn't concerned. Her husband wouldn't dare complain today. These were the pictures that would mark the years and milestones somewhere down the road.

On the porch, Ashley handed baby Cole to Elizabeth, who hung back with John while Daisy, the photographer, helped the five siblings through a series of snapshots. The tension from earlier seemed gone, as if everyone had together agreed that regardless of personal issues or thunderstorms, today was going to be good, after all.

While Daisy snapped photos of the kids, Elizabeth rocked the baby and lifted her eyes to John. He was still every bit the love of her life, and as her gaze held his, Elizabeth could almost see herself blush. This was the way he had made her feel since the first day they met. He stood tall and handsome at her side. "My love . . . that tux looks dashing on you." She took his hand. "You are easily the best-looking father of the bride of all time."

He leaned close and kissed her lips. "And you . . .

Elizabeth, you're not supposed to outshine the bride. But look at you."

"John and Elizabeth?" Daisy was smiling. "Time for the whole family. Or at least the ones here."

"Yeah, Mom . . . Dad . . . come on." Luke rolled his eyes in their direction. But this time he was only kidding. The look on his face told them that much. Their kids had commented often on how they appreciated their parents' love. How it felt right and secure knowing that they were still crazy about each other.

Even after all these years.

Ashley took Cole again, and the photographer set them up a dozen different ways looking for the perfect family picture. Halfway through the shoot, Elizabeth locked eyes with John again. And suddenly she knew without a doubt what he was thinking.

One was missing.

Their firstborn, the one they had talked about earlier on this same porch. Elizabeth kept smiling, kept enjoying the moment. Still she couldn't help but wonder about him. Was he out of school by now, working in some big city? Had he taken up medicine like his father or did he live in another country?

Lord, I don't know where our oldest son is. But You know. She lifted her eyes to the stormy sky. *So please, Father, wherever he is today, would You guard and protect him, please? And would You let him know that he is loved.*

Even if we don't ever meet him this side of heaven.

Another smile, another photo. Another repositioning of the ten of them. In the process, Elizabeth noticed Ashley, the way she looked holding Cole. The two of them seemed more comfortable together. As if Ashley was suddenly more aware of her little son.

Good for you, Ashley. Elizabeth smiled at her middle daughter and then back at the photographer. No matter what terrible events had led to Ashley coming home pregnant with Cole, at least she came home. Elizabeth and John had opened their door and hearts to her, and they had welcomed little Cole.

Something Elizabeth's parents had never dreamed of doing all those years ago.

Ashley would never have to wonder what happened to her firstborn. She would never have to cry alone at night, longing for even the slightest detail or imagining where he might be. No, Ashley had her firstborn son.

Something Elizabeth could never say. And on a day like this, the questions burned deeper than usual. Questions that would never get answered, short of a miracle. If only Elizabeth could find him, talk to him. Explain what happened. How she hadn't been given a choice about keeping him.

Elizabeth faced the photographer and remembered to smile. And like she'd done thousands of times before, she asked God for one thing in particular. That before she drew her last breath she might not only learn the whereabouts of her son.

But that she might actually meet him, face-to-face.

Take him into her arms and tell him the truth. That no matter what had happened the week after he was born, Elizabeth and John loved him.

They loved him more than their own lives.

• • •

THE CAST AND crew of Dayne Matthews' latest film were in Casablanca, Morocco, this time, taking up residence in the heart of the city for a movie shoot that would last another month. At least.

Dayne shrugged into the motorcycle jacket and slipped on the helmet. Every inch of his six-foot-three frame was dripping in sweat. He stared at his director, Kent Barrett. "Why did we film this in the summer?"

Standing just in front of him, Barrett adjusted Dayne's helmet and studied his look. "Sweat makes you glisten. The girls love it, Matthews. Don't knock what works."

"Yeah, yeah." Dayne tried to take a full breath. Inside the helmet the air was suffocating. "And how come I agreed to do my own stunts again?"

Barrett laughed. "Because you love it."

True. Dayne grinned. "You got me." He took a few steps to the motorcycle parked nearby. "Let's do this."

The movie was an action film, one in a series that had made Dayne Matthews the most popular, most recognized actor of all time. He would turn twenty-eight next week and already he had been at the top of his game for three years.

His life before becoming Hollywood's most-loved heartthrob? That . . . well, that was something he tried not to think about.

A quick glance at the sidewalk across the street and the proof was there for anyone to see. Paparazzi from Morocco and the United States and ten other countries fought for position on the heated curb. Security men tried to keep them at bay.

It was like this everywhere Dayne went. Paparazzi, security, people screaming his name. Anything for a picture or an autograph. Dayne could block them out. He was used to navigating his life around them.

"Get on the bike, Matthews." Barrett moved off to his spot behind the camera. "Let's get it this time. Everyone's on board."

Dayne didn't care how many takes it took. He loved racing the motorcycle down the busy city street, dodging cars and trucks while the cameras rolled.

He climbed on the machine and grabbed the handlebars. *Deep breath, Matthews,* he told himself. *Give it your best.*

"Camera speed." The director of photography yelled above the noise of the busy street. "And . . . action."

The motorcycle shot out with Dayne hunkered over the handlebars. *Stay low. One with the machine. Let's do this.* Leaning one way and then the other, Dayne ripped down the avenue and around every car and truck in his way. At the end of the block he skidded his back tire to the left and veered the bike to the right. Just before he would hit the curb, he threw the machine into park, hopped off and tore his helmet from his head.

"Jaynie!" He screamed her name.

At the same time his costar Margaret Ellen came running from the nearest building. She ran into his arms and the two clung to each other, desperate, clearly aware that their minutes were numbered. And then they kissed.

A kiss that would be watched and replayed for all of time.

Seconds later, when the kiss ended, Dayne stared into Margaret's eyes. "That was fun," he whispered. "Glad we practiced last night."

"Gotta get the shot." She looked like she might kiss him again but she took a step back.

At the same time they heard the director. "Cut. Got it! Matthews, Ellen, that was fantastic." He was jogging their way, yelling through a megaphone. "Everyone take ten, then let's move on. We're burning daylight, folks."

Dayne slipped his arm around Margaret's shoulders. "Best kiss yet." He grinned at her. "Let's hit the craft table."

Cast and crew had the same idea, so Dayne changed his mind. "There's a street vendor at the other end. Juice and ice cream." He released his hold on her and took her hand instead. "Come on."

In every movie Dayne had filmed, he'd had a deep friendship with his leading lady. This time with Margaret Ellen was only slightly different. He really liked Margaret. If they weren't both superstars he might've dated her. Maybe even married her.

They slipped away from the crowd and bought a couple of juices. This was his drink of the day—morning and night, actually. Dayne didn't imbibe when he was filming a movie, not ever. He saved his partying life for between films. The precious little time when he wasn't working.

Dayne took another guzzle and faced Margaret. "I think it's possible." He could feel his lazy grin making its way up his face.

"What's that?" She flirted with him. "We might need to reshoot that kiss scene?"

Across the street, paparazzi had made their way closer. Anything to get a picture of Dayne and his costar. Dayne nodded to the empty storefront a few feet away. "Let's check out the local wares." He led the way to the building.

Then without looking back at the myriad of photographers, Dayne ushered Margaret inside. It was even muggier in here, but it wasn't the first time the two of them had slipped away. Found a quiet place where no one could bother them.

Dayne figured their producer and director knew he needed alone time now and then. Otherwise why were all the storefronts empty for the shoot? The production company had rented every single one—in case they needed the space.

Or in case Dayne needed it.

He slipped out of the leather jacket and worked his fingers into Margaret's hair. "I think it's possible you're the most beautiful girl I've ever kissed."

"Hmmm." She let herself get lost in his eyes. "You've kissed a lot of girls."

Another grin. "Exactly." Dayne closed the distance between them and kissed her, long and slow. "It's okay, right?" He kissed her again.

"This?" Now she took the lead and this time their kiss lasted longer. "Practice, you mean?" She eased back and laughed. Then again she kissed him. "Best part of the job."

Three seconds of bliss and the door to the storefront swung open. Barrett stood there, eyebrows raised, clipboard in hand. "Your ten minutes is up." He contained a chuckle. "I need Margaret."

"Just practicing, boss." Dayne saluted. Then he cast a long look at Margaret. The two of them would've practiced a whole lot longer if they'd had the chance. Maybe later. Her look said she felt the same way. Dayne turned to Barrett once more. "I'm here when you need me, boss."

"You've got another ten at least." He headed for the door with Margaret. Before they left Barrett glanced over his shoulder. "Don't make me come looking."

"You got it." Dayne leaned against the storefront window and watched the two leave. A hundred cameras were aimed at the door, so for now Dayne would stay here. However hot it was.

What a day. Best job any guy could ever have. He

breathed out, allowing himself to relax for the first time in hours. Moments like this were rare, just him and his thoughts. No one asking his opinion about a scene or telling him where to stand and how to talk and what to do.

No one aiming a camera at him.

He stared down the busy street and a memory came to mind. His family visiting a city like this one when they were on furlough fifteen years ago. Back when Dayne was just thirteen years old.

As if they were standing in front of him, he could see them again. His dear parents, the kind missionary couple who had adopted him and raised him. Only when they were on furlough did his parents spend much time with him. They had believed that God's work came first— before family.

Which left Dayne with the same question every time their one-month breaks ended. Why had they adopted him? Why take on a child if you didn't plan to spend time together?

One year after another, Dayne had been raised by teachers and counselors and guardians at the boarding school for missionaries in Indonesia. He studied math and English and history, but his favorite class was drama. He loved the idea of playing someone else, someone whose parents hadn't abandoned him.

And all during those schooling semesters, Dayne's adoptive parents spent their days flying around in a twin-engine plane telling people about Jesus.

Dayne narrowed his eyes, the memory still crystal clear. His parents had been like kind relatives. An aunt and uncle, maybe. Certainly not parents. They missed far too much of his childhood for that.

Meanwhile, nearly everyone they came in contact with found faith in Christ.

Everyone but Dayne.

A deep breath filled his lungs. The news had come to him at the strangest time. Dayne was eighteen, taking a final in history when the door to his classroom opened. Eleven other students were in the room, and all of them looked up.

There in the doorway was the headmaster, his face red, his eyes filled with alarm.

"Dayne." The man stared at him. He was out of breath. "We need to talk."

Right then? Dayne remembered thinking. In the middle of his history final? But the headmaster wasn't leaving so Dayne set his pencil down and followed the man. Down the hall and to the office in the next building.

When they were both seated, the man shook his head. "We just received terrible news, Dayne. I'm so sorry."

Dayne tried to imagine what could possibly have happened, something so bad that the man would interrupt a final exam. He waited.

"There was a plane crash, Dayne. Your parents' plane." His eyes welled up. "They were both killed."

The headmaster rambled on, something about recovering their bodies from the wreckage and next steps. How his parents had life insurance and how Dayne could go to any university he wished. Wherever he wanted to go.

Something like that.

The next few weeks—the deep conversations and important details, the funeral and memorial service—all of it was like a nightmare, one Dayne couldn't wake up from. He knew from the minute the headmaster gave him a choice, the perfect place where he wanted to go to school.

Exactly what he wanted to do.

He applied to UCLA and a few months later he received his acceptance letter. From his first day on campus he studied acting like it was his lifeblood. Like his next breath depended on being the best actor to ever grace the halls of UCLA.

His first film took the movie world by surprise. The second took the world by storm. Who was this Dayne Matthews? Where had he come from? His face dominated the cover of every gossip rag in the grocery checkout lines.

Dayne Matthews wasn't only a leading man, the media announced. He was an acclaimed actor. Wildly talented, beyond handsome. The accolades filled the pages of magazines and newspapers.

Everyone loved Dayne Matthews. Every language. Every nation.

But none of his fans really knew him. No one did. The fact was, Dayne had survived the unimaginable. The details he found himself rehashing day after day.

Dayne had been orphaned not once, but twice.

He literally had no one. Not anywhere in all the world.

A quick breath broke the moment and Dayne shook the drops of sweat from his hair. His break was almost up. Time to jump on the motorcycle again and film the getaway scene. The one that came after the kiss. He clenched his jaw and looked long at the hazy sky. He didn't miss his adoptive parents, really. They were never around, anyway.

Rather he missed the parents he had never met. Whoever they were. The ones who had given him up when he was just days old. They were from the Midwest. That's all he knew. But sometimes, on days like this, he would be tearing down a street in Morocco on a motor-cycle and he wasn't heading to the end of the scene.

He was racing as fast and hard as he could to find them.

Yes, days like this Dayne was consumed by two ques-tions. Questions that had followed him and haunted him and ripped at his heart the way they had since he was old enough to know he was adopted.

Who were his real parents?

And where in the world were they?

At least he had a lead now. Money wasn't an issue, so months ago Dayne had hired a private investigator. And just yesterday the guy had emailed with one bit of information. One piece of news.

The man had finally linked Dayne to his birth mother.

This bit of truth had consumed Dayne since the message landed in his in-box. "It won't be long," the investigator had written to him, "till I find her. Till we can arrange a meeting."

A chill ran down Dayne's arms. It wouldn't be long. Because now Dayne had a name. The name he couldn't stop thinking about. The name of his birth mother.

Elizabeth Baxter.

13

The rain stopped long enough for them to climb into the limo. Kari's sisters helped keep her dress from getting wet or muddy and once they were situated inside, Daisy took more photos.

A few seconds later the driver set out. Kari surveyed her family seated around her. Ashley was still holding Cole, who was awake now. Wide-eyed and handsome in his baby tux. Ashley spoke up first. "You look beautiful, Kari. Really."

"Thanks." The earlier tension between them was gone now. "You, too. Those dresses are perfect." She looked at Brooke and Erin and back to Ashley. "Just like I pictured them."

"Can I just say . . ." Luke was sitting across from Kari. He reached over and took her hand. "I'm honored to be your brother, Kari. You deserve this today."

Peace filled her heart the way it filled the air around them. Whatever reservations her family may have had about Tim Jacobs, they had faded. Maybe because they could see the certainty in Kari's face.

On the way to the church, their dad told stories

about when Kari was little. How when she was just eleven she had organized her siblings to throw their mother a surprise birthday party.

Everyone uttered a quiet laugh. "I remember like it was yesterday." Kari smiled at Ashley and Erin and Brooke and Luke. "We wanted everything to be so perfect."

Brooke leaned forward. "I was in charge of cooking. What was it? Chicken?"

"I think so." Their dad chuckled. "Not that any of us ended up eating it."

At the other end of the car, Erin smiled at Kari. "It all started with that cat clock you had us chip in on."

"True." Kari sat back and smoothed her hand over her wedding gown. She loved this, being surrounded by her family on her way to the wedding chapel. Telling stories about when they were little. "It was plastic orange and black and the tail moved with every second, if I remember."

"That was it." Their dad laughed a little harder. "It was hideous. But then Luke stepped on the tail."

"He did everyone a favor." Ashley giggled and she bounced Cole a bit. "We were busy hanging decorations in the front of the house and everyone was talking about the cat clock and how Mom would love it."

"And then this loud crunching sound." Erin leaned against Luke. "You thought you were in so much trouble."

The driver was getting closer to the chapel. Kari

hoped he would take his time. This together moment was too precious to rush.

Luke patted Erin's knee. "I think even back then I knew Mom would never hang that thing anywhere in the house." He smiled at the youngest of his sisters. "But you were very nice about it, Erin. I remember you putting your hand on my shoulder and saying everything would be okay."

"And now it is." Their mom looked happy, like this time together was exactly what she needed, too. "Of course . . . it was all fine back then, too. The idea was what mattered."

"The chicken caught fire while we were analyzing the broken cat." Brooke shook her head. "I'll never forget how much smoke filled the house."

"Remember?" Kari leaned forward and looked at each of her siblings, one at a time. "The smoke alarm was going off just as Mom walked through the door."

"Surprise!" All five of them said the word at the same time. Kari laughed hard at the memory. "The look on Mom's face . . . I'll never forget it."

Before they could talk about how they had spent her birthday dinner that night at a restaurant, the limo pulled up in front of the chapel. The driver was out of the car in an instant, opening the door for them.

"Here we are." Their dad looked at each of them. "I like this. Everyone laughing, remembering way back when." He hesitated. "Let's have more of this, okay?"

They all nodded and Kari felt a rush of emotion. She

would miss this, being part of her family on an everyday basis. But as they exited the limo, Kari noticed how Luke and Ashley didn't make eye contact, even as Ashley carried Cole out of the vehicle. She sighed. At least they'd been laughing for the last few minutes. That was a start. And good things tended to happen on a wedding day.

Kari needed to believe the best.

Her dad helped her out of the limo, and under the darkest clouds, again her sisters carried her train. Not until Kari and her family were through the back door of the chapel did the storm hit in earnest.

Lightning and thunder rocked the building at almost the same time, and Kari caught her breath. Her hands trembled at the fierceness of the wind outside. "Hopefully this is the last of it."

Her mom came to her and touched her shoulder. "I'm sure it is. You still have half an hour before you walk down the aisle."

Kari tried to imagine saying her vows over the deafening sound of this thunder. The idea was almost laughable. *Please, Lord, make the storm pass. So that my wedding can go on without thunder interrupting us. Please.*

And sure enough, over the next half hour the storm let up. By the time they lined up at the back of the church, a ray of sunshine was even piercing the stained-glass windows.

Kari's friends Liza and Mandy were the first to walk down the aisle. They were girls Kari had known since sixth grade. The year the Baxter family moved to Bloomington. Each of the friends gave Kari a hug and then headed toward the front of the church.

Erin was next to head down the aisle. Before she started off, she took hold of Kari's shoulders and gazed all the way to her heart. "I've always looked up to you, Kari. Always wanted to be like you." She blinked back tears. "This is the right thing today. It is." She paused, like she was fighting to find her voice. "God brought you Tim. The two of you are going to be so happy."

For all the times when Erin seemed too young to understand Kari or too distant for the two of them to be very close, this moment was all that mattered. Kari hugged her littlest sister. "Thank you, Erin. You don't know how much that means to me."

They shared another look, and then Erin made her way to the front of the church, her small bouquet of white roses in front of her.

Brooke was next, and like the others she hugged Kari. "I'm happy for you. Your wedding is already so beautiful."

"Thank you." Kari smiled at her older sister. "It helps . . . having your support, Brooke."

Her sister smiled and then turned and walked down the aisle.

Finally the only bridesmaid left was Ashley—her maid of honor.

No matter what difficulties they'd shared, no matter how their faith and views didn't align today the way

they had all the years they were growing up, Ashley remained Kari's best friend.

She always would be.

"You did a beautiful job with the flowers." Kari
looked to the front of the church. "You really are the
best artist, Ash."

"Thanks." Her sister's eyes softened. She never broke
eye contact. "All those seasons, summers and winters,
talking late into the night. Dreaming about tomorrow."
Ashley's eyes glistened with tears. "So many memories."
Her voice caught. "I can't believe you're getting married."

"I know." Kari felt tears sting the corners of her eyes.
"I love you, Ash."

"Love you, too." She smiled. "You and Tim . . . it's the
right thing. I believe it."

"Thank you." There could be no greater gift for Kari
than the support of her sisters. Especially Ashley. The
fact that they all accepted Tim made this day even better. Her heart even more sure.

Ashley set off down the aisle and with all the
bridesmaids gone, it was time for little Maddie. The
child didn't want to walk by herself, so her daddy—
Peter—walked next to her while she scattered flower
petals. The child was only two. She was utterly
adorable in her flouncy white dress and patent leather
shoes.

Then, inside the chapel, the music changed.

Kari had requested the traditional wedding march. Pachelbel's "Canon in D Major." As the familiar music played, Kari's father took her side. "Okay, little girl." He had tears in his eyes and one on his cheek as he held his elbow out to her. One last time. "I remember when you were three years old. We were at the zoo and you didn't want to sit in the stroller. We were leaving the monkey exhibit and you looked up at me. 'Daddy, hold my hand, please. I don't want to take this walk without you.'"

"I said that?" Kari positioned herself beside her dad.

"You did." He smiled at her. "I told myself I'd remember that day forever, so that when it came time to walk you down the aisle I'd feel the way I did then." He kissed her cheek. "Like I wouldn't want you to take this walk without me." He blinked back tears. "Kari, no father has ever been more blessed than me."

"Dad." Kari blinked a few times. "That's the sweetest thing."

"Okay." He took a long breath and stared straight ahead. "Let's do this. Hardest walk a dad will ever take."

Kari hesitated. "Well . . ." She took his elbow. "I'll say what I said when I was three. Hold my hand. Please, Daddy."

So he did, and like that they were heading down the aisle and suddenly she saw him, at the front of the church. Her groom, her Tim. The one she loved. He was standing there dressed in a black tux with tails, his eyes locked on hers.

They were almost to the end of the aisle when her dad leaned closer. "He's the one, Kari. Look at him."

She could feel her father beaming beside her, feel the way he approved of this marriage. And of course. Because up ahead of her Tim wasn't just smiling, looking at her like she was the only girl in the world.

He was wiping tears. Which could only mean one thing. Tim felt the same way she did.

Like this was the greatest day of his life.

• • •

ANOTHER DRAMA WAS playing out in the church that day, one that Elizabeth noticed from the moment Luke seated her in the front row. The drama between Ashley and Landon Blake.

As the guests turned to watch the bridesmaids walk down the aisle, Elizabeth could see Landon. He was four rows away, watching the back doors like everyone else.

But there was something different about the look in Landon's eyes.

Elizabeth had known the boy since he and Ashley were kids. He had always been tough, a competitor on the sports fields and in the classroom. Everyone liked Landon Blake, and he had a smile for each person he met.

Still, as long as Elizabeth had known Landon, when he looked at Ashley his expression changed. Every time.

Something dreamy filled his eyes and the depth of his soul was easy to see. That was how Landon looked now, waiting for Ashley to appear.

One bridesmaid at a time, Elizabeth could see Landon nod and smile the way most people did. But always his eyes returned quickly to the back of the church. Elizabeth tried not to be distracted by the situation. But clearly the young man had come to the wedding in hopes that he and Ashley might find the love they'd lost long ago.

Elizabeth smiled at her beautiful daughters as they approached the front of the church. First Erin, then Brooke. Finally, it was Ashley's turn.

As much as Elizabeth wanted to watch her middle daughter and nothing else, it was impossible not to be distracted by Landon. Because there it was, the way it had been for so many years. That look of his.

A look that showed how he felt about Ashley. How he would maybe always feel.

Elizabeth studied Ashley, her hair cut to her shoulders, her pretty face high and proud. All her life, Ashley had been strikingly beautiful. Quirky. Funny. Mischievous. Yes, all those things.

But the expression on Ashley's face was different from those on Elizabeth's other girls. Despite her pretty features, she looked harder, defensive. Elizabeth knew why. Ashley was probably thinking that everyone was judging her and talking about her and wondering how she could've gone off to Paris and gotten pregnant.

A Baxter girl, of all things.

Please, Lord, help her let it go. Just for today. Elizabeth wanted to pause the moment and whisper truth to her middle daughter. *No one is judging you, my precious daughter. No one. If you only knew how loved you are.*

Elizabeth glanced back a row at baby Cole sitting with Elaine Decker, Elizabeth's longtime friend from church. Earlier, Elaine had to get up to walk him a bit. But now that the wedding was underway, Cole was quiet. Watching like everyone else.

Little Maddie walked alongside Peter, scattering rose petals along the white linen that lined the aisle. And then the bridal procession began to play and at the back of the church . . .

"Kari." Elizabeth uttered her daughter's name in the softest whisper. "You look absolutely perfect, honey."

Elizabeth wished she could freeze time. Wished she had three hours or three days to remember every wonderful memory with Kari leading up to this point. From the first time she held her in the hospital, to her first teeth and first steps. Her first day of kindergarten and every milestone and happy time that followed.

Since she couldn't stop the clock, Elizabeth allowed the brief montage of images to play in her mind as John walked their daughter down the aisle. Kari had always been the easiest of her daughters. She was smart and independent, but she was also a dreamer.

When they couldn't find Kari, the first place Elizabeth looked was the front or back porch. Almost always there she would be. Journaling. Staring at the Blooming-ton sky. Writing down her hopes and prayers and goals for the future . . . a future with Ryan, no doubt. But all of that was behind her now.

As John and Kari neared the front of the church, Elizabeth glanced over her shoulder at Tim.

And what she saw made her certain Kari was right. Tim was the man she was supposed to marry.

He was standing there, tears streaming down his face even as the biggest smile tugged at his cheeks. The way he watched Kari wasn't exactly the way Landon looked at Ashley. But there was no denying the ocean of love Tim had for their second daughter.

Pastor Mark Atteberry from Clear Creek Commu-nity Church stepped forward. "Who gives this woman to be married?"

John smiled at their daughter. "Her mother and I." He kissed Kari's cheek and then placed her hand in Tim's. With a single nod, John turned and took his spot next to Elizabeth.

He let out a small exhale and grinned at her. A look that told her he had done it. He had given away another of their daughters. Even if it had just about killed him. They turned their attention to the ceremony beginning in front of them.

Their stunning daughter was looking so deep into Tim's eyes, her expression so full of hope and love for the lifetime ahead. Of course Tim was the right one for her.

Like her daughter, Elizabeth no longer had even the slightest doubt. In fact she was as sure as Kari. Tim Jacobs would stay by Kari's side, loyal and true, till they were both old and gray.

Forever and always.

14

Throughout the ceremony, the last thing Ashley wanted to do was catch Landon's eye. Instead she focused on the wedding. The stunning floral arrangements, the beautiful way her family looked. The expression of love on Kari's face.

But that wasn't much better.

There was Kari, her sister and best friend, promising her life to a man Ashley still wasn't certain about. Oh, sure, Tim fit the part today. Teary eyes, beaming smile. His gaze locked on Kari alone. Ashley had even given Kari her vote of support for Tim.

But didn't every guy seem happy on his wedding day?

What about the arrogant Tim, the one who talked down to Kari far too many times? How was Kari ever supposed to feel smart with a husband who demeaned her? And how come she could feel Landon staring at her?

Ashley breathed out. *Focus on Kari and Tim,* she told herself. They were saying their vows, promising forever to each other. Something Ashley couldn't imagine doing for any man. Not with her past. Especially not Landon Blake.

Without meaning to, Ashley glanced out at the guests in the pews and stared directly where she didn't want to look.

Into the captivating eyes of Landon Blake.

She wanted to ask him a million questions, starting with this one: Why was he here? What was he hoping would happen? But the questions fell flat in the warmth of his gaze. She dropped her look to her pale-pink heels.

Inches away or across the room, Landon had that effect on her. He took her breath, even when she was positive she would never date him again. Then, before she could stop herself, she looked at him again. The corners of his mouth lifted.

That same hint of a grin that had belonged to her alone for half her life. Ashley returned the smile before she could remind herself of the truth. Landon wasn't an option. Not tonight.

Not ever.

Ashley avoided him for the remainder of the ceremony and as Kari and Tim were introduced as husband and wife. She didn't look at Landon or find herself anywhere near him while the guests left the chapel and headed next door to the reception hall.

For the next half hour, Ashley made sure the floral centerpieces were just right in the dining area, and that the cake display also had the correct flowers scattered around it.

After that Kari and Tim and the bridal party were introduced to the guests and they found their seats and ate dinner. All that time Ashley steered clear of Landon. She would not allow herself to be Cinderella tonight. Prince Charming would have to find someone else. Especially once the dancing started.

Besides, she meant what she had promised herself earlier. If Landon tried to break down her defenses, she would go home. She could help her family get ready for the after-party but she wouldn't stay here. Across the room, her mother's friend Elaine still had Cole. The plan was for Elaine to watch him throughout the wedding and reception.

So Ashley could play her role as maid of honor.

As she finished eating at the head table with the other bridesmaids and groomsmen, Ashley kept an eye on Cole. In case she needed to take him from Elaine. For that matter, maybe she should take her son home early, so he could get a good night's sleep. These thoughts were going through her head as the band began to play. Kari and Tim danced first, of course, and then they invited their parents to the floor. The bridal party came next.

Ashley had no one specific to dance with. Most of the groomsmen were Tim's friends, married and already dancing with their wives—all except her brother, Luke. And he wasn't talking to Ashley.

She stood near the center of the floor while everyone around her found a partner. Even Erin seemed to have connected with a friend of Tim's. Ashley felt her heart beat hard in her chest. What was she doing? This was em-barrassing. A quick turn and she headed back to the table. But before she reached it, she felt a hand on her shoulder.

"May I?"

Ashley would know his voice anywhere. She blinked slowly and turned around. And suddenly she was at prom again and he was her date and in all the world Ash-ley couldn't think of a happier girl.

"Landon." She froze, and her eyes became lost in his. "I . . . I should go watch Cole."

"He's good." Landon smiled. "I checked on him first. Elaine says everything's fine." He held his hands out to her. "Dance with me, Ash. Please."

Nothing she could've done would've given her the strength to say no to him. Not when all she wanted was to feel his arms around her, to sway and twirl and move to the music while he led her across the dance floor.

She nodded, and every promise she'd made to herself disappeared. "Okay."

And like that they were in their own world. She slid her arms loose around his neck and he put his around her waist. They shared no fancy waltz-type moves, no spins or dips. Rather, this dance was just the two of them, swaying to the music, trying to remember they weren't still eighteen and in love.

The whole time the band played, through the first verse and chorus, Landon looked at her. Wouldn't glance away for a single moment. His eyes found their way through her, to the deepest parts of her. Like he had never stopped loving her. His hands on her back, his breath on her cheek. The familiar smell of his cologne.

Don't let go, Landon. Don't ever let go. Her traitorous heart couldn't get enough. No matter what she had told herself about this night in the weeks leading up to Kari's wedding, Ashley had just one thought now. She didn't want the music to ever end.

Halfway through the song, Landon whispered close to her face. "Why do you keep running, Ash?"

She held on to him a little tighter. Because if this was the last time she was ever in Landon Blake's arms she wanted to make the most of it. Her face tilted up to his. "I'm sorry."

He put one hand along her cheek. The way he used to do before he kissed her. With the slightest movement, he shook his head. "You don't have to be sorry. Just . . . stop. Stop running." His face brushed against hers as the music played. "We can have this again. Don't you see?"

How could she tell him he was wrong? That they could never be together. She had changed and besides, if he knew Cole's dad was a married man he wouldn't want her. Was that what it would take to get him to move on? Did she finally have to tell him?

Ashley let her head fall to his chest. When she looked up, she could feel tears gathering in her eyes. "We can't, Landon. It's over." This time she put her hand on his face, she worked her fingertips into his hair. "It is."

Darkness shrouded his eyes, a mix of hurt and anger. "You're wrong." He looked like he might kiss her.

Which he absolutely couldn't do. Ashley would be his all over again if he did. And for this single moment it would be heaven—for both of them. But heartache would soon follow.

He caught a single tear as it slid down her face. "Why the fight?" His voice was warm with love, the darkness in his expression from a few seconds ago, gone. He ran his thumb along her cheek, his touch like silk. "No one will ever love you the way I do, Ash. Never."

She squeezed her eyes shut. If that was true, Ashley would spend the rest of her life alone. "You need a good girl, Landon. Someone like you."

The song wasn't over yet, but Landon took a half step back. "What's that even mean? A good girl?" He laughed once, hurt filling his voice. "No one's good. You know that. We all have something."

"Not you." Ashley closed the gap. This wasn't the time to talk it through. If she had it her way that time would never come. Better they live their own lives without a closing argument. But if she had to tell him the truth, she would. Maybe later tonight.

She remembered to smile. "You're always good, Landon."

A flicker in his eyes told her he didn't agree. "You don't know everything."

His answer surprised her. "What?" She found her familiar teasing smile. "Did you break curfew at college?"

Frustration flashed across his face. "You're making fun of me? Is that it?" He still held her, still ran his thumb along her cheek with his other hand. "You're not the only one who makes mistakes, Ash."

Part of her wanted to know what he was talking about, what the handsome, clean-cut Landon Blake could ever have done to mar his perfect image. But a conversation like that would lead nowhere. Whatever it was, he had never slept with someone who was married.

She moved her hand to the back of his head, feeling his hair against her fingers. The music was coming to an end. "The two of us . . . whatever we've done or not done . . . we're in the past, Landon." She felt her eyes fill with light for all the days gone by. "Thank you."

"Thank you?" He hadn't let go, hadn't made a move to leave the dance floor. Another song was beginning, a line dance. He studied her, clearly confused. Again he moved closer, his face inches from hers, his words so hushed she almost didn't hear them. "That's it?"

Ashley wanted him to kiss her, desired it the way she hadn't since her senior prom. But before that might happen, she leaned in and kissed his cheek. "I'm sorry." She felt the sadness in her smile, even as she eased away from him and walked off the dance floor.

At the same time she heard a baby crying. She turned and saw Elaine bouncing Cole, tending to him. The woman cast Ashley a helpless look. Ashley wasn't the best mother, she would be the first to admit that. Normally in a situation like this she would be happy to have someone else take care of Cole.

So she could dance and laugh and pretend she wasn't a young unwed mother.

But here and now Cole was the perfect distraction. She hurried to Elaine and took her baby from her arms. "Thank you." She held her little son close and kissed the top of his head. "Does he need a bottle?"

"Maybe." Elaine looked relieved. "I made one a few minutes ago. He didn't want it." She handed the still-warm bottle to Ashley. "Could just be too loud in here for him."

"Yes." Ashley felt herself kick into mom gear. She sat down at Elaine's table and put the bottle to Cole's lips. He took it with gusto, as if he were starving.

Elaine smiled. "I guess he just wanted you." She looked out at the dance floor. "I think I'll join my friends for a while."

"Please. Go ahead." Ashley nodded to the woman. "Thank you again."

When Elaine was gone, Ashley sat back in the chair and held Cole close. Poor baby. She really did love him. It's just . . . she wasn't ready. Her mom was so much better at being a mother. The more Ashley left him at her parents' house, the more she enjoyed her time away.

All of which was wrong. She knew it.

Warm in her arms, Cole settled down. Halfway through the bottle, he sighed, his eyes still on hers. Once more he seemed to have a certain look about him. This time as if he wanted to ask her one burning question. "Mommy . . . why don't you hold me more?"

"I'm sorry, Cole." She ran her fingers over his soft wispy blond hair. "You deserve better. Like everyone else in my life."

Until now she hadn't looked up, hadn't checked to see where Landon had gone. Now, with Cole finally content and finishing his bottle, Ashley lifted her eyes just enough to scan the room. It took a minute, but she finally spotted him at one of the tables in the back. He was sitting with her brother, Luke, and one of Luke's friends.

Perfect. She rolled her eyes and looked back at her little boy. Frustration flashed in her heart. Didn't Landon know how rude Luke had been? How he had barely talked to Ashley since she returned from Paris, and how he hadn't held Cole even once?

She thought about that. No, of course Landon didn't know. Ashley had barely spoken to him since she'd been back. Again she studied Landon, his easy smile and the way Luke laughed at something Landon said.

And suddenly she wasn't frustrated. *I should be there*, she told herself. *Sitting between them. Talking about something funny that happened last week and letting Landon back into my life. We should be here together and we should leave together.*

Why was she so stubborn?

Her gaze landed on the flowers at the center of the table. They really were beautiful. Maybe one day—if the painting thing didn't work out—she would be a florist. In fact, the room looked like something from a fairy tale, twinkling lights draped over the dance floor and a couple hundred guests dressed in their wedding best.

But even that couldn't keep her from finding Landon across the room again. Ashley was glad for the shadows. She was pretty sure Landon didn't know where she was sitting. The band started playing a slow song, one that she and Landon had loved back in high school.

Before she could turn away, from across the room Landon looked over his shoulder and caught her eyes. He started to smile, but as quickly as she could she stared back at Cole. A strange heat made its way through her cheeks. What was she doing? If she wanted him to leave her alone, then she needed to do the same to him.

Ashley watched Cole finish his bottle, and everything faded. The music and laughter, the thoughts of Landon. Suddenly she could picture herself, traipsing around Paris with a married man, no care for his wife or for the consequences—whatever they might be. She may not have believed in God the way she had when she was growing up. But the way she lived in Paris was wrong. No arguing the point.

For a long moment she tried to imagine again what would happen if she talked to Landon about Paris. Later tonight, even. She could pull him aside out in the parking lot and really talk to him, so that everything was once and for all out in the open. Landon would watch her, no doubt, and listen, and then when Ashley reached the part about the artist being married, he would squint a little.

"You . . . were with a *married* man?" he would ask. And his tone wouldn't be rude or condescending. Just shocked. Completely shocked.

Gradually it would dawn on him that Ashley really had changed. That the girl he had fallen in love with no longer existed. He would make polite conversation for a few minutes more and he'd tell her he was sorry, but he had to go. And that would be that.

If only Landon knew the truth.

And so Ashley let her resolve grow and build until she knew exactly what she was going to do. Sometime tonight, before the celebration was over, she was going to find a quiet spot with Landon and she was going to tell him everything. The whole ugly truth. Then she wouldn't have to worry about him falling in love with her again. And this time Cinderella wouldn't have to worry about fleeing the ballroom at midnight.

Landon would be gone long before that.

*   *   *

ELIZABETH WAS DANCING with John, moving easily in his arms as he twirled and spun her across the floor. The day had been marked by dark clouds and thunder, fears and deep concerns for Kari's future. But ever since Elizabeth watched her say her vows, a peace had come over the entire event.

Everything was going to be okay.

Tim and Kari had been on the dance floor since the music started two hours ago. Every time Elizabeth looked at them, they were within an arm's length of each other. Like they couldn't be closer together if they tried.

Another good sign.

"You look happy." John slowed the pace, and took her hand in his. "The wedding was beautiful."

"Yes. It was." Elizabeth exhaled. "I worried about nothing." She loved this, moving to the music in John's arms. "Out here . . . dancing with you. It always takes my heart back."

"To that college mixer at University of Michigan." He smiled, his eyes sparkling. "You look just as beautiful now as you did then."

"And you. My handsome John." She moved closer to him. "Kari's happy. I can see it in her face."

"Mmm." John shot a quick look in the direction of Kari and Tim. "I'd say she looks giddy."

"I like that. Giddy." Elizabeth smiled. They were barely dancing now, their focus on only each other. "God even held back the big storm."

"He's always good."

Elizabeth leaned her head on his chest as the song wound down. Yes, God was always good. All the time. There hadn't been any need for worry or doubt or hesitancy. Okay, so Kari's life hadn't worked out the way Elizabeth had expected. But that didn't mean it hadn't worked out.

The song ended and Pastor Mark took the mic. He asked the guests to come to the double doors at the back of the room. Time for the bride and groom to say their goodbyes. Just then, Kari and Tim hurried up to Elizabeth and John.

"Mom . . . Dad . . ." Kari still looked radiant even after spending hours dancing. She hugged them both. "Today was perfect. The wedding of my dreams. Thank you."

Tim shook John's hand. "I'll take the best care of your daughter, Dr. Baxter." He grinned. "Happiest day of my life."

People were lining up on either side of the doors. Kari glanced that way and then back at Elizabeth. "I love you, Mom. Thanks for everything. For talking to me." She didn't say more than that, but Elizabeth understood.

Kari was clearly thankful she had gone through with the wedding, glad she hadn't allowed irrational fears or the terrible storm to stop her from marrying Tim. Elizabeth hugged her daughter once more. "Have a wonderful time, honey."

"We will." She took Tim's hand and the two of them waved. Then they were off through the pathway of wedding guests. Tim was taking her on an Alaskan cruise. The two of them would have a beautiful week together and then a lifetime of love.

Today was only the beginning.

15

None of the other guests was leaving the wedding, so Landon made his way back to the table on the far side of the room. The band was playing a line dance, and most of the bridal party was on the floor.

Even Ashley.

Her parents had Cole at their table, and Ashley was doing the Electric Slide beside her sisters—Erin and Brooke—and a few of their friends. Landon watched her, the way she moved in her pink dress. Laughing like she hadn't just shared the deepest few minutes with him.

Landon had longed for her every day since things fell apart. And now as he watched her it was easy to see the girl she'd been. Before the accident. The spirited, sometimes headstrong girl who had eyes only for him.

Maybe it was the music or being alone at a wedding table while everyone else was dancing, but Landon could sense the years slipping away, remember the way it felt to go by her house on his way to college that summer after the accident.

Like old times they had sat on her parents' porch

and then they had walked to Ashley's favorite place on their ten-acre property—the giant rock near the pond. The spot where all five Baxter kids had left their handprints in white paint the day they moved in. Ashley loved to go there to think or pray or dream.

Her best artwork seemed to come out of moments spent at the rock.

And there, dressed in a tank top and shorts, Ashley told him what they both already knew. He could still see her sitting beside him, still hear the water in the stream a few yards away. Tears spilled onto her cheeks before she said a word.

"Just say it, Ash." He had leaned back on his hands so he could see her better. "I leave for college tomorrow, so tell me. Why did you want to talk?"

For a long time she only shook her head. When she could find her voice she turned and faced him, sitting cross-legged the way she had when they were kids. "It's over, Landon. I . . . I can't do this."

The breakup didn't make sense then and it still didn't now. That day he had lifted his face to the sky. "Do you ever just . . . you know, just go over everything that's happened since the accident?"

A few soft sobs came from her, but she didn't say anything.

"You have the most horrific accident." He looked at her. "Not your fault, but Luke's friend is killed." He turned so he could see her better. "Horrible. Worst thing a person could go through."

Another river of tears spilled from her eyes. "Landon . . ."

"Wait." He sat up taller and put his hand on her knee. His voice fell. He wanted to be sensitive, but she needed to hear this. Before they said goodbye. He took a breath. "Hear me out, Ashley. Please."

She squeezed her eyes shut, and another few sobs trembled through her.

"For whatever reason, you survive." He gave the slightest shrug. "Who can know these things? Why one person dies and another lives. But you live, Ash. You're here because God isn't finished with you."

Ashley turned her face away, her eyes still closed.

"So you come home to rehab and figure out life again." He slid closer still, and moved his hand to her shoulder. "And somehow between my hospital visits and a dozen stops by your house, you stop loving me."

Her eyes flew open at that. "It's not that, it's . . ."

Landon gave her time to finish. But no words came. "It *is* that, Ash. And I'm just saying . . . help me understand why?"

"I still . . . I . . . l-l-love you." She shook her head, an ocean of sadness twisted into her expression. "I just . . . can't do this."

Nothing like Ashley's accident had ever happened to Landon. He couldn't argue with her, not then or now. If she felt unable to stay in the relationship there was nothing he could do to change her mind.

That day at the rock, Landon had put his arm around

her. He waited until she wasn't crying anymore. His fingers on her bare arm, he tried to imagine life without her.

He couldn't.

Ashley had pulled her knees to her chest and buried her face in them, all while Landon sat quietly, not saying anything until finally he took a deep breath. "I go to school tomorrow and when I come back . . . you and I . . . we'll be just friends?" The words were the hardest he'd said in all his life. He ran his hand along her back. "Is that what you want?"

"Yes." Her answer spilled out. She lifted her face and looked at him. "I don't know who I am anymore, Landon. I just know . . ." She gave the smallest shake of her head. "I can't do this. I can't . . . be who I was. With you. With anyone." She looked out at the stream. "I want to go to Paris and paint and be single. Love hurts too much."

Landon started to debate the fact. He thought about reminding her of the beautiful months when they were in love, before the accident. But something in her voice told him the topic wasn't open for discussion. *Love hurts too much.* Her words ran through his mind again then and now.

While he watched her dance with her sisters.

Love hurt too much because she lived and Jefferson Bennett died.

There hadn't been more to say that day, so she had walked him to his car and hugged him—for a long time. Then she stepped back and crossed her arms tight in front of herself. "Goodbye, Landon. You'll do great at school."

On the inside Landon was screaming, dying to tell her she was wrong and that the two of them had always been meant only for each other, and that she couldn't possibly break up with him because she'd been through a hard time. But it was too late for any of that.

So he had only nodded, climbed behind the wheel, and driven away.

Ashley went to community college that fall while Landon started his freshman year at Baylor. He thought about her every day, literally walked around campus with an ache in his chest from missing her.

But college wasn't all bad. Second day of school Landon met Jalen Hale, a guy who happened to sit next to him in English Lit. On the way out of class Jalen fell in beside Landon. "You play football?"

"I did." Landon laughed. "Didn't quite make the cut here at Baylor."

The guy's eyes lit up. "I'm putting a flag team together. Intramural." He pulled a flyer from his backpack. "Give me a shout if you're interested."

Landon was. He called Jalen that night and added himself to the team. Suddenly Landon's Saturdays and Wednesday nights were full of more fun than he planned to have his first semester.

After the second game, Landon met Jalen's twin sister, Hope. She had the same dark hair as Jalen, but her brown eyes and smile took Landon's breath. It was the first time another girl had turned his head.

By the end of October, Landon and Hope were hanging out a few times a week. He had told her up front there was someone back home. "I need time. This won't be easy."

She didn't mind. "I promised myself I wouldn't get a boyfriend until my junior year." Her answer was just what Landon wanted to hear. "Too much to do, too many people to meet."

At Christmas break, Landon went home with every intention of making things right with Ashley. Instead, she refused to see him. He went to her house with a Christmas present, a sketchbook like the one she'd had when he first met her.

Her mother greeted him at the door and apologized. "Ashley . . . asked me to tell you it's too soon." Mrs. Baxter looked troubled. "She needs space, Landon. Pray for her. Please."

When Ashley finally talked to him, it was only to tell him she had made up her mind. She was moving to Paris.

After the break, Landon found something else to take his mind off Ashley Baxter. Firefighting. It happened because Jalen had joined the local volunteer fire department. "I won't do it forever," Jalen had told him. "But I love the idea of fighting fires. Saving people. The adrenaline rush." He grinned. "You should join me."

And Landon did. He wasn't sure if he wanted to be a firefighter. But he had a blast hanging out with Jalen. Besides, working ten hours a week with the local department was good for his college résumé. Either way.

The memories lifted and Landon watched Ashley

again. He would never forget how much he missed her at Baylor. Some days he would sort through letters she'd given him, reminding himself how much she had loved him.

How much she *used* to love him.

He didn't see her until her going-away party—a week before she left for Paris. She was kind to him, but the distance between them was so vast she practically felt like a stranger. Even the way she talked was different. Less enthusiasm, less . . . Ashley.

Despite all that, the chemistry between them was palpable. Like her body had the sense to know she belonged with him. Whether she admitted it or not. There were times when he would catch her watching him. And at the end of the night when they hugged, neither of them wanted to let go.

But Landon left the party thinking one thing about the girl he still loved: The darkness was winning. He saw her just once more, the night before her flight to France. And even then he couldn't convince her to stay. Half a year later she came home from Paris pregnant and alone. He would always remember how he felt when he heard the news.

What happened that day was so awful he hadn't told anyone back home. Landon looked out at the dance floor again. The song was coming to an end, but Ashley and her sisters seemed happy to stay on the dance floor. Whatever the band played next.

Tonight was supposed to be different, Ash. He sighed.

You felt it when we danced. I know you did. He had hoped to ask her out for coffee after the reception. Or just find a place where they could finally and fully talk. That didn't look likely now. He pushed his chair back. Maybe it was best just to leave, not make an attempt at good-byes.

He was about to stand when he felt a hand on his shoulder. A quick turn and there was Mrs. Baxter. She looked like an older, more genteel version of Ashley, with one exception. Her eyes were warm and full of welcome. "Landon." Her smile could ease the most troubled heart. "There you are."

"Mrs. Baxter." Landon was on his feet, hugging the woman. He raised his voice so she could hear him over the music. "I hoped I'd get a chance to thank you. The wedding was beautiful."

A depth shone in her expression. "I'm glad you joined us. I know . . ." She glanced across the room in Ashley's direction. "I know it's never . . . easy."

"No." He chuckled. "Definitely not."

"Anyway"—she took a quick breath and a smile filled her face—"join us after the reception back at the house. We're having a small party, some food and a chance to catch up." She raised her eyebrows and laughed. "Where it's a little quieter."

Back to the Baxter house after the reception? Landon had never considered such an idea. He shot a quick glance at Ashley and he didn't need time to process the offer. This was the moment he'd been hoping for. A time when he could talk to Ashley for more than a few minutes. "You're sure?" Much as he wanted to join them, he didn't want the situation to be forced. "Won't it just be family?"

"Landon Blake." Elizabeth took his hand and gave it a gentle squeeze. "You are family. You always will be." Her eyes told him she meant every word. "Join us."

"Okay. I will." He gave her another hug. "Thanks."

As she walked away, Landon looked at his watch. It was only just after eight o'clock. Which meant there was still plenty of time left to make it to the Baxter house and spend an hour with Ashley.

He only hoped she would be okay with her mother inviting him.

With this new plan, Landon settled back in his seat. He doubted the reception would go much longer. The bandleader had announced he was playing a final set of songs. The music changed and a familiar tune filled the room. "In the Mood." The perfect number for swing dancing.

A memory filled Landon's heart and he smiled. Ninth grade at their middle school, he wound up in the same PE class as Ashley. Only instead of the usual running or kickball or calisthenics, Mrs. Bell was obsessed with swing dance.

Third day of school she announced that the first PE unit would be spent learning the great ways to move their partners across a dance floor. Landon could see again the looks on his friends' faces, the horrified groans that came from most of them. Swing dancing? Paired up with some girl they barely knew?

But somehow Mrs. Bell actually made the class fun. Landon and his friends looked forward to PE every day. And so did Ashley. There had been no question that Ashley would dance with him. She ran to him the first time Mrs. Bell asked them to partner up. "I can't do this with anyone else." She giggled. "You won't let me fall, right?"

He might've only been fourteen, but Landon could still see himself, grinning down at Ashley and shaking his head. "Never, Ashley. I'll never let you fall."

Turned out they were both pretty good at it. By the end of the ten weeks, Landon and Ashley were asked by Mrs. Bell to demonstrate a proper swing dance for the rest of the class.

The song she played that day in PE class was the same one playing now. "In the Mood."

Landon watched to see what Ashley was going to do, whether the song triggered the memory for her the way it did for him. And sure enough. She turned and their eyes met. Then, like she'd done that first day of PE class, she hurried to him and held out her hand. "Come on, Landon. For old times' sake."

And like that they were holding hands on the dance floor, swing dancing as if ninth grade were just last week. "You still remember?" He kept his eyes on hers. Was this really happening? The two of them out here dancing this way?

"Of course." She looked more relaxed. Maybe because the song took her back the way it did for him. "I had the best partner in the whole PE class."

As the music played, most people danced to the edge of the floor so they could watch Landon and Ashley and two other couples who knew the various moves. Landon wanted to freeze the moment, Ashley laughing and dancing, her hands in his, their bodies and feet moving in perfect rhythm with each other.

With her so close, with yesterday alive again, it was impossible not to see the Ashley he had first met in fifth grade, the one giving her report on the octopus at the front of the class . . . or the Ashley walking across the stage at ninth-grade graduation, when she found him after the ceremony and told him she was afraid.

"Why, Ash? We're done with middle school!"

"Yeah, but"—she searched his eyes—"what if we're not friends next year. There'll be so many new kids."

And Landon had laughed and shook his head. "I'll always be your friend, Ashley Baxter. You can't get rid of me."

Then they were sophomores and learning to navigate a new school. But they found out that long after the music of PE class had stopped, the song continued. Through every year of high school right up until the accident.

"They're all looking at us." Ashley pushed her hair back from her face. She was still laughing. "Are we that bad?"

"No, Ash." They did a spin and faced each other again. He looked deep into her eyes. "We're that good."

The song ended and the other wedding guests clapped and hollered their approval. By then only Landon and Ashley remained on the floor. They were still holding hands, and together they did a slight bow. She leaned close to him and whispered. "Thanks, Landon. That was fun."

They walked off the dance floor and she released his hand. Both of them were breathless as Ashley turned to him. "I'm sorry. How I acted earlier." She gave a slight shrug, like she still had no answers. "Being with you, in your arms, dancing like that. It confuses me."

He had a hundred questions for her. Couldn't she see what was happening? If she was confused, then maybe it was because she actually wanted to be with him. Did she ever consider maybe she was making things difficult for no reason? So she had a baby, so what? Was that her problem? If so, Landon didn't care. He loved her as much now as ever. And who wouldn't love little Cole?

If only she would let him.

Landon didn't ask a single question. Instead he felt a half smile lift his lips. "At least the swing dance didn't confuse you. We would've tripped over each other and landed"—he moved his hands away from each other, like an ump declaring a runner safe—"splat. Right across the floor."

A giggle seemed to take her by surprise, and her eyes sparkled. "You still know how to make me smile."

He winked at her. "Remember that, Ash."

A depth layered the moment. "How could I forget?"

She took a step back and waved. "See you, Landon. Thanks for the dance."

"You, too." Clearly she didn't know about her mother inviting him over after the reception. But she was already walking away. Which was maybe for the best. He didn't want to lose the chance to talk to her back at the house.

If he had it his way they would go deep this time. She would tell him why she thought she had changed too much to ever make things work. And he would tell her about Baylor and the one thing no one but his parents and a few school friends knew.

The only thing he wouldn't tell her was the part that scared even him. The fact that after tonight he knew one thing for sure. He could never date Jalen's sister, Hope. Because he could never love another girl the way he loved Ashley Baxter.

Even if it meant being alone the rest of his life. She was practically out the door headed to Baylor, ready to study art and live out four dreamy years as Landon's girlfriend. Couldn't God have stopped the truck from crossing the line?

16

The ride home with her parents was light and full of a happiness Ashley had missed. The music of the evening still rang in her heart and soul. Ashley sat next to Erin, Cole strapped in his car seat between them. Their parents in the front seat.

Outside, another storm was building. Lightning flashed in the far distance, and on the radio there was talk of a tornado coming later that night. Ashley wasn't worried. For now it wasn't even raining.

She leaned back in her seat and sighed. "That was actually a lot of fun."

"Kari looked happy." Her mom angled herself so she could see Ashley. "Seems like it all worked out after all."

"I knew it would." Erin smiled. "Kari really loves Tim."

"She does." Ashley nodded. The idea was growing on her. "I always pictured her with Ryan Taylor. But maybe it was just me wanting that for her."

Their dad grinned at them through the rearview mirror. "We all prayed for Kari, that she would know whether Tim was the one." He returned his gaze to the

209

road ahead of them. "God made the answer clear. To-night was proof."

Even now, with not a bit of tension in the air, Ashley had to resist the urge to remind her dad of one thing: They weren't *all* praying. Ashley hadn't prayed in for-ever. She still hadn't found a reason to believe in God again. She didn't need one. Life was better without Him.

But she kept that to herself. No need to spoil the mo-ment.

"By the way." Ashley's mom looked back at her again. "I asked Landon to come by the house for the after-party."

And just like that the mood was ruined.

Shock worked its way through Ashley. "Are you kid-ding?" She leaned forward. "Mom, why? You didn't even ask me."

On the other side of the seat, Erin looked out her passenger window. Cole was asleep, but he stirred at the sound of Ashley's angry voice. *Deep breath*, she told her-self. She forced herself to be quieter. Nothing about this was okay.

"Landon is like family, Ashley." Her mother didn't back down. "There was no time to catch up at the wed-ding. I asked him to stop by. It's no big deal."

No big deal? Anger seeped into her veins like a drug. "You know how things have been between us. I really can't believe this, Mom."

"Watch your tone." Her dad's voice remained calm. But he gave her a sharp look in the mirror. "Let the guy be your friend, Ashley. He never did anything to deserve the way you treat him."

"The way I—?" She didn't finish her question. What was the point? Landon was coming to the house and obviously expecting to spend the next few hours visiting. As if they hadn't been apart nearly every day for the past three years.

A thick tension hung in the car now, the lighthearted air from earlier gone for good. Ashley looked out her window and dropped the conversation.

Her dad tried one more time. "Your mother is only doing what she feels is best, Ashley. You have to see that."

"Fine." She didn't want to get into it. Her parents couldn't understand how desperately she wanted to avoid Landon, how terrified she was that if they spent an evening talking, they might somehow wind up back together.

They got home before the rest of the family, and Ashley hurried upstairs to her parents' room. How could this happen? Her mother should've known better. She laid Cole in his crib, then went to her old room and shut the door behind her.

Never mind the lights.

She found her bed, the one near the window where it had been ever since they moved to Bloomington. The room she had shared with Kari until Ashley moved out just before Cole was born. She sat on the edge of the mattress and stared out the window at the distant lightning.

What did Landon Blake know of the life she had lived in Paris? Or how it had been to come home pregnant? To the Baxter family, of all people? Her family was marked by a strong, consistent faith. Sure, as kids they made mistakes. They lied about finishing their math homework or cheated on an occasional test.

But those moments were big to the Baxters.

Each of those times eventually came to the surface with long talks and meetings and encouragement to be honest and kind, tell the truth and work hard. Every other kid in the family seemed able to do that.

Everyone except Ashley.

Okay, so Brooke was no longer the Sunday-school poster girl she once was. She had moved on to a more scientific understanding of life. Progressive, she called herself, which made sense. As children, they were all taught to believe in God. Blind faith, really. Based only on their parents' beliefs. Brooke had simply made progress since then.

Kind as their mom and dad were, they were wrong about the existence of God. Ashley knew that now. The thoughts of His presence she had held onto in Paris were only because she was afraid and alone. Now? Now she could see life for what it was. She had no tangible reason to put faith in God. No proof, no reason to believe.

What good had God ever done for her? She was practically out the door headed to Baylor, ready to study art and live out four dreamy years as Landon's girlfriend.

"If only I'd stayed home that night," Ashley whispered in the dark. As if in response, a lightning bolt sliced the sky. The storm was moving closer.

Of course.

After all, Landon was almost here and then there would most certainly be a tornado. Her heart would be picked up and spun around and dropped to the floor. Whether the wind actually grew stronger outside or not.

She leaned her shoulder against the cool wall and the memories came unbidden. Memories of the last year, so many months she would rather forget. And she could see herself in Paris, alone and afraid.

Once she had decided to keep her baby, she knew her days in France were numbered. Two weeks after she ran from the abortion clinic, the gallery owner found out about her affair and fired her.

The same day, her landlord must have gotten news about what happened, because she was waiting when Ashley came home. "You are pregnant." The woman sneered at Ashley. "You will need to find other arrangements. Immediately."

Ashley could hardly believe it. She didn't even have time to say goodbye to her neighbor friend, Celia. Running low on money, Ashley found a sketchy hostel in the neighboring district, where she paid for a single bunk and a shared shower.

After that she found a job at a small bakery. The place was in an undesirable part of Paris, but it allowed her to survive. Ashley worked on her feet and when waves of nausea and exhaustion hit, she would lean against the counter and steady herself.

And somehow during those long, frightening days, Ashley seemed to find her way back to God. Not to the faith of her family, but to a God who loved her even after all she had done. At least it felt that way at the time. She even shared that momentary faith with another pregnant girl at the bakery, a French woman who had battled drug addiction.

Ashley was maybe six months along when a couple of older women came into the bakery and ordered coffee. One of them pointed to Ashley's belly. "Congratulations, dear," she said in English. "When are you due?"

Until then Ashley had thought she was hiding her pregnancy well. She was lean and long, and with her loose-fitting, artsy shirts she figured no one would ever know. But if a stranger could walk in and see that she was expecting, Ashley knew she didn't have long before she made a plan. Her baby would be coming soon.

On top of that, shady men had been following her to and from work. At times, she had a sense her life was in danger. Throughout it all, she never once called home. Not even after her decision to keep her baby. She couldn't bear to hear her mother's concern on the other end of the line. But one night after working at the bakery, Ashley finally dialed the familiar number.

"Ashley, you haven't called us in so long." Her mother's relief was as tangible as the tears on Ashley's face. "We were worried."

Ashley had squeezed her eyes shut. "I know. I'm sorry." She didn't dare mention the baby. "Mom ... I want to come home."

And like that, Ashley's failed time in Paris was over. Because of her own choices, she was pregnant, broke, and desperate. Her dream of being an artist had failed in a way that defied Ashley's understanding.

"I can't afford the flight home." She squeezed her eyes shut. "Please . . . can you help me? I'll pay you back."

There was a pause on the other end and Ashley's heart sank. The news of her financial troubles would've been hard for her mother to understand. Ashley's parents had arranged for their attorney to give Ashley a portion of the settlement money from the accident up front. For her time in Paris. The rest wouldn't come till she turned twenty-one.

But now those funds were gone.

"Ashley. You ... you're out of money?" It was the only time her mother had sounded surprised.

Ashley wasn't sure what to say. "I am." Ashley hung her head and pressed the phone to her face. "I'm sorry. I'll explain everything later."

Of course, her mom didn't hesitate, and didn't ask questions beyond that. She arranged for Ashley's flight and the next day she boarded a 747 for New York City.

She didn't cry until her layover at JFK, just hours from Indiana, and the inevitable news. News that she had known would crush her entire family.

Ashley blinked a few times. The wind was picking up outside, but she still saw no sign of Landon's car. Maybe he wasn't coming. He had probably thought it through and realized seeing Ashley again was a waste of time. For both of them.

Tears blurred Ashley's vision, and she blinked again. She wouldn't cry. Not now, not when Landon still might be coming to see her. She closed her eyes and lay back on her childhood bedspread.

As she got off the plane that afternoon at the Indianapolis airport, Ashley had a used maternity book in her backpack. She was seven months pregnant by then, and according to chapter 12 she should've been over being sick. Which could only mean one thing.

She was nauseous not because of the baby growing inside her. But from what faced her at the end of the Jetway.

Like always those days, Ashley wore a loose flouncy top, long enough to hide her unzipped jeans. But she had always been skinny and now her thin frame did nothing to hide her basketball-size bump.

Forever she would remember watching her parents' faces as she walked off the plane. They were waiting for her at the gate, of course. Because they really did love her that much. Whatever had caused her to cut short her time in Paris, they would be there. That was the Baxter way.

Ashley watched their faces light up as they spotted her. But as she approached them, as the other passengers peeled off in their own directions, and Ashley's entire body came into view, she saw both their gazes fall to her pregnant belly.

Her dad took a step back and stared at the floor. Then barely a second later he lifted his face and returned to the spot next to her mom. He straightened his shoulders and waited for her.

At the same time, her mom's eyes welled up with tears. She brought her hand to her mouth and then let it fall to her side again. As Ashley came closer her parents closed the gap. In all the times Ashley had imagined how they might respond to her pregnancy, the one thing she didn't expect was what happened next.

Her parents drew her into a hug. Ashley began to cry then, and the embrace lasted until the final people were off the plane. Her mom and dad wouldn't let go. They just held her and ran their hands over her shoulders and back.

When they were finally alone at the gate, her dad led them to the three closest seats. He had tears by then, too. "Ashley . . . my precious girl. What happened?"

The details were so ugly, so completely sordid, but she had to share them. From the moment she left Paris, Ashley had promised herself she would tell her family the entire truth. So there would be no dark secrets to cover up, no lies to carry.

Ashley kept the story brief, while her parents listened to every word. Not once did anger flash in their faces. They weren't disgusted with her. They were heartbroken. Which was maybe worse.

Once she finished talking, her dad put his arm around her. "We'll stay by your side, Ashley. Your mother and I, we aren't going anywhere."

Her mom took her hand. The tears on her cheeks were drying now. "We're so glad you're home. We'll get through this." She stood and put her hands on Ashley's shoulders. "We will. Everything's going to be okay."

Then her dad did something Ashley hadn't done since before the accident. He put his other arm around Elizabeth, and he prayed. For God to protect Ashley and her baby, and for their family to be supportive and come alongside her. "I know Ashley regrets her choices, Father. Please, give her Your healing and forgiveness. Show her Your grace. In Jesus' name, amen."

But if her parents had given Ashley a welcome greater than she had expected, the opposite was true for her siblings. When she walked through the door, she hurried to her old bedroom and changed into a sweatshirt. Her clothes hid her baby bump as the family gathered in the living room.

No one expected her to be pregnant, so no one noticed.

But once everyone was in the same room celebrating Ashley's return, she spoke up. "I'm pregnant. I'm due in two months." She took a deep breath and told them the same story she had told her parents earlier.

She didn't spare a single detail.

When she was finished her parents jumped up to hug her but as soon as they sat down, everyone waited in silence, not stirring. Erin's mouth hung slightly open. She was the first to move as she stood and came to Ashley. "I'm so sorry," she whispered. It was all she said before she returned to her seat.

Kari's face was pale. She crossed her arms and looked down. When she lifted her gaze to Ashley again she shook her head. "I can't believe it. So your baby won't have a dad?"

"He doesn't need one." Ashley's response was quick. By then she had decided the baby was a boy. Just a feeling she had. "I'm enough all by myself."

At that, Ashley saw her parents exchange a knowing look. Like Ashley had no idea what was involved in having a baby.

Ashley's oldest sister, Brooke, was married to Peter by then and the two had just brought home baby Maddie. Their family lived across town, so they would have to find out later.

Finally it was Luke's turn to say something, do something. Ashley looked at him, the boy who had been one of her best friends when they were little. Anger built in his eyes until Luke looked like he might blow up. He stood and stared at her. "You had an affair with a *married* man? Are you kidding me?"

Then he turned toward the doorway and waved her off, like he was finished with her.

"Luke!" Their father was on his feet now. "Get back in here."

"Why?" Luke stopped and faced their dad. "She trashed our name and now she's back here pregnant with some married guy's kid." He glared at Ashley. "God gave you a second chance, Ashley. This is what you do with it?"

He ran upstairs before anyone could stop him. And he'd been angry with her ever since.

Ashley heard a car pull into the driveway. One look out the window told her who it was. Landon had come after all. She stood and pressed her hand against the glass. How would she survive the next few hours without falling in love with him all over again?

She imagined herself dancing in his arms a few hours ago, his face close to hers. Everything in her wanted to go to him, hold on to him and tell him she was sorry for being rude and unkind these past three years. She would tell him she loved him still. She always would.

But that could never happen. None of it. If the night ended like that, it would be disastrous for them both.

Stay strong, she told herself. *He's totally wrong for you. You're wrong for him. You have to tell him what happened in Paris.*

Yes, that was it. She would find a moment tonight to make the details painfully clear. So he would walk away knowing the whole truth about her time overseas. She sighed and found her bag on the floor. She had brought a change of clothes for the after-party, both for her and for Cole.

A minute later she was dressed in dark jeans and a white scoop-neck T-shirt. She slipped on a pair of tennis shoes and took a deep breath. For the next few hours she had one goal: to tell Landon Blake what she'd really done, and to keep her heart as far from him as possible. Before she changed her mind.

She had to go deep when they talked tonight. No more chatting about school and paintings and what used to be. No more memories of life in the fifth grade. Tonight they would share their first honest conversation since she came home. And that would be that. Otherwise she would do the one thing she had promised she would never do.

Run into Landon Blake's arms, and never, ever let go.

17

After the wedding Landon stopped by his house to change. Jeans and a T-shirt were more fitting for the after-party. When his parents asked him where he was headed, Landon only smiled. "Catching up with some friends."

If he told them he was spending the late evening at the Baxters', they would think he needed counseling. Which maybe he did. Either way, he was going. But not without a gift for Cole.

The idea of getting something for Ashley's baby had dawned on him as he left the wedding. He'd never been allowed this close to Ashley, and so he'd never properly welcomed the little guy into the world.

Another severe thunderstorm was closing in around Bloomington, and the city was still under a tornado watch. Landon didn't care. He was thrilled at the chance to go out and buy something for Cole. Maybe the gift would be a peace offering, and Ashley would see he was okay with dating her—even if she had a baby.

He drove to the bookstore while thunder sounded overhead. A cold front was moving in and by the looks of the swaying trees on either side of the road, the after-party would be inside.

Maybe even in the basement.

Landon walked to the children's section and found a baby devotional. Short stories and basic Bible verses. Something Ashley might read to Cole in their quiet time at home. He looked the book over and flipped through a few pages.

But maybe not. Ashley's views on God hadn't changed. She still didn't share her parents' faith, didn't want Landon's love for the Lord or for Scripture. If there was a God, she had told Landon, He didn't care about His people.

That's the way she saw it.

Landon stared at the sweet baby devotional and slowly set it back on the shelf. It was the perfect gift. But not right now. Ashley wouldn't read it to Cole, anyway. He moved to the Dr. Seuss section. *Horton Hears a Who!* Landon flipped the book over and read the back cover copy.

A person's a person, no matter how small.

Yes, that would be better. For now, anyway.

Landon grabbed a blue gift bag and tissue paper and at the last minute a blank card with a picture of yellow flowers on the front. So he could write Ashley a letter. Then he headed for the cashier. All the while he couldn't keep his thoughts anchored in the here and now. He paid for his purchase and was walking back to his Toyota when lightning cut through the sky in the distance. A few seconds later thunder shook the ground. He stared at the clouds overhead. No rain.

But that was coming.

As soon as he was behind the wheel he assembled the gift. But like earlier his mind was a million minutes back in time. Christmas break of his freshman year. He had come home expecting Ashley to be there, ready to talk and figure things out. Never mind that she had barely spoken to him when he called or that she never responded to his letters.

Christmas was coming, of course she'd talk to him. They would get together and break the ice that had built up since the accident. And then they'd hug for a long time and life between them would begin again. That's how he saw it happening.

But he had never been more wrong.

A few days after getting home Ashley asked if they could meet. This was it, he had told himself. The moment when she would tell him she was making strides toward healing. That she was at least believing she could move on from her grief.

Instead she had used the time to tell him two things. First, she was moving to Paris. And second, she could never be his friend. The two of them were over. For good.

He could picture her that Sunday afternoon—more beautiful than ever—her heart frozen solid. Her eyes told the story. Ashley was no longer the girl he had fallen for in Mr. Garrett's fifth-grade class. She wasn't his prom date from less than a year earlier. She was different. Completely.

And nothing was going to fix that.

Landon saw her a few more times that break. The chemistry was still there, he could feel it, and he was sure she did, too. They still gravitated toward each other and made eye contact across any room. A few times they had awkward conversations—at his family's Christmas open house and again when they ran into each other at Luke's high school basketball game.

Toward the end of break, Landon attended Ashley's going away party, but she turned in early and never said more than a quick goodbye to him. The next night – just before her flight – Landon went to her house in a blinding snowstorm. Anything to change her mind.

But in the end, she held her ground. She left for Paris and didn't look back.

So with Ashley wanting nothing to do with him, Landon poured his attention into his new friends. Jalen and Hope. It was spring of his sophomore year when he returned to school and the three of them became inseparable. But always there was Ashley. There in the corner of his mind, woven into the depths of his heart.

Another flash of lightning jolted him back to the present as Landon pulled into the Baxters' driveway and found his familiar parking spot. How much time had passed since he'd been here? He killed the engine, grabbed the gift and then reached for the door handle.

But something wouldn't let him get out of the car.

He set the gift down on the seat beside him, and leaned back. The card for Ashley. He needed to write her a letter. In case tonight didn't go the way he planned. In case he didn't have the chance to tell her how he still felt.

Landon pulled the card from the bag and found a pen in the glove compartment. Then as if his heart had sprung a leak, for the next five minutes he poured his feelings onto both sides of the blank paper and slid it into the envelope.

His lungs filled and he clenched his jaw. Was he out of his mind? Here in the same place he'd parked more times than he could remember? Landon stared at the card in his hand. Why was he here? What was the point?

He hadn't even told her he was stopping by. Because if he had, he knew how she would have responded. She would have shaken her head and begged him not to come. *It can't work*, she would have told him. *It's over between us.*

So why stay? His head asked his heart the question, but neither could make a move. Landon fiddled with his keys. No, he couldn't leave. Not when this would be the only time he'd had with Ashley in years. Maybe if he told her what happened when he first heard the news about her.

Maybe if she knew about his college drinking.

A ribbon of frustration wove itself through him. He had never been a drinker. Not in high school when most of the football team downed six-packs of beer every Friday night after the games. And not when he moved to Texas and began taking classes at Baylor.

Lots of kids partied. Not Landon. His faith in God was enough to keep him on track, alone on Saturday nights if that's what it took. At first Jalen agreed with him. The two would round up a group of guys and go bowling and out for pizza. Landon figured maybe God had him at Baylor to help his friends see they didn't need to drink to have fun. Besides, none of them were of age. So it was illegal, no matter how many college kids drank.

But by the time they reached the second semester of their sophomore year, Jalen had joined the crowd that hit up the kegs at their college parties. "It's no big deal, Blake," Jalen would tell him. "I'm not like those other kids who get wasted all the time."

He was right. Some kids were out of control with their drinking. Couldn't take in a day of classes without downing a few shots of Jack Daniel's. Jalen wasn't doing that. But still it frustrated Landon that his friend partied at all. And it frustrated Jalen that Landon didn't.

"Come on, Blake, loosen up. Pop a top, already," Jalen would tell him when they were out. He would grin and poke Landon in the shoulder. "God won't be mad at you."

Landon had held his ground. He wasn't afraid of making God angry. His conviction was about honoring the Lord, living a life set apart from the world. Landon remembered a Bible verse that had kept him on track during those years.

Do not conform to the pattern of this world, but be transformed by the renewing of your mind.

The Scripture was Romans 12:2, and it kept Landon focused. He didn't want to be like everyone else. They still weren't of legal drinking age at that point, and Landon had no intention of breaking the law. Let alone getting drunk.

But all that changed when he heard about Ashley.

It was a Saturday that fall. His mom called to tell him the news. "Ashley Baxter is home, Landon. I ran into her mother at the market."

At first his heart soared. Paris hadn't worked out. As hard as that must've been for her, at least she was home! Which meant maybe the two of them might get back together after all! But before his internal celebration could take root, his mother exhaled. Whatever she was about to say, Landon sensed it wasn't good. "Mom? Tell me." He swallowed hard. "What is it?"

"There's no easy way to say this." She hesitated. "Landon, Ashley is pregnant. She must've met someone in Paris."

Met someone? Landon's mind raced right past the fact that Ashley was expecting a baby and straight to the more terrible possibility. "Is she . . . is she married?"

"No." His mom sounded sick about the situation. "The baby's father . . . he isn't involved at all."

A few hours after the phone call, the news was still decimating Landon. Ashley was pregnant. That meant she'd been with some guy . . . some jerk who had slept with her and walked away. Otherwise why didn't she marry the guy, right?

The more Landon thought about the situation, the darker he felt. He and Ashley had been meant for each other since they were kids. And now . . . now everything had changed.

When Jalen asked him to go to a party that night, Landon didn't hesitate. And for the first time he didn't avoid the keg in the kitchen. He parked himself by it. One cup of beer became two, and two became four.

Landon had never drank, never felt what it was like to be buzzed, let alone drunk. But that night he finally understood the draw. Alcohol eased the pain. It changed reality into a hazy happy place where troubles grew dim.

Halfway through the party, Jalen found him leaning hard against the kitchen counter, a fifth beer in his hand. "Blake, what are you doing?" He chuckled, but his expression looked startled. "Someone told me you were in here getting hammered."

Much of that night was outside the scope of Landon's memory. But he remembered Jalen talking to him in the kitchen. Landon had laughed, his words slurred. "Hammers up!" He stumbled a bit and caught himself. "You always tell me to be loose. Drink a little." He raised his red plastic cup. "Just doing what you said, Jalen, old buddy, old pal."

"Yeah, well, cut it off." Jalen took the cup from Landon and dumped the beer in the sink. "You've had enough."

After Jalen left the kitchen, some kid walked in with a bottle of whiskey. Or gin, maybe. Landon still wasn't sure. The guy lined up a few shot glasses and asked Landon if he wanted to play. "Most shots wins." The kid laughed. "You're first."

All Landon could see was his beautiful Ashley, his childhood friend and high school love, alone and pregnant with some other guy's baby. He gritted his teeth and ignored the sick feeling in his stomach. Jalen was right. He'd probably had enough.

But Landon was angry. Furious with Ashley for ruining things. They were supposed to get married and find a small house where they would start their life and their family. Her first baby was supposed to be his.

Only now everything was wrecked.

Landon had pushed back from the counter that night and reached for the poured shots. "Sure," he mumbled as he took the first drink. "I'll play."

The last thing Landon remembered was hitting the floor. His head smacked against the cold tile and in the recesses of his mind it registered that he'd been hurt. That he might even be bleeding.

But he couldn't make his hands and arms move. And then there was nothing but the darkest black night.

When he woke up, he was in the hospital, hooked to an IV and pain medication. Jalen was sitting in the chair at the end of his bed. "Thank God." His friend clearly meant the words. He stood and came to Landon's side. His face was pale. "Blake . . . you almost died."

Nausea welled up in him and his head felt like it had been hit with a baseball bat. "Where . . . what happened?"

The story made him sick still today. As the shots hit his bloodstream, Landon fell to the floor and his head split open. But worse than that, the alcohol had nearly killed him. Jalen had rushed him to the hospital, where doctors pumped his stomach and stitched up his head, a gash just into his hairline near his right ear.

Later that morning, the doctor came to see him. "You were barely breathing when your friend brought you in." He frowned at Landon. "Son, you can't drink like that." He grabbed hold of the railing that ran alongside Landon's bed. "Kids like you don't get it. It takes half an hour for alcohol to make it from your stomach to your bloodstream. That's why you keep drinking, long past when it's safe." He sighed. "I'm going to refer you for counseling. I think you need it."

Landon was embarrassed, disgusted with himself. "Yes, sir." He looked up at the doctor. "I won't drink again."

"I hope not." The doctor jotted something down on his chart. "We're keeping you another day to make sure your head's okay. You suffered a minor concussion in the fall."

Jalen had waited in the hall while the doctor talked

to Landon. Now as the man left, Landon's friend returned. "Bad, huh?"

"How could I be so stupid?" Landon stared at Jalen.
The gravity of the situation was still hitting him. "Jalen,
man. You saved my life."

"I never should've told you to drink." He didn't
laugh. There was nothing funny about the situation.

After that, Landon kept his word. He told his parents what had happened, attended the counseling sessions, and most of all he hadn't touched alcohol since.
Not a sip. No interest. Landon was positive he would
never drink again. Sure, his heart was broken from the
news about Ashley. But that wasn't license to nearly kill
himself. Even if he hadn't almost died, Landon had
turned to the wrong source to comfort his pain. Alcohol could never help him navigate the loss of Ashley
Baxter.

Only God could do that.

Landon bid the terrible memory good riddance.
Again. Then he grabbed the gift for Cole, slipped the
card inside, and climbed out of his car. Maybe he
shouldn't be here. Maybe the magic of the wedding was
all the two of them would ever have. Or maybe tonight
he would find the answer to the question that had
haunted him since the accident.

Why had she stopped loving him?

He started on the pathway leading to the door and
hesitated. He had no way of knowing what was about to
happen or how things would go with Ashley. Just that he

loved her and he had to talk to her. Maybe this was their chance. A gust of wind blew against his back, as if God were pushing him toward the house. He needed to get inside. There was a reason he was here tonight.

Now he could only beg God to show him why.

18

So far the after-party was nothing but awkward bits of conversation and strange moments of silence. Exactly the way Ashley had pictured it. Brooke and Peter and little Maddie sat at one end of the table.

Their parents anchored the other end, and in between were Erin and Luke on one side and Ashley and Landon on the other. Before Landon got there, Brooke had asked their mom why he was invited. "It's just family tonight."

Her mom had been adamant. "We haven't spent time with Landon in forever." Her tone was slightly defensive. "He's like family to all of us. Or at least to me and your father."

Brooke shot Ashley a look, as if to say she had tried. Ashley nodded her thanks and rolled her eyes. It felt good to have her oldest sister on her side. They weren't always this close when they were growing up.

Now Ashley looked around the table. No telling which storm was worse—the one brewing outside or the one here in the dining room. Luke seemed extra grumpy, as if the charm of the wedding reception had completely worn off.

Cole was hungry, off his sleep schedule and wanting to eat. Elizabeth set him in his high chair and was feeding him carrots and turkey from a couple baby food jars. Ashley watched her mom open a small bottle of juice, pour it into his sippy cup and hand it to him. "I loved seeing you all dance tonight." She glanced at Landon and then Ashley. "You two looked as good as you did back in high school."

A quiet cough came from Brooke, as if she was not so subtly cautioning their mother against doing this. Reminding her not to push Ashley toward Landon. Not to say things that would only add to the tension.

Ashley would thank Brooke later.

The meal was more of a snack, or maybe with the dark cloud hanging over the table everyone had lost their appetite. After a painful half hour, Ashley stood and grabbed a glass of water from the kitchen. Landon took her lead and helped clear the table.

After that everyone got up, and Ashley found Brooke at the sink rinsing her plate. "Hey . . . thanks for that, earlier." She shook her head. "Sometimes I don't think Mom knows how she sounds."

"Whatever happens or doesn't happen between you and Landon, it's your choice." Brooke seemed as frustrated as Ashley felt. "This whole thing is ridiculous. Him being here."

Ashley was about to agree when Luke walked up and stood a little too close to her. "Look over there." His voice was quiet and angry. He pointed to their mom still feeding Cole. Luke glared at Ashley. "How do you expect your son to know who his mother is? When you do none of the work?"

"Mom wants to feed him." Again Brooke stuck up for Ashley. Her tone was louder than Luke's, and she seemed to catch herself. "Never mind." She stared at Luke. "One of these days you're going to have to get off your high horse, little brother. No one can stay perfect forever."

Brooke didn't wait for Luke to respond. Instead she gathered her purse and Peter and Maddie and bid the family goodbye. "We want to get home before the sirens go off." She glanced back at Ashley and then cast a quick smile at her parents. "Thanks for the food. The wedding was great."

A round of hugs and kisses and Brooke's family was gone. Erin went up to her room, probably because she could sense things weren't headed in the right direction.

Great, Ashley thought. Now Luke could take verbal swings at her all night long. Ashley watched her mother resume her spot near Cole's high chair, feeding him the last of his meal.

This time her brother didn't have to say anything. As Landon worked on the dishes, Luke simply tossed a sarcastic glance in Cole's direction and then raised his eyebrows at Ashley. In a voice only she could hear, he muttered, "Some mom, Ashley. One of the best."

That was it. Ashley slammed her water glass down and walked to her mother. "Move, please."

Her mom looked up, confused. "Ashley. What's wrong?"

"Just let me do it. Please." She shot daggers back at Luke. "My brother thinks I should be feeding Cole. Every time. Always."

From where she was standing she could see Landon in the kitchen. He looked over his shoulder and hesitated. For a moment Ashley wondered if he might say something to her, try to calm her down. But apparently he knew better because he shifted his focus back to the dishes.

John returned to the dining room just then. "What's happening here?"

"Luke." Ashley waved an angry hand in his direction. "He accused me of being a bad mom, never doing the work. He said my son won't even know me when he's older." She turned to her mother again. "Please, Mom. He's my son. I want to feed him."

With no choice, her mother stood and gave Ashley the chair. She took it with gusto, slamming herself into the seat and pulling the high chair closer. "I can feed my own baby. Just trying to let Mom be a grandmother. But whatever, Luke." She glared over her shoulder at her brother, who was helping Landon in the kitchen now. "Just so you know. You're a terrible example of a Christian. All judgment and hatred. Really nice, Luke. You never even—"

Before Ashley could finish talking, Luke slammed a plate down on the counter and it shattered into a hundred pieces.

"Luke!" Their dad stepped forward. "That is completely—"

"Not now, Dad. Please." Luke stormed toward Ashley and suddenly he seemed to notice Cole. The child's eyes were big, like he was very aware of everything happening around him.

"Watch your tone." Ashley hissed. "If you have something to say, don't yell."

"Whatever." Luke dropped his voice. "My point is, you leave your kid with Mom and Dad constantly. For what?" He pointed at her. "So you can hit the town with your friends?" Every word dripped with venom and disapproval. Luke leaned on the table so he could get closer to her. He grabbed the cap to Cole's juice bottle and pointed it at Ashley. "I just want to go on record saying I think you're pathetic. A pathetic example of a mother."

Landon was drying his hands, headed their way. "Luke, take a breath." Landon's voice was calm, quiet. Probably because he was stunned that the fight was happening now, while he was visiting. He nodded at Luke. "You don't mean that."

"Actually, I do." Luke slammed the cap on Cole's tray.

"I should go." Landon looked at Ashley and then at her parents. "I'm sorry. This is . . . I shouldn't be here."

As Landon left the room, Ashley watched her dad step closer and grit his teeth. He pointed to the back door. "Both of you, outside on the porch. Go make things right and don't come in till you do."

Ashley couldn't believe this was happening. She was on her feet, trying to make sense of it all. First, Landon had witnessed the whole thing, and now this? Was her dad serious? Go outside and talk things out? Just then Erin came down and stared at Ashley and Luke. "Are you two for real? Fighting like this . . . with Landon here? I can hear you all the way in my room."

"It's not your business." Luke was clearly still hot, like he wanted to punch his hand through a wall. He turned to their father. "With all respect, Dad, I don't want to talk to Ashley. Not now." He shot her another mean glance. "Not ever."

"Same." Ashley didn't want him to have the last word. All of this was his fault.

Luke shook his head, his expression proof that he had nothing but disdain for her. He headed toward the stairs and on his way he caught Landon at the front door, just leaving. "Why in the world you still love my sister, I'll never know." He released a single mean laugh. "She isn't worth it."

"Luke, hold on!" Their father's voice was angry now, too. "Don't you leave this—"

Before he could finish his sentence a coughing sound came from Cole. Ashley turned to him and panic seized her. Her son's face was bright red, his eyes strangely wide.

He made the sound again. A tight raspy noise like he wasn't getting any air.

"He's choking! The juice cap!" Ashley screamed the words, but she couldn't move.

"Dear God, no!" Her mom raced for Cole and took him out of the high chair. Her father was there, too, and both of them began patting Cole's back. Hard. "Come on, baby, cough it out. Come on, Cole!" Her mom had never sounded so desperate. She patted him again. "Dear God, please."

"No!" Ashley screamed. "Cough it out, Cole!" She turned to her sister. "Erin . . . call 9-1-1."

Their dad took firm hold of Cole and tried again, hitting his back harder this time. "Come on, Cole. Please, baby."

Ashley still couldn't move, couldn't breathe. Her baby was choking. He couldn't draw a single bit of air and now the sounds he'd been making earlier were gone. His mouth hung open, his cheeks purplish.

She put her hands to her face and paced a few steps in each direction. "Someone! Help us!" she screamed. "Dear God, don't let him die! Please!" And suddenly she knew the one person who could save her baby. Landon had mentioned it over dinner a few minutes ago. He had just finished taking an infant CPR course as part of his volunteer firefighter training.

"Landon!" His name was a shrill scream on her lips. "Landon, come back. Hurry!"

· · ·

THE FIGHT WAS more than Landon could take. He had never seen any of the Baxters act this way, and he wanted only to get away from them. He left the gift bag near the front door and slipped outside to the porch.

It wasn't raining, but the wind had picked up. Which

helped dim the noise of the angry voices inside. What had happened to the people he loved? Luke's attitude was completely out of line. No wonder Ashley didn't want to return to her family's faith, with Luke acting like that.

He wanted to talk sense into them, tell them to stop it. Force them to listen to themselves. But the moment he tried to say anything, Luke had jumped on him, too. Landon looked at the sky, at the fast-moving clouds, and he drew a calming breath. It was time to go. He could apologize later. But clearly this wasn't the night for him to be here.

Halfway down the porch steps and headed for his Toyota, Landon heard Ashley scream his name. What could possibly be happening inside? Her parents were there, and Erin. Someone else should be able to help settle down tempers.

Still, Landon didn't hesitate. If she needed him, he would go. He ran back up the steps and into the house. What he found as he reached the dining room was pure chaos. Luke was on his knees in the adjacent kitchen, his face in his hands. Erin and Elizabeth and Ashley were weeping, and—

It took Landon that long to realize what was happening. Cole was choking. The child's face was deep purple, his mouth open at an unnatural angle. His eyes rolling back in his little head. Dr. Baxter held him, patting his back, but clearly nothing was helping.

Ashley's father turned to Landon. The man's voice

was loud and thick with shock. "He . . . he can't breathe. We've called for help." He hit the baby's back again. "He swallowed the juice cap."

"Give him to me." Landon took Cole from the man's arms. He had just done this, just learned what to do. Moving as fast as he could, he sat in the nearest chair, turned Cole upside down and braced him against his knee. Using his forearm for support, he cradled the baby's face in his hand. Then with the other hand, Landon gave six quick jabs at the upper center of Cole's back. He called out as he worked. "Please, God . . . help me."

Again he repeated the same motion, all while Cole's face was aimed at the floor. They couldn't lose Ashley's son, not like this. Not in the middle of a huge fight. *Please, God . . .*

Then, on Landon's third attempt, the juice cap came flying out of the baby's mouth. Landon turned him upright and gave smaller pats to his back. "Breathe, baby. Come on. Please, God."

All at once Cole gasped and coughed and screamed. For another few seconds he made a series of hiccups, like he couldn't get air fast enough. Ashley was at his side, taking him in her arms. Landon could easily read the desperate tears of gratitude in her eyes. Like she would never live long enough to repay him.

Ashley held Cole as close to her chest as she could. "Cole, breathe, baby. It's okay. Everything's okay." She rocked him and soothed him, and after a minute she gave him some juice from his sippy cup.

"Just a bit. To help his throat." Her father came to her. "You don't want him to inhale it. He's too upset to drink much."

Landon watched as Ashley nodded. "Okay." She had never looked more scared. Even now her face was more gray than white. She closed her eyes and kissed the top of Cole's head. "Thank You, God. Thank You."

Landon was still trying to make sense of the near disaster. And now Ashley was talking to God? He exhaled and took a step back. As he did, Mrs. Baxter, Erin and, finally, Luke circled around Ashley and Cole.

Dr. Baxter looked at Landon. "Thank you." He mouthed the words. Then in barely a whisper he explained something that hadn't made sense till now. "I've never done the Heimlich on a baby. I just . . . I forgot about holding him facedown."

"It's okay." Landon took a seat at the table a few feet away and watched the Baxters as they huddled around Ashley. He had asked God to show him why he was supposed to be here tonight.

And now he had his answer.

"Landon, if you'll call 9-1-1." Dr. Baxter cast him another look. "Please. Tell them we're okay."

Landon did as he was asked. When the call ended, he turned to the family he loved so well. He watched Luke put his arms around Ashley and Cole and pull them close. "I'm so sorry. This was all . . . all my fault." He wasn't crying now. He was sobbing.

With one hand, Ashley held Cole close to her, and

with the other hand she held on to her brother. "You didn't mean to." Fresh tears sounded in her voice. "It was an accident, Luke."

Their parents and Erin stepped back, as if they could sense this moment wasn't only important. It was critical. The baby was whimpering now, his voice raspy from the ordeal. But the danger had passed.

"I've been . . . awful, Ashley." Luke put a hand to his face and shaded his eyes. "I can't believe the things I said."

Ashley didn't respond. Instead she kissed Cole's cheek and did something Landon didn't see coming. She held her baby out to Luke. "Here." A quick couple sobs shook Ashley's shoulders. "Love him, Luke. He needs men in his life. Please."

Landon wondered if Luke might faint on the ground. He watched as disbelief seemed to work its way through Ashley's brother. Then, without holding back another second, Luke took Cole in his arms. Tears streamed down his face as he cradled the baby close to his body. "I'm so sorry, Cole. Forgive me." He gave Ashley a plead-ing look. "Please . . . forgive me."

No words were needed. Ashley nodded and she wrapped both arms around her brother and baby boy. Landon noticed that their parents and Erin also wiped tears. Landon thought about the class he'd taken. Cole wouldn't have made it if they'd had to wait for paramed-ics. They lived too far out of town.

And just then something occurred to Landon. He

had been right where he was needed and with his training he had saved a life. Which was why the whole firefighter thing wasn't some passing hobby or a strong
extracurricular to build his college résumé.

"I put that juice cap on his tray." Luke sounded
shook, like he might never get over the fact. "I was so
angry I didn't pay attention to it."

"He's okay." Ashley looked into Luke's eyes. "God
saved him."

Luke handed Cole back to Ashley, and excused himself. On his way past Landon he apologized. "This was all
me, the fight. All of it." The deepest regret flashed in his
eyes. "I'm sorry, man. Completely me."

"You're good." Landon nodded and Luke left the
room.

Erin wasn't far behind. "Good night." She patted
Cole's back and hugged Ashley. "Thank God . . . I was so
scared."

"Me, too." Ashley's tears had stopped, but her expression was more broken than before. More distant.

When Erin was upstairs, Ashley handed Cole to her
mother. "Please. Take care of him for a few minutes." She
turned to her dad and back to her mom. "I need time."

Without glancing Landon's direction, Ashley jogged
to the back door and left. As the door slammed behind
her, Landon looked at her parents. "I think she's in
shock."

"Maybe." Mrs. Baxter held Cole close, and her husband put his arm around them both. "Sometimes a scare

like this can be life-changing." She turned her eyes to Landon. "For the good."

Landon walked to Ashley's parents and ran his hand over baby Cole's back. "Poor little guy. Must've been terrified."

"I don't . . ." Ashley's mom shook her head. She looked at Landon and seemed to wait till the words would come. "I can't thank you enough."

"I should've known." Dr. Baxter was obviously still frustrated with himself. "Upside down, heel of the hand between the shoulder blades. Face and neck braced. Then thrusts to the back." He shook his head. "It all happened so fast."

Landon held out his hands. "May I?"

"Of course." Elizabeth handed over Cole. "I don't know what I would've done if . . ."

"God had me here." Landon nuzzled his face against Cole's. "You okay, little guy?"

Cole looked at Landon, really studied him. "Ba-ba."

"Is that 'bottle'?" Landon looked at Ashley's parents.

"Yes." Dr. Baxter hurried to the kitchen. "I'll make it for him."

Landon waited until Mrs. Baxter was sitting in a living room rocker, feeding Cole his bottle. Then he motioned to the back door. "I have to find her."

Mrs. Baxter ran and found a flashlight. Breathless, she handed it to Landon. "Go. She wants you to follow her. No matter what she tells you."

That was all Landon needed to hear. He crossed the

room and stepped onto the porch. In the windy dark night, he couldn't see her. But he had the flashlight. He knew where she was going, and he knew how to get there. There was just one place Ashley would go tonight.

She was headed for the rock.

19

Ashley ran until she couldn't breathe and then she kept running. She would've known the way to the back of their property in her sleep. Through the clearing at the back of the property and past another line of trees and there it was. Even beneath a dark sky, she could see it.

The rock.

Never mind the approaching storm or the way the wind howled around her. She didn't care about the small branches that flew about and brushed against her arms. She needed to be alone, needed to process what just happened. Along the top of the rock were white painted handprints. Faded from the years of sun and rain, but they remained all the same. Handprints belonging to her siblings and her, the day they claimed the spot as their own.

She climbed a few feet up the side of the rock, and sat on the flat surface. Then she pulled her knees close to her chest.

Ashley tried to catch her breath, but her sides were heaving, her entire self still scared to death. Baby Cole had almost died. That had really just happened. If Landon hadn't still been there, if he hadn't come when she screamed his name, Cole could be . . .

She couldn't let herself go there. He was alive and breathing. Her baby would be just fine. He was alive. He was still alive.

But what about her?

Sure, Luke had apologized for his bitter words. Telling her she was a bad mother and questioning Landon for sticking around for someone like her. Luke was sorry. She believed that.

Still . . . didn't her brother have a point?

What sort of mom was she, after all? Luke was right about how often she went out with friends and dropped Cole off with their parents. Right about the way she treated Landon, and even the lack of interest she had shown to her own child.

And how come she'd spent three years denying God, but when Cole was choking to death, she cried out to Him first? That was more the definition of hypocrite than anything she had accused her brother of being.

She closed her eyes. *Precious Cole. I almost lost you, baby. How could I have walked away from you with a juice cap on your high chair tray? I'm so sorry, Cole.*

The truth was her son shouldn't be alive. If Landon had left any earlier, well . . . this would have been a very different night. Not only that, but Cole shouldn't be here for another reason.

Because she, herself, shouldn't be alive.

The sound of the wind moving through the trees faded, and Ashley opened her eyes. She felt herself going back to that time. The accident three summers ago. Maybe if she allowed herself to remember those terrible days, the details surrounding the tragedy, she would find her way back to herself.

Back to God and her family.

Maybe even back to Landon.

Ashley didn't look at photos from the crash scene till a month after she was home from the hospital. By then her family had hired a lawyer, and she and her parents were at a hearing. The deceased truck driver had been working for a national construction company at the time of the accident. His blood alcohol level had been nearly three times the legal limit.

"There's nothing to discuss here." The truck driver's attorney looked around the table. "We'd like to offer a settlement."

At the same time, amidst the police reports and insurance documents lying on the table, there were pictures of both vehicles. Photos passed around like so much matter-of-fact evidence.

Ashley was only eighteen. She took the photographs from the table and stared at them for the first time. Even now she could remember the panic that consumed her. Neither the truck nor Ashley's car was recognizable. Just twisted metal and shattered glass, strewn parts and bent tires.

An intense nausea took hold of her and her forehead became cold and clammy. Her mother had noticed what was happening. She turned to Ashley, her expression suddenly concerned. "Honey . . . are you okay?"

Words wouldn't form. Ashley could only stare at the pictures and imagine herself and Jefferson caught up in the tangle of twisted steel. "How . . ." She tried to finish the question, but nothing came.

With her mother at her side, she ran from the conference room to a bathroom down the hall and threw up. As if her body was trying to remove the images the only way it knew how. It took half an hour before Ashley felt strong enough to return to the proceeding. By then the photos had been tucked away in a file.

While the lawyers talked about the settlement amount, Ashley could only imagine the accident. How violent it must've been. How horrific.

What had allowed her to live? Why?

Ashley blinked, and memories of the proceeding faded. This wasn't helping. The details made her just as angry and confused now as they had back then. She lifted her eyes to the sky and watched the clouds. They were low and fast-moving. Dangerous.

The change in her heart had happened the moment Ashley woke in the hospital, right after she found out about Jefferson. Until then, her days with her family, with Landon, had been predictably wonderful. Sure she had trials and concerns. Arguments with friends at school, the awkward growing pains of adolescence. Something might go wrong, and then she would talk to God about it, share her struggles with her parents and pull out her sketchbook and draw.

Before the accident, she had anchors in her life. Absolutes she could depend on. The fact that God loved her and that He had sent Jesus to die for her. The constant support of her family and friends.

And always, Landon Blake.

Ashley squinted. She could still see the look on Landon's face when she had learned the truth about Jefferson. That the boy hadn't made it and that his memorial service had already come and gone. For the first time since Ashley knew him, Landon's eyes had filled with something unfamiliar. Something she had never seen there before.

Complete and unfiltered fear.

Ashley learned later that Landon had been afraid the news would traumatize her, destroy her.

He had entered her room that day and taken the seat beside her. And in his typical Landon way he had tried to speak hope and life into the situation. Jefferson was a hero, he had jerked the steering wheel and taken the brunt of the crash. All to save Ashley, Landon had told her.

But she could barely hear him. The voice in her head was so much louder. Jefferson hadn't done anything to deserve death. He was a nice kid who had his whole future ahead of him. And now he was dead for one reason.

Because God didn't protect him.

That's what she had told herself then, and it was how she still felt today. Remembering the details didn't change anything. Ashley was different. She didn't want to be the same naïve person she'd been back then.

The truth was, God had allowed Jefferson to die and that single reality changed everything for Ashley. If God had done that, then maybe He wasn't so good after all. And maybe Landon was simply misinformed. Her parents, too. Just sadly ignorant, basing all their life's existence and the sum of their futures on a Being who—in the end—didn't care about them.

Ashley spent time every day beating herself up back then. If only she hadn't asked to go to the store. If only Jefferson's mother had picked him up instead. If Ashley hadn't offered to take the kid home, he would still be alive.

But since he wasn't, since he had done the heroic thing in his final seconds, then Ashley better make her life count. That's how Luke felt about the situation. And with Ashley making one bad choice after another, Luke had been angry. Then and now.

Ashley couldn't blame him.

Her troubles with family hadn't stopped with Luke. After the accident Ashley quit going to church, something her parents brought up often. "Come with us,

Ashley," her father would say on his way out the door each Sunday morning. "Healing won't truly begin until you give this over to God."

"Really?" Ashley could remember the sarcastic responses she had shot her father. "So God is up there keeping score? Taking attendance?" Her tone had been ruder than she intended. "And He won't let me get over this accident till I show up at church?"

Times like that her dad didn't push. He would come to her, put his hand on her shoulder and, without asking for Ashley's permission, he would pray. "Father, let her know You love her. Please. In Jesus' name, amen."

Once when he did that, Ashley waited till her dad finished before turning angry eyes toward him. "Please don't do that. I never said you could pray for me."

Her words sounded petulant and immature now, but they were how she had felt at the time. It was the one occasion when her father resisted her attitude. "Listen," he had told her. His voice had been stern. "As long as you live under this roof, your mother and I will pray for you."

"And when I move out?" Her response had been fast and mean.

"Don't take that tone with me, Ashley." Her dad had faced her, his arms crossed. "You were in a terrible accident. Jefferson was killed. We all get that." His tone softened a bit. "But you've been treating us differently since you got home. That needs to change." He hesitated. "And just so you know, I'll pray for you after you move out, too." Tears shone in his eyes. "As long as I have breath in my lungs. I'll never stop praying for you."

That morning Ashley had watched her family pile into their van and leave for church. Her parents along with Kari and Luke and Erin. Then she had grabbed her sketchbook and drawn the only thing she could think about.

A tombstone and a single name: Jefferson.

She pictured herself once more, running up the stairs of her parents' porch after her talk with Landon the night before her flight to Paris. The rest of that evening she stayed in her room. Her parents tried to talk to her, but she refused. She needed to be alone with her broken heart.

Not because she'd had any doubts about her flight the next morning or because she thought she'd made a mistake by ending things with Landon once again. But because nothing she was doing made sense. Landon was the best guy she'd ever known. Yet in that one moment it was really and truly over with him.

Ashley let the memory die there.

Until tonight.

Earlier this evening, dancing with him had changed something. For her, anyway. That single dance with his arms around her again, hearing his voice soft against the rough edges of her soul, all of it had shattered her resistance.

On top of that, Landon had just saved her son's life. He was strong and kind and compassionate. He loved her even now, after all she'd done to him. So of course she needed to get away.

Needed to rehearse the words she would finally tell him when she returned to the house. The truth about Paris. Because she was wrong for Landon on every level. She could never make him happy. She wasn't a good mother and she'd never be a good wife. Also, no matter how she had called out to God minutes ago, she didn't really believe in Him. Not enough to go to church with Landon.

And Landon deserved someone who would.

Of course, Landon wouldn't agree about any of that. Not until she told him about Cole's dad. She took a deep breath. Yes, it was time to go back to the house and tell him. Then it would be over. No need to drag both their hearts through the mud of her mistakes and misfortunes one more time.

So, yes, she had needed to run.

Because if Landon tried to talk to her now, if he found her out here or if she looked into his eyes after all they'd gone through today, she would keep her secret as long as she lived. And that was one chance she simply couldn't take. Not for her sake.

But for Landon's.

20

Landon used the flashlight to make his way across the open fields toward the stream at the back of the Baxters' land. Lightning was getting closer, and the wind was even sharper than before.

Whatever talk they might have out here, the weather wouldn't give them long.

Even still, Landon wasn't in a hurry. Ashley needed the quiet maybe more than she needed him—if she needed him at all. At the first line of trees, he found his way through to the clearing, and then he slipped between another couple oaks and some shrubs until he reached the stream on the other side.

Sure enough, she was there. At the top of the rock. Sitting with her knees pulled up, face to the sky. This was the Ashley he knew and loved. The one who had to process, had to be alone to sort through the shattered pieces of her heart.

Especially today.

Landon walked closer and put his hand on the rock. "Ashley."

She didn't hear him over the wind. So he climbed up and when he was a few feet from her she gasped and turned to him. "Wha—" A loud breath came from her. "You scared me."

"Sorry." He took the spot beside her and stretched out his legs. For a minute he didn't say anything. Then he looked around and remembered the last time they were here together. "Familiar spot, huh."

"Yes." Her eyes found his and she didn't blink, didn't look away. "I'm sorry, Landon. For how I've treated you. All the breakups. The way I avoided you." She straightened her legs in front of her and stared into the night. "You didn't deserve that."

"You were hurt." The wind died down a little, so his voice was soft. Marked with a vulnerability he felt only around her. "I knew you didn't mean it."

"I never wanted to be unkind." She glanced at him. "But I *did* mean it, Landon. I had become a different person. And I'm worse now."

"You're not worse." Landon wanted to take her hand, put his arm around her and love her back to the girl she used to be. Until she believed it, too. But it wasn't the time. He needed to get through this conversation first. "You keep saying how bad you are. But here's the thing. How can you move on in life and be happy when you beat yourself up all the time?"

A sad laugh came from her and again she looked out at the stream. "Haven't you been paying attention? Everything Luke said is true." She took a sharp breath. "I'm a terrible mother—I mean, who would walk away from their baby and leave a juice cap on his tray?"

"That was a mistake." Landon wasn't getting anywhere. Frustration built in his gut. "You love Cole. Anyone could've seen that today."

"But Luke's right." She put her hands behind her and leaned back. "I drop Cole off at my parents' house all the time. It's hard for me . . . being a single mom."

This time Landon waited. There was more she wanted to say. He could feel it.

Ashley shifted so she could see him. "I guess I figure my mom and dad want to spend time with him. As much as possible." She hesitated. "He likes them better, anyway."

Landon only raised his eyebrows. "Do you hear yourself? You used to be the girl with the most gumption, ready to tackle any problem. And now you're talking yourself into believing every possible negative thing. All of it lies."

A smile lifted Ashley's lips. "Okay." She angled her head. "We won't talk about that." She crossed her legs and faced him. "Tell me about you, Landon. Your time at Baylor . . . there must be something interesting you can tell me."

It was the first time she'd asked about his college days, something Landon hadn't expected tonight. He faced her and pulled one knee up. "College." He chuckled. "Where to begin?"

Guilt flashed in her eyes, like she was realizing, too,

that she had never asked him about Baylor. She waited, ready.

"My best friend is a guy named Jalen Hale." He paused as something else shone in her eyes. Jealousy, maybe. Until the accident she had been his best friend, and he had been hers. Landon let it go. "His twin sister, Hope, hangs out with us a lot. She and I . . . we get coffee or dinner sometimes."

"Wait." Ashley leaned forward. She definitely wasn't expecting this. "You and Hope?" Her expression held no anger, of course. She would have no right to that. But he recognized the hurt in her voice. She seemed to force a smile. "You mean . . . you have a girlfriend?"

"I didn't say that." Landon allowed a quiet laugh. "Don't twist my words, Ash."

"I'm not. You said you and Hope get dinner some-times. That's called dating." She found her rhythm, her voice more cheerful now. "You should've told me, Landon."

This was ridiculous. "I don't have a girlfriend. Hope and I are . . . we're talking. That's all."

Ashley gave a slow nod. "Talking." She looked at him for several seconds. "Well, then, everything is going to work out just fine. You have Hope and I can get on with my life. Do things my own way."

"Look." He hated this. "I've been away for a long time, Ash. Of course I have friends. I take eighteen credits a se-mester and I play flag football on Jalen's intramural team.

My volunteer work at the fire station has turned into a passion."

She raised her brow. "The reason you took the child-lifesaving course?"

"Yes." Landon relaxed some. It had killed him not sharing his life with her. Now that she wanted to know, he couldn't wait to color in the details. "Spring semester of my sophomore year we got to respond to an actual fire. Not all volunteer firefighters get to do that." He shrugged, searching for the words. "It was incredible, Ash. Being there on scene, rushing into a burning house looking for victims." He grinned. "I loved it."

"So that's what you're going to do?" Ashley looked stunned. "My safe, predictable Landon Blake? Fighting fires? Wow." Her tone sounded impressed, but he couldn't be sure.

Either way, her words got to him. "You always say that, how I'm safe." He clenched his jaw. "It bugs me."

"I'm sorry." She leaned back on her hands again. "I just mean . . . you never do anything wrong. I guess fighting fires falls in line with that. Still being the good guy. Landon Blake, the boy every girl had a crush on back in high school."

The boy who only had eyes for you, Ashley. That's what he wanted to say. But he kept the words to himself. "I've already talked to the Bloomington Fire Department. Once I graduate and pass the physical, they're ready to hire me."

"Tell me about the physical." She seemed genuinely interested. "I've missed so much."

"Yes." He let that hang there for a long moment. Then he told her about his training regimen and how difficult the test would be.

With every additional detail, her eyes grew wider. "I'm impressed." Her expression grew somber again, more serious. "And grateful. The timing. You taking the class." She shook her head. "I can't imagine what would've happened if you hadn't still been here. I can't."

"When your mom asked me to come tonight, at first I was all for it." He smiled. "I even picked up a present for Cole. Since I never got him anything when he was born."

"A present? Where is it?" Ashley was starting to look like the girl he remembered, the one who hung on his every word, the one whose eyes shone when he was around.

"I left it in the foyer." He shrugged one shoulder. "I wasn't sure if I should give it to you right away or if I needed to . . . wait till I left."

She nodded. "I get that." A long sigh came from her. "You never know how I'll respond. Right?"

Another quiet laugh filtered over his lips. "I guess."

"So . . . you're going to be a firefighter. And Cole's was the first life you saved." Ashley leaned forward again and took his hand. "I'm happy for you, Landon. Your life is going to be just perfect. The way you deserve."

Was she really so dim? Didn't she get it? This wasn't why he had come out here to find her. "I want to hear about you."

"Okay. I need to tell you something." She glanced up. "But let's get back to the house." She shivered. "The night feels weird all of a sudden. Too quiet."

She was right. But he had so much more to say. He hadn't asked his question, the one that had been burning a hole in his heart since she woke up in the hospital. "Before we go . . . just tell me one thing, Ashley. Please."

"Later." She stood and helped pull him to his feet. She still had hold of his hand. "Come on. This is tornado weather. Can't you feel it?"

They climbed down and once their feet were on the soft dirt below, Landon held his ground, his back to the rock. "Ashley." He didn't move, didn't let go of her hand.

She had no choice but to stop and turn to him. And suddenly, the way it had so many times before, the air between them became charged with an electricity that had nothing to do with the weather.

In a few quiet steps, she came to him until they were face-to-face. He could feel himself breathing harder, unsure where this was going or what she was going to say or do. She traced her thumb over his brow and looked straight to his heart, to a place that was hers alone. A place that always would be. "Hold me, Landon. Please."

Moving slower than he'd done earlier on the dance

floor, more intentional, he put his arms around her waist and drew her close. "This is all . . . all I wanted, Ashley. A chance to be us again. Like before."

For the first time in so long, she didn't argue with him. Instead she put her head against his chest, her arms around his neck. For what felt like minutes, they stayed that way. Landon wanted desperately to kiss her, but more than that he wanted his answer.

Why? Why had she stopped loving him?

Finally she eased her head back enough to look at him, deep into his eyes again. "Remember ninth-grade PE? You said you'd never let me fall." Her voice was a whisper, a balm to his aching soul.

"I meant it." He ran his fingers down the side of her face.

"And tonight, when we were out there. I kept thinking I was crazy to be dancing like that in those shoes. But then . . ." She hesitated. "I remembered what you told me back then, and I knew. You'd never let me fall. Not then . . . or now."

"Right, Ash." He brushed his cheek against hers. "I'd never let you fall. Not ever."

She searched his eyes, his face. "You know what I want?" The wind was picking up again, and thunder rolled nearby.

"What?"

"I want a do-over. July fifth. Weeks after high school graduation." She blinked back fresh tears. "I want to never even think about going to the store, and I want Jefferson's mom to come pick him up."

Tears stung at his eyes, too. "I want that for you. If I could give it to you, I would."

"I know." She traced his cheekbone with her thumb. "I love your face, have I ever told you that? You have the most handsome face, Landon."

He couldn't think, could barely find the words to talk. Holding her in his arms, her body against his, her fingers on his face. "You know what I want?" He was intoxicated by her closeness, the warmth of her. "I want to know why you stopped loving me."

"Why . . . ?" Her breathing was faster now, too. She searched his eyes. "I never stopped loving you, Landon. I changed." She squeezed her eyes shut. "And in Paris . . . I have to tell you what happened. About the guy I—"

"Stop." He moved his thumb over her lips. "Ashley . . ."

Neither of them said anything after that, because they both knew what was coming. He couldn't stop himself any more than he could stop his pounding heart from beating. And before they could take another breath his lips were on hers and they were kissing the way they hadn't done in forever.

The way he never thought they would again.

"I . . . still need to tell you." She muttered the words even as she kissed him again. "We shouldn't be . . ."

Landon framed her face and cradled her head in his hands. Then he kissed her once more. "Yes, we should."

Another kiss and another, even as the wind whipped into a roar around them. "Don't you see? We're supposed to be together, Ashley."

"You need to know the truth." She drew back, breathless, intense.

Landon searched her eyes. "For what?" His voice grew louder, his words fast and panicked. "So I can go back to Baylor and date Hope? So I can marry her someday?" He shook his head. Then he forced himself to be calm as he kissed her lips one more time. "I don't . . . want that, Ash." He grabbed a quick breath. "I want you."

"But you haven't heard what—"

"Don't." He worked his fingers into her hair and the kiss continued, deeper this time, marked by too many seasons of unspoken desire. "I love you, Ashley. Not Hope. Not anyone else." His eyes found hers, his voice soft against her ear. "I don't care what happened in Paris."

The passion between them was too hot to play with. Ashley blinked back tears and she found his lips again. This time he couldn't think of anything but her, the way she felt, the way the kiss grew and built.

He needed a break, but he couldn't pull away, couldn't force himself to put distance between them. "Ash . . . hold on."

"Yes." She put her hands on his shoulders and forced herself to step back. "We can't . . . You need to know."

Like him, she was clearly caught up in the passion of the moment. But she was equally determined.

"I have to tell you . . . when I got pregnant . . . the guy . . ." Then, just when it looked like she might blurt out whatever she was trying to say, a wailing sound blared through the air.

Tornado sirens!

They cut the night sky, screaming and rhythmic, ominous and deafening. Fear seemed to seize Ashley and she took hold of Landon's hand. "I knew it!"

They were both out of breath from what had just happened, but there was no time to wait. The night air did feel strange, and Indiana was tornado country. Some of the worst twisters in history had come through this part of the Midwest.

"Come on." He pulled the flashlight from his back pocket and used it to lead her out of the woods and into the field behind her parents' house. Together they ran through the grass, faster and faster, all while the sirens wailed.

"I feel it, Landon! There's a tornado!" Ashley sounded terrified. "Right behind us!"

Move faster, he ordered himself. *Help us, God. Please.* "Stay with me, Ash!" Landon shouted, and he shot a look at her over his shoulder. "I won't let you fall."

She stayed with him as they ran. The wind sounded like a train behind them, a sure sign of a tornado. As they reached the porch steps, Landon was still consumed by their kiss. All he wanted was to find a place where they could pick up where they'd left off. But that moment was gone now. And Landon had just two thoughts on his mind as they raced through the door. He and Ashley had to get to the basement. And a question that was in many ways even graver.

If she still loved him, why in the world would she push him away?

21

This was the disaster Elizabeth had been fearing all day. As soon as the sirens went off, she was certain. A tornado was headed their way and Ashley and Landon were somewhere at the back of the property.

"John!" She had been holding a sleeping Cole, but now the baby woke up. Cole started to cry as the sirens blared. She stood and motioned to the stairs. "Get Luke and Erin."

"On it." He hurried up, calling for them. "Luke . . . Erin . . . to the basement."

In some parts of the country people took tornado sirens for granted. Elizabeth had a cousin in Nashville, and they had compared storm notes once. Her cousin said they almost never had tornadoes in Tennessee. In fact, she said they slept through tornado sirens the couple times a year they happened.

That was definitely not true for Indiana.

This was EF5 territory, and after the storms throughout the day, the radio had warned that any tornado tonight could be a big one.

Yes, this was the ominous moment Elizabeth had

dreaded. She could feel it. "John?" Her voice sounded shrill, desperate. "Hurry!"

He jogged back down the stairs, Luke and Erin behind him. John motioned to the basement door. "Everyone get down to the corner." He looked at Elizabeth. "I'm going after Ashley and Landon."

It was what she wanted him to do, but at the same time she was terrified something would happen to him. "Hurry. Please." She hesitated. "I love you."

"I love you, too." He waited till they were safely at the bottom of the basement stairs, and he shut the door behind them.

They had pillows and a couple old mattresses set up in the corner of the storage room, the safest place for storms like this. The area had cement-block walls and room for a dozen people.

Luke went ahead of the others and adjusted a few pillows. "Here, Mom. You and Cole sit here." He and Erin took the spot next to her. "I don't like Dad being out there. Landon and Ashley could be anywhere."

Her son was right. *Lord, please be with them. Bring them back, Father. Keep them safe.*

A few minutes passed and Elizabeth heard the basement door open. "They're here," John yelled down. "We're on our way."

She could hear the sirens, still loud and constant. Warning of the danger ahead. Ashley and Landon came into view first, and then John. Landon had hold of Ashley's hand as they found spots in the storm room.

Before Ashley sat down, she took Cole from Elizabeth's arms. "Thank you, Mom." She gasped for air. "We . . . we got here as quickly as we could."

"Thank God you made it!" She watched her daughter take a spot on the opposite wall, Cole in her arms, Landon at her side.

The picture they made was perfect, and Elizabeth wondered if life would ever really look like this for Ashley. If she would find it in herself to let her guard down long enough for Landon to love her. The way he so clearly longed to do. At the same time, Elizabeth was plagued by a pang of guilt. She had worked too hard to get Landon here tonight. Ashley had to make her own decisions.

Elizabeth had never wanted to meddle, but tonight she'd done just that. She would apologize to Ashley later.

Lord, I was wrong tonight. Inviting Landon here. I'm sorry. But here we are, and You've saved us again. Elizabeth closed her eyes. Whatever happened next, at least they were safe. She thought about Brooke and Peter and Maddie. *Lord, keep them in Your hands, too. Please.*

In the quiet of the cellar, Elizabeth felt something special happening, something deeper than the seven of them fleeing from a storm. Luke had his arm around Erin, and Landon still had hold of Ashley's hand. With his other hand, he ran his fingers over baby Cole's soft hair.

The child was falling back to sleep, and Landon was helping.

Beside Elizabeth, John took a slow breath. "I don't

know if we'll get hit by a tornado tonight." He looked around the small room at each of them. "But I know this. We're going to be okay." A half smile lifted his lips. "Since we don't have anywhere to go, maybe we can make *this* a family meeting."

Groans and laughter came from Luke and Erin and Ashley. But mostly laughter. And suddenly Elizabeth had one hope for this moment. That by some miracle this terrible night might become a time of healing. Because of God's grace there would not be a disaster inside or outside the walls of the Baxter home tonight.

But rather, a disaster averted.

• • •

ASHLEY'S CHEEKS FELT hot and she wondered if her face was still red. Whatever had happened out there by the rock, it had only left her more confused. Confused and infatuated all at the same time.

She nestled in close to Landon and listened to her father. Earlier this evening when everyone was fighting, Ashley never could've imagined the night ending this way. Her baby son had nearly died and in the hours since Landon saved his life, things between them had changed.

Between all of them.

"We've been through a lot tonight." Her dad leaned back against the cement wall. "Landon. We will never have enough words to thank you. For saving Cole."

Landon nodded. "Glad I was here." He narrowed his eyes. "I keep thinking, what if I hadn't just taken that class?" He looked at Ashley. "What if I would've been halfway down the street when you called my name?"

"We can't think of the what-ifs." Her father sounded strong, confident. "But about the fight that happened earlier." He turned to their mom. "Your mother and I were crushed. We've never . . ." He looked at Luke and then at Ashley. "Never heard you talk that way to each other."

"It was my fault." Luke was quick to speak up. He caught Ashley's eyes. "I'm sorry, Ash. The things I said . . . you could hate me forever for that."

"I don't." She cradled Cole a little closer to her chest. "It was like . . . we both forgot who we are."

Her response resonated through her heart. Wasn't that her problem, after all? She sighed. *I've forgotten who I am. In every area of life.* But tonight . . . tonight in this basement shelter she remembered. And for this one moment of clarity she felt like the girl she'd left behind.

"I guess I just wanted to remind all of you of the truth. Who we are." Her dad put his arm around their mom. "Being a Baxter means something. To us, as your parents, and to each of you. Because you alone know what it was like growing up in this family."

This wasn't a lecture. It was her dad baring his heart, reminding them of what he and their mom had spent a lifetime teaching them. Ashley liked that. She appreciated that her dad would make the effort. Even though on so many levels Ashley no longer believed the way her parents did.

"Baxters are believers—in God, in His Word—the Bible—and in being kind to each other above all." He took his time, like he was being careful to make this a reminder and not a reprimand. "We respect each other and people outside of our home. And we cherish the time we have together."

Ashley didn't know about the whole God part, but she nodded anyway. Her dad was right. These were the things that had defined them through the years, and they mattered. She remembered that now, too. Even if she didn't agree with every point.

Beside her she felt Landon approving, moving his head as Ashley's dad spoke. Landon had always respected Ashley's father. On the other wall, Erin and Luke nodded, too. Their eyes were soft, like they were hanging on every word their dad spoke.

"But let me be clear on one thing." Dad looked around the storm shelter. "Baxters aren't perfect. Tonight was proof of that."

He continued. "We will make mistakes . . . and say things we don't mean." He paused. "But when that happens, this family makes things right. Before a single day passes. We apologize and forgive and hug each other. So that before too much time goes by, we're laughing again." He looked at Luke and then Ashley. "Sitting in the same room and supporting each other again. Even in the midst of a terrible storm."

Outside, the sirens stopped their wailing. The worst of the storm must be over. Ashley glanced toward the stairs. No telling how bad things looked outside, but down here the family was still in one piece.

Ashley looked at Cole, sleeping in her arms. Then she lifted her gaze to her family and Landon.

Her father glanced around the room again. "I'd like to pray for us, for all of us." He stood and the others did the same thing. "It'd be nice if we all held hands. The way we used to pray when you all were little."

When they were all on their feet, Ashley held Cole close and took her mom's hand. Beside her, Landon put his hand on her shoulder and he took hold of Luke's hand with the other. When the circle was complete, Dad bowed his head and closed his eyes. "Let's pray."

Then he did what he'd done for their family on more occasions than Ashley could count. He asked God to protect them and guide them, train them and use them. "We want to be a light for this world, Lord. Help us keep our eyes on what matters. And help us love You and each other. And anyone else You might bring into our lives. In Jesus' name, amen."

"Amen." Ashley didn't think twice about saying the word. It was an honor to be in the same room as her family, their father praying over them the way he had when they were younger.

The room grew quiet except for the sounds of everyone hugging each other. After a minute when the sirens stayed silent, they climbed the basement stairs back up into the house. The walls were still standing and everything seemed to be in order. They had survived one of the wildest days in all their lives. Stronger for it, better.

And for the first time in a long time Ashley felt something she hadn't thought she'd ever feel again.

She felt like a Baxter.

• • •

FOR LANDON, THE worst thing about the storm passing was the moment Ashley let go of his hand. Landon could've stayed in the basement forever, listening to John Baxter, sitting beside Ashley, her fingers soft between his.

Now, he watched Ashley pass Cole to her mother. She turned to Landon. "I'll walk you out."

"Okay." Landon sighed. He walked with her to the front of the house. "Here." He took the blue gift bag from the floor and handed it to Ashley. "It isn't much." He paused. "Oh . . . and there's a card inside. For you, Ash."

A familiar softness came over Ashley, something he hadn't seen in such a long time. It made her even more beautiful, if that were possible. She took the bag and peered inside. "So nice of you, Landon."

"Like I said, I meant to send him a gift before this." He pressed his shoulder into the door and studied her.

She looked at him, for a long time. "I still have them. Every letter you ever wrote to me."

"You do?" His heart felt suddenly lighter. "Really?"

"Mmm." She nodded. Her eyes held a shy look. "Every one."

Landon remembered the last letter he sent her. After he'd sobered up and been released from the hospital, he had decided not to be angry or hurt or devastated about Ashley's place in his life, the times they'd shared. Until now, he wasn't sure she'd received it.

"I never wrote back." She put her hand on his shoulder. "Something else I'm sorry for. It was . . . the sweetest letter." Her smile started in her eyes. "All those times we shared. I practically memorized it."

Landon's heart lifted. That meant she had read it more than once. Often, even. He let her comment pass. It was enough that he knew without making her feel possibly awkward about caring too much. "You amaze me, Ashley Baxter." He took her hand again. The passion from earlier was gone. But what remained was powerful. "I'll just leave it at that."

She laughed and pulled the tissue paper from the bag. "I better open it." Then she pulled out the book *Horton Hears a Who!* She set the bag and paper down and thumbed through the book. "I love this story."

"Seemed to fit." He grinned at her. "Because you really are a good mother, Ashley. Give yourself a chance. I think you'll be one of the best."

Their conversation was quiet, just the two of them. Everyone else was in the living room, laughing about something. The mood was so different than when Landon had arrived hours ago.

She reached back into the bag. "The card? It's in

here?" She pulled it from the bag. "Should I read it now?"

"No." Again Landon didn't want Ashley to feel awkward. "Read it later."

"Okay." She put the book back in the bag. "I need to get Cole home to bed."

"Yes." He nodded toward the front porch. "Come with me? To my car?"

The sky was clear now, and stars shone bright over the countryside of Bloomington. Across the front yard, tree branches lay scattered over the grass. There would no doubt be more visible damage when the sun came up. But here he was with Ashley Baxter.

Nothing else mattered.

When they reached his Toyota, there was no kiss, none of what they'd shared earlier. Ashley was happier, less burdened. Her eyes shone with a light that hadn't been there before. Even still, her mind was set.

Landon could feel it.

"So . . ." Ashley faced him, leaving more distance between them than before. Her smile was colored by a mix of embarrassment and tenderness, and her tone filled with a familiar depth. "About the rock."

"No one ever said we didn't have chemistry." He slid the toe of his shoe against hers a few times. "If it wasn't for the sirens, I'd still be out there."

"Me, too." She lifted her eyes to his. "But I feel the same way, Landon. You and me . . . it could never work."

He looked at her for a long time, his gaze never leaving hers. "Tell me, Ash." He wanted to know. Whatever it was that had mattered so much to her before. "What were you going to tell me?"

Ashley's smile faded a bit and she looked at the ground for a long minute. When she lifted her face to his she shook her head. "It isn't important anymore." She looked at peace. "We have our separate lives now. Let's just let it go."

"What if you're wrong?" Landon moved closer. Just an inch or two. "Maybe you take the next year and ask God if He's real. Ask Him if He has good plans for you, Ashley. The way I believe He does."

"Why?" Her voice fell a notch. "God's moved on from me."

"Not possible." He wanted to push, but this wasn't the time. The night they'd shared would have to be enough for now. He took a slow breath. "One of these days we'll have to swap stories, you and I." He touched her cheek. "You're not the only one who's ever messed up, Ash. That's the whole point."

She angled her head, like she didn't quite get it.

"Christians aren't perfect." He desperately wanted her to hear him, really hear him. "They're just a group of broken people who know they need a Savior." He took her hands in his. "Because we're such a mess."

A glimmer in her eyes told him maybe—just maybe—he had gotten through to her. She nodded, and looked across the vast front yard, her expression distant. "I don't know."

"All I'm saying is ask." He shrugged. "Ask God to show you if His grace is enough. If there's still something very good that can come from all this." He thought for a moment. "Other than Cole. Because your little boy is good. And because every baby is a miracle. No matter what the circumstances."

That was all. Landon didn't want to linger here, lecturing her. He just wanted her to stop running.

She breathed deep and faced him again. "Go back to school, Landon. Take Hope on a date." She shook her head. "Don't wait for me. We're just friends."

"Ashley, you can't—"

She released his hand. "Don't. I mean it. I can't promise you anything. Not now, and probably not ever." She moved closer and took his face in her hands. For a long beat she looked at him, like she was lost in his eyes. Then she kissed him on his lips. Not the kiss of longing and desperation from earlier. This was a goodbye kiss.

There was no mistaking the difference.

She stepped back. "You matter to me, Landon. No matter what I've said or done." She brushed her thumb over his brow again. "Ever since you stuck up for me in fifth grade. There's never been anyone else."

She hadn't said she loved him, not in so many words. But she had told him she had never stopped caring. In a friendship sort of way. But still, it was more than he had expected for tonight. He nodded, and he felt a smile come over him.

Tears welled in her eyes. "I could do no wrong back

then. You defended me to everyone." She let her voice grow soft again. "Even myself."

"Someone needs to . . ." He hugged her. Like he might never see her again—which was always possible with Ashley Baxter. "I love you, Ash." He looked into her eyes once more. "I always will."

She only smiled. When he released her, she stepped back and crossed her arms. "I'm glad we had tonight. And I'll never forget what you did . . . for Cole." She paused and looked over her shoulder at the front door. "Which reminds me. I really need to go."

He nodded. "Okay." With all his strength he forced himself to back up toward his car. "You're a good mom, Ashley. You are." He winked at her. "See you around, Ash."

"See ya, Landon."

He turned to his Toyota and climbed behind the wheel. She stood there until he drove down her driveway and turned out of sight. The last thing he saw was her in his rearview mirror. Landon felt the sting of tears again, but he refused them. He had to take his own advice. No need grieving this goodbye or telling himself he'd never see Ashley Baxter again.

Tonight was a win. She was a happier person now than she'd been when he got to her house earlier. And despite the drama of the night, they had found their way back to each other. *You can say what you want about the future, Ashley.* He smiled to himself. *I choose to see the good ahead.*

One day Ashley would remember her faith in God and she'd fight to find her way back to her old self. When that happened Ashley wouldn't only be his girlfriend. She'd be his wife. He kept his eyes on the road ahead. God wasn't finished with Ashley Baxter. One day they would be together, and this season would be only a distant, painful memory.

Yes, Landon would believe that. Now and next year and as long as he lived.

22

The house was quiet again, Erin and Luke upstairs asleep in their rooms and Ashley and Cole back at their place. Elizabeth was cleaning up in the kitchen, John at her side.

"What a day." She looked at her husband, the only man she had ever loved. "This morning seems like a week ago."

"You thought something bad was going to happen." John raised one eyebrow. "I won't doubt your feelings again."

She laughed. It felt good to be on this side of everything that could've gone wrong. "In the end I didn't need to worry. God had us, all along."

"He always does." John closed the dishwasher and turned to her. "Let's make tea."

Elizabeth opened the wooden box on the counter and pulled out two tea bags. She put the water on to boil, and when it was ready, they each poured a cup and carried them to the living room. They sat in their favorite chairs, side by side. From this spot they had a view of their kids' framed portraits. All but one of them, anyway.

Elizabeth sank back in her chair. "If you'd asked me

five years ago, I never would've imagined life the way it is today. Kari married to Tim, Ashley and Landon broken up. Little Cole." She shook her head. "But I learned something today."

"What's that, my love?" John looked relaxed. He breathed in the steam from his tea, his eyes on her.

"God alone can write their stories." She stared at the photo of Ashley. "I apologized to her before she left. About inviting Landon. I never . . . never want to be pushy."

"Mmmm. I like that." He nodded, a grin forming at the corners of his lips. "Seems like something we've talked about before."

"We have." She held her cup in her hand and breathed in the rising steam. "But today was different. God really taught me something. Our family's story, our kids' stories . . . they're just beginning. I can't say things aren't working out just because of how they look today."

"Ashley and Landon, you mean?" John lowered his cup and looked at the same photograph on the wall in front of them. "How can she not see it?"

"She will." Elizabeth nodded. "I believe that, John. One day she will. And then she'll wish she'd never spent a day away from that boy."

"They're only twenty-one. Still so young." He sighed. "And God even forced us into a family meeting."

"I loved that." She reached for his hand. "What you said, John. It was perfect. Exactly what we needed to hear. Especially after everything that happened tonight."

They were quiet for another minute. Elizabeth ran her thumb along the side of his hand. The feel of his fingers intertwined with hers was as familiar as her own heartbeat. He was part of her. He always would be.

But she had a sense something was troubling him, even now. After the happy way the day had ended. She looked at him, his concern as he studied the portraits of their kids. His brow was slightly lowered, and shadows gathered around his eyes.

Elizabeth shifted so she could see him better. "Okay. What is it?"

"Hmm." John turned to her. He seemed to try to smile, but it never quite took hold. "I need to let it go." He sighed, and ran his other hand through his hair. "What happened with Cole today, I should've known what to do." His voice was quiet, more thoughtful than upset. Still, there was no denying his frustration. "I'm a doctor, Elizabeth. Do you know how that felt?"

Once or twice since Cole's choking ordeal, Elizabeth had wondered how her husband was handling it. How he must've wanted so badly to save their grandson. "You oversee the ER, John. A dozen doctors report to you." She leaned closer and looked straight at him. "When's the last time you gave a baby the Heimlich?"

He shook his head. "Never." Fear darkened his eyes. "Still . . . I'm sure I was trained on that in med school."

"More than twenty years ago?" She paused. "You're being too hard on yourself. It was a terrifying moment." The picture of Landon running in and taking over filled her mind again. "God provided. That's all that matters."

A sigh rattled his chest. "I guess we're both in the same boat." His concern lifted some. "You can't write their stories, and I can't fix them. That's why we need the Lord."

"Yes." Elizabeth settled back into her chair. After a while her eyes focused on the framed picture of their youngest son. "You think Luke will be less critical now? Treat Ashley with more respect?"

"I hope so." John thought for a minute. "Tonight could've ended so . . . differently. The guilt Luke would've lived with . . . the rest of his life."

"No." Elizabeth shook her head. She took a sharp breath. "I can't go there."

"Me, either." John seemed to let the possibility fade. "Did you hear what Brooke told Luke? In the kitchen?" John took a sip of his tea. He watched her, waiting for her response.

"I was with Cole. I missed it."

"Brooke told him that one of these days he'd have to get off his high horse." John looked at her again. "Because no one can stay perfect forever."

"Hmmm." Elizabeth drank her tea and nodded. "She's right."

"Honestly? I've been worried about that for a while with Luke." John set his cup down on the arm of the chair. "He's young. Somehow I think he has a few big mistakes ahead. Lessons only God can teach him."

"Let's pray not." Elizabeth never wanted to expect the worst with their kids. "Maybe he's learned his lesson." She paused. "I know God's still teaching me." For a while she didn't complete her thought. The way she had early that morning, she pictured the little baby boy in her arms. She and John hadn't been married, so her parents gave her no choice. But tonight she had even learned something about him. "Our firstborn . . . so often when I think about him, I feel . . . an urgency, I guess. Like I have to find him and help him, make sure he's okay."

A slow breath seemed to fill John's lungs. "That's me. Way too often." His smile barely lifted his lips. As if the burden of not knowing their oldest son was too great to carry.

"The situation with Cole made me realize something." Elizabeth leaned back, her eyes still on John. "God has the son we gave away. Just like He had Cole tonight. Wherever he is, whatever he's doing. I can't help him." A supernatural peace soothed her heart. "Not if he were a million miles away or right here under the same roof with us."

"God knows we want to meet him, find him." John clearly understood. "And like everything else, that's something we can trust Him with."

"Exactly." Elizabeth finished her tea.

Finally, John stood and helped her to her feet. "It's been a long day, my love."

"I needed this. Time to debrief." She walked with him

to the kitchen and they set their cups in the sink. The dishwasher was halfway through the wash cycle, the swishing sound a familiar part of their nighttime routine.

"It's past midnight." John faced her. "Which means it's tomorrow." He kissed her forehead. "We can put the good and bad of this day behind us."

"Yes." She pictured Kari, so beautiful in her wedding dress. "Tim and Kari are halfway to Seattle by now. If they didn't get delayed."

"I think they must've made it." John smiled. "We were between storms when their flight was scheduled."

Taking a red-eye hours after their wedding wasn't something Elizabeth would've wanted. Better to have their first time together unrushed, at a nice hotel near the airport. But the honeymoon plans had all belonged to Tim, the late flight and the cruise to Alaska. Every detail.

"Did Kari ever tell you she wanted to honeymoon in the Caribbean?" Elizabeth leaned against the counter. "I feel like that's all she used to say, how one day she wanted to visit the Bahamas or Aruba. Someplace sunny."

John hesitated. "Yes, actually. I remember her saying that." He looked long into Elizabeth's eyes. "Instead they're going on an Alaskan cruise."

For a few seconds, they were quiet again, letting those simple facts sink in. Elizabeth closed the distance between them and put her hands on his shoulders. "You think she made the right choice?"

"It's not the choice I expected." John's voice was raw

with honesty. "But it's the choice she made." He paused, searching her eyes. "And if I know our girl, she will make the most of her marriage to Tim. She's in it for life. I'm sure."

For life. Elizabeth smiled and nodded. "You're right. She'll work every day to make her marriage beautiful. And I'm sure . . . well, I hope he'll do the same."

John turned off the kitchen light and they headed upstairs to bed. Before Elizabeth fell asleep, she pictured the way Kari had looked, walking down the aisle toward Tim. Her eyes shining with love for her groom, her heart inclined toward him alone. And of course Tim, waiting for her, tears in his eyes. Those were reasons enough to believe Kari was making the right choice.

Definitely.

And something else, something she hadn't spent a lot of time thinking about today. The wedding had been too beautiful to dwell on the uncertainty from hours earlier. Still, here in the dark it was the events of the morning that made Elizabeth even more sure about Kari and Tim.

Not just because of how they had looked at each other or the intensity of love in their vows. But for one more obvious reason.

Ryan Taylor had come to see Kari on her wedding day. And Elizabeth's middle daughter had done something no one would've expected in a million years.

Kari had sent him away.

If her daughter could do that, then she could love Tim for the rest of her life.

Elizabeth closed her eyes and smiled. She was absolutely sure.

• • •

THE FLIGHT WAS taking forever, but Kari didn't mind. She leaned in close to Tim and rested her head on his shoulder. He'd been asleep since they took off around ten o'clock.

Kari had tried to drift off, but she couldn't. Her heart was too full. She was married to Professor Tim Jacobs, and her joy practically consumed her. Every few minutes she glanced down at her wedding band, the other half of the set Tim had chosen months ago.

They were traveling in the very back row of the plane, discount tickets Tim had found through a travel agent at the university. That didn't bother Kari, either. As long as Tim was beside her she could've ridden down in the cargo area with the bags.

She looked at her husband, and at the ring on his left finger. Already he was taking care of her, watching their budget. Making sure they didn't spend too much. He had explained the accommodations they would have on the one-week cruise.

"It's not a balcony room." He'd chuckled. "But at least there's a window." They had been boarding the plane. Until then he'd kept details of the trip a secret. So he could surprise her. "I figured we didn't need a balcony. We'll make better use of the room than that."

He had kissed her neck and grinned at her.

A chill ran down Kari's arms then and now. She was about to share a bed with Tim, share her body with him. This was the beginning of the rest of her life. There were other surprises. He had planned for the two of them to take excursions at every stop along the inner passage of the coast of Alaska.

A Jeep tour, a day hike, whale watching.

Tim had it all scheduled. Which was one more reason she loved him. Organization and details were his strong suit. With him, she would never have to worry if the light bill got paid or the mortgage was up to date. Things she could sometimes forget.

He would watch over her and care for her with his whole being.

Kari had the window seat and now she looked out at the night sky. Tim had been impressed that the back row had any view at all. "Usually all you see is an engine or a solid wall." He laughed, and leaned in to kiss her. "It's a good sign, baby. You and me, we'll always have a beautiful view. As long as we're together."

With the wedding behind them, and their long flight ahead, Kari had wondered if he might wait till they were settled in their seats to talk to her about Ryan. Why he had come by the house and what they had talked about.

But he never once brought it up.

Kari thought she understood why. Tim was more confident than that. So what if Kari had dated Ryan through high school and most of college? Ryan was the past, Tim was the future. Tim had no doubts about that. And clearly Tim trusted her.

Which only added to the wonderful way Kari felt about marrying him.

Once in a psychology class, Kari had learned about the behavior of guilt. The textbook had explained that people often tended to get upset about the very thing they were guilty of doing.

If a man was cheating in his marriage, he was typically all the more suspicious of his wife. Assuming the same behavior of her. If a girl hated being talked about behind her back, chances were she had a problem with gossip. That sort of thing.

The rule wasn't foolproof, of course. There were exceptions. Kari still remembered the teacher's final word on the subject. "Bottom line, if someone you know is extremely jealous, look a little closer at whether he's being faithful."

Kari had tucked the lesson away, and until today she hadn't remembered it. But the teaching seemed to apply here. Tim literally had expressed no struggle with Ryan coming to the house this morning. Sure, he told Ryan to leave. That made sense. But he never once questioned Kari. She smiled and turned to her sleeping groom again. According to the textbook that could only mean one thing.

Other than her father, Tim was the most faithful man she'd ever known.

She rested her head on his shoulder again and closed

her eyes. Sleep would be nice. But her thoughts kept coming back to the cruise. When the topic of a honeymoon came up one afternoon at her family's kitchen during the wedding planning, Kari had been quick with an idea. "The Bahamas!" She had practically squealed. "Please! I've always wanted to honeymoon in the Caribbean."

Tim made a face and shook his head. "I hate being hot." He smiled and tapped the tip of her nose. "You know that, honey bunch."

At first his response left an empty feeling in her heart. He could've at least taken a few minutes to think about what she wanted. Her expression must've given her away because he reached for her hand. "Hey . . . don't be sad."

"I'm not." She tilted her head. "It's just . . . you didn't actually think it through. Where I wanted to go."

His smile was kind, proof that he hadn't meant to upset her. "Look, baby. If it means that much to you, we'll go there for our five-year anniversary. We can save up till then and take the best Caribbean vacation any two people ever had."

"Sure." She nodded and tried to smile. "So what's your idea?"

He stretched his arms out to both sides. "An Alaskan cruise! On the biggest ship in the Pacific!"

It had taken Kari a few minutes to come around to the idea, but by the end of their conversation she had started to see why Tim was excited. This honeymoon wouldn't be on a sandy white beach.

But it would be an unforgettable adventure.

Sleep began to take over. An adventure. That's exactly what being married to Tim would be. The two of them celebrating each other's victories, sharing each other's struggles and sorrows. Raising a family someday.

One incredible adventure of love.

And nothing could be a better adventure for the two of them than the week ahead, sailing along the coast of Alaska on a cruise.

Kari smiled to herself. She could hardly wait.

23

In the quiet of the dark night, Ashley sat in the plush rocker and held Cole close. Midnight had come and gone, and still she couldn't lay him down in his crib. Not when she'd almost lost him earlier.

What would she be doing right now if Landon hadn't been there? Would they be at the hospital still? Home planning a funeral?

She shuddered. "Cole . . . I love you, baby." Her whisper was the same. Over and over again. "Mommy loves you."

Why hadn't she said those words more often? Before today? Ashley thought about the past year, and her months as a mother. Babies were a lot of work. Before Cole's birth, Ashley had made every decision with just one person in mind: herself.

Her parents had encouraged her to stay at their house for the first few months. "You'll need help after the baby is born," her mother had told her several times. "We're here, Ashley. Whatever we can do."

But that same stubbornness that had sent her running from Landon and flying off to Paris kicked in hard.

Especially later in her pregnancy. One afternoon in her third trimester, Luke came home from school and found Ashley in the kitchen making soup.

"Please tell me you're moving out before the baby comes." He brushed past her to the refrigerator and made himself a sandwich. "I won't get any sleep with a screaming kid around."

Comments like that weren't typical for Luke. He wasn't always so mean. Once in a while during her pregnancy he had even asked her how she was doing, whether she could feel her baby moving. But too often his snide comments stayed with her.

The way they had that day.

By then she'd received all of her settlement money from the accident. So the next week she contacted a real estate agent and in two days she had put a down payment on a small house near downtown Bloomington. It was in the heart of the city, and ten minutes from her parents' home. Not too far, but enough so that when she brought Cole home from the hospital after his birth she was truly on her own.

Her mother offered to stay with her for a week or two, but Ashley refused. "I have to do this by myself, Mom," Ashley had told her. "Getting pregnant was my mistake. I can't expect anyone else to carry me."

And so trial and error had taught her everything about being a mom. How often to change Cole's diaper, when to feed him, and what to do when he wouldn't stop crying. All of it was work, to Ashley. Like a checklist of daily duties. And if she could drop Cole off with her parents, she was happy to let someone else take care of him for a few hours.

Her attitude had stayed that way right up until today, when she almost lost him.

Now, looking back, she was sure of one very sad truth. She hadn't had enough moments like this. Times when she sat in the dark and stared at her miracle boy, memorizing the lines of his sweet soft cheeks and the feel of him in her arms. She held him a little closer and whispered again, "I love you, Cole. Mommy loves you."

Tonight he could've died. And she would never have had this second chance, never had the opportunity to really love her baby boy. Tears filled her eyes and spilled onto her face. "I'm sorry, baby. I love you." She caught her tears with the back of her hand. "I didn't act like it, but . . . I always have."

Things might not change right away. She had her art groups at night, people she painted with and dreamed with. Friends who understood her. But when she was here, bedtime with Cole would never be the same again.

She would slow down, take her time. Notice the little changes from one week to the next as Cole grew from a baby to a toddler. He was her very own son, and he was alive. By God's grace or some crazy amazing chance, he was still alive. Here in her arms.

Ashley studied him. What about her family, the Baxters? The people everyone else always wanted to be like? They each had their own lives now. Brooke and Peter busy working and raising little Maddie. Kari had Tim. Erin and Luke were still in school and too young to understand.

Since Cole's birth, she had never felt more alone. But after today she wondered if maybe that was her fault.

Ashley drew a long breath, and the sound made Cole stir in her arms. Poor little guy. His throat probably hurt from the plastic juice cap. Her dad had suggested she take him to his pediatrician on Monday to be checked. Just in case he'd injured his windpipe. Given the ordeal, Cole needed his sleep more than ever.

Ashley couldn't hold him all night.

With quiet movements, she stood and carried him to his crib. Gently she laid him down, and ran her hand a few times over his back. He wore his navy one-piece jammies, the ones with the white snaps. Ashley tucked his baby blue blanket around him and she crept out of his room.

Of all the people to rescue her baby today, how could Landon Blake have been the one? Ashley hadn't wanted him to come to the house at all. And now . . . now Cole was asleep in his bed because Landon showed up.

She tiptoed to the kitchen and the blue gift bag Landon had given her. The guy was thoughtful to the core. Even when she'd done nothing to deserve his kindness. Staring at the bag, she remembered something.

The card.

She pulled it from the bag and stared at it, at her

name across the front of the envelope. Whatever the card held, Ashley knew she'd keep this one just like the others. Forever.

Ashley pulled the card from inside and opened it, careful not to bend it. One day when Cole was older, she might share cards like this with him. She would tell Cole about Landon, the man who had loved her for so long.

The one who had saved his life.

She found the first line and started to read. After spending the last several hours with Landon, it was easy to hear his voice between the lines.

Dear Ashley,

I meant to send you this a year ago. But this is better than waiting another day. I remember when my mother called and told me you had your baby. She and your mom keep in touch, of course. At first I thought I'd give you a call, congratulate you over the phone. So you could hear my voice and know how happy I am for you.

But I figured you wouldn't take my call. I mean, you haven't let me get through to you for a few years now. Sure, we danced at the wedding. But for all I know you won't let me talk to you tonight. So I decided to write.

Ashley, it's overdue, but congratulations on the birth of little Cole! Congrats on having him in your life. After today, after seeing more of him, I can say he is the most beautiful baby in the world. He looks just like you, Ash. Your face, your blue eyes. I hope I have the chance to watch him grow up because I know he'll be an amazing boy.

Because you're an amazing mom.

I guess I just wanted to say that I know this isn't how you saw your life going. Whatever happened in Paris, you didn't plan to get pregnant. Obviously.

But if you'll let Him, God can make good out of every situation. I promise, Ashley. Every child, every life, is a miracle from Him. As if God is saying, "Here, Ashley. I'm trusting you with this tiny child."

Ashley stopped there and closed her eyes. Maybe God shouldn't have trusted her with Cole. Her carelessness had almost cost her baby his life. She squeezed her eyes shut. *Stop,* she told herself. *Don't talk to yourself like that.*

Landon was right. She needed to believe she was a good mother if she was going to take her job more seriously. Her negative talk had never helped anyone, least of all herself.

She blinked her eyes open and finished the letter.

Now that Cole is nearly one, you probably see how fast time flies. His high school gradua tion will be here before you know it. So raise him to the light. Make God proud that He picked you for baby Cole.

I haven't given up on us, just so you know. You having Cole doesn't change the way I feel, the way I believe that somehow, someday we'll find our way back together. Tonight, dancing with you in my arms, made me remember just how much you matter to me. How deeply I feel for you. If things go right, I might share all this in person tonight. We'll see.

Either way, give me a chance, Ashley. Please, give me a chance.

This past year I wish I had been there to help you, to hold Cole when you needed sleep or feed him when you were tired at the end of the day. But I guess that part wasn't meant to be.

Until I see you again, I'll pray for you. And for Cole. And maybe we can spend a few hours together before I head back to Baylor for my senior year.

Love you still. Love you always,
Landon

Her hands trembled as she stared at the card. Then, as if his words quenched a thirst deep inside her, she read the letter again. Then she held it to her chest.

Landon really did love her. Would he really run if he knew the truth about Paris?

She had decided not to tell him, once the storm passed. The moment seemed unnecessary since her mind was made up. She couldn't shut him out of her life entirely. Sitting in the basement with her family she'd realized she would be forever indebted to Landon for saving Cole's life. They would always be friends, so there was no need to ruin his memory of who she once was, no reason to give him a reason to be disgusted with her.

Ashley returned the card to the envelope and took it to her room. There, she placed it in her drawer. Landon deserved the girl she used to be before the accident. The one he had saved himself for. Ashley's wild living and rebellion against God and her family had changed everything.

But she was glad she had spared him the sordid details.

The morning hours were coming, and Ashley needed sleep as badly as her baby did. She changed into sweats and a nightshirt and tugged a pair of socks over her feet. A few minutes to brush her teeth and wash her face and Ashley was in bed.

Only she was still wide awake.

She kept thinking about Landon's last words to her before he left tonight.

Maybe you take the next year and ask God if He's real. Ask Him if He has good plans for you, Ashley. The way I believe He does.

Was it possible? That God was real and somewhere down the road He had good plans for her? So she wouldn't be the family mess-up? The one who'd gone astray?

What if she took Landon's advice and actually asked God if He was real?

Landon had said something else, another few lines that played in her mind again. *Christians aren't perfect. They're just broken people who know they need a Savior. Because we're such a mess.*

Growing up she had never thought of Christianity like that. She had always done her best to be good. Church on Sunday morning, time during the week to help her family. And if she told a lie or went against her parents in any way, it wouldn't be long before she'd apologize.

Make things right.

So she'd be perfect again.

That's what she thought it meant to have faith in God. Just enough perfection so a person could be better than everyone else. Not quite arrogant, but definitely critical. Judgmental. Like Luke had been—until after the choking incident, anyway.

Again, she considered the idea. Could it be that Christians really were just broken, everyday people? And the only thing that set them apart was their faith in Christ to forgive them? To accept His grace and His offer of heaven?

The idea seemed unlikely, but it stayed with her.

She remembered the night, every minute with Landon. His face filled her mind and heart. His words comforted her and his kiss stayed with her. The familiar passion between them stirred her again. No matter how hard she tried to stop herself, she would always love Landon Blake.

His final words on the subject came to her one more time. *All I'm saying is ask. Ask God to show you if His grace is enough. If there's still something very good that can come from all this. Other than Cole. Because every baby is a miracle . . .*

Her thoughts swirled and collided until she couldn't take them anymore. All she could picture was her baby boy down the hall, asleep in his crib. Alive . . . still alive.

And suddenly she threw the sheets back and padded across her bedroom floor and into the hall. In no time she was at Cole's door, and she opened it without making a sound. As she reached his crib, he stirred and looked up at her.

"Mama." He started to cry . . . and she did, too.

What was this? He had called her "Mama"! For the very first time! She picked him up and grabbed his blanket and pacifier. Then she carried him back to the chair and sat with him, rocking him. "Mama's here, Cole. I'm right here."

He had started babbling lately, but he had never said her name. She'd never taught him to say it. But here . . . in the wee hours of the morning with a voice still raspy from earlier, Cole had called her by name.

"Mama loves you, baby." She whispered to him over and over until he fell asleep again. Then she closed her eyes and leaned back in the chair. Because this was her baby, her precious son.

And she would hold him as long as she wanted.

• • •

FOR THE PAST week, Ashley had kept her word. She'd gone out with her art friends just a couple times, and she only took Cole to her parents' house when it was absolutely necessary. And always . . . always she was the one to put him to bed—whether at her house or her parents'.

Other times, grocery shopping or a trip to the bank, Ashley brought Cole with her. She couldn't get enough of him. He was trying to talk more, saying her name constantly. As if even he understood that something had changed.

Because it had. Ashley truly cared more deeply than before.

That Friday morning, Ashley had thought about asking her mom to watch Cole. She had something she wanted to do, somewhere she needed to visit. And at first she didn't think Cole should go.

But when Friday dawned, Ashley made up her mind. Cole would come. Maybe it was better that he did. She dressed him in a lightweight gray jumper and darling canvas shoes, and the two of them set out.

On the way, she stopped at the grocery store and bought a bouquet of purple carnations. Always purple carnations. The color of Jefferson Bennett's wrestling jersey at Bloomington High.

The cemetery wasn't far from the edge of town, and Ashley knew the way. Before the accident, she'd had no reason to go there. Since then, though, she had come occasionally. More during the first year—four or five times. Now it had been six months since she'd stopped by.

She parked near his tombstone, unbuckled Cole from his car seat and held him on her hip with one arm. With the other, she grabbed the flowers from the front passenger seat. *Okay, God.* She looked up at the sunny sky overhead. *I'm doing this. I'm taking Landon's advice. I hope you can hear me.*

"Mama." Cole put his hand on her face and pulled at her hair.

"Yes, baby. Mama's here." She kissed his cheek and snuggled him close. Then she walked along the cement path until she spotted Jefferson's grave marker.

Deep breath, she told herself. No matter how many times she came here, the visit was never easy. But she had to do this today. She was going to ask God to show Himself to her—not in random miracles or wondrous events, but in the deep places of her soul.

She stopped directly in front of his tall stone and read the words again. The way she did every time she was here.

Jefferson Bennett, forever 16.
Loving son, best brother, loyal friend.
Champion wrestler at Bloomington High.
Until we see you again, baby. We miss you and
love you always.

Ashley blinked back her tears, but she couldn't stop them. She pictured him, happy to take a ride with her, glad to spend a few minutes with Luke's older sister. The kid was pale-skinned with big brown eyes. Bushy dark hair that never quite laid flat on his head.

No one ever noticed that about Jefferson, though. They noticed his smile, his laugh. He would be nineteen now, heading into his sophomore year at college. If only he hadn't jerked the wheel.

But he had. The police reports made that clear. And so Jefferson died and she got to live. There was nothing she could do about that. She laid the flowers alongside Jefferson's tombstone. Then she ran her hand over her baby's back.

She would never understand, why some people lived and some died. Jefferson was a Christian. His mom and dad loved God and prayed for their children. Yet Jefferson was here, in the ground. Two tears made their way down her face and she sniffed.

"I'm putting myself at the crossroads here, God." She whispered the words, her eyes turned upward. "You took Jefferson, and you left me behind."

Cole was quiet, as if he were listening. He rested his head on her shoulder.

"Landon gave me a challenge." She dabbed at her tears. *Stay strong, Ashley. Come on.* "I love him, God. I respect Landon Blake. So . . . here I am."

A whippoorwill sounded in a nearby tree. Ashley shifted her gaze. A summer breeze stirred the branches, and Ashley remembered something her father had taught them. "Trees are like people," he said. "God breathes the wind and the trees move and sway in response. Just like we're supposed to do."

Despite her failed faith, Ashley had always liked that picture. Wind in the trees, branches raised to heaven, responding to God.

She took another jagged breath. "So here's my question, God." Her hesitation didn't last long. "Are You real? Do You see me?" Jefferson's tombstone caught her eye again. "Did You save me for a reason?"

Cole stirred, and Ashley soothed him again. "Almost done, baby. Hold on."

Once more she lifted her eyes to the distant sky. "Landon says You did. You let me live because You have plans for my life." The words were hard to say, hard to voice over her doubts. "Good plans. So I'm asking You . . . if You're real, if You have plans for me . . . then please, God . . . show me."

With that she reached out and touched the grave marker one final time. "Take care of Jefferson, God. You must have some very important reason why You need him more than his mama does."

Then she stood, stared up at the sky again and walked back to the car. Once Cole was buckled in and Ashley was behind the wheel, she noticed something she hadn't felt in a long time. Something she could only describe one way.

Freedom.

As if by taking Landon's advice, she had melted some of the ice from her soul. She wouldn't come here every time she talked to God. And she couldn't promise she would bring the question to Him each morning. But she would make it a point to ask as often as she could for the next year.

Even if doing so didn't quite make sense.

She pictured Landon, dancing with her, holding her hand. Kissing her. Ashley still loved him, still ached for him. It had taken all her strength not to call him this past week.

He would go back to school and probably move on, and she might never see him again, never kiss him again. Still, she could at least do this one thing. Not because she believed God would answer her or that He would make this year different. But because—no matter what happened next—the request came from a boy she would love as long as she lived.

Landon Blake.

ACKNOWLEDGMENTS

As always, a book like *The Baxters* doesn't happen without a team of passionate, determined people working behind the scenes. On that note, I can't leave this story and the deeply emotional journey it has been without thanking the people who made it possible.

First, a special thanks to my amazing Simon & Schuster publishing team, including my talented editor, Trish Todd. You have a wealth of experience, Trish, and an extraordinary eye for story and detail. I am so very blessed to be working with you and my publishing team, including the wonderful Libby McGuire, Suzanne Donahue, Lisa Sciambra, Isabel DaSilva, Paula Amendolara, Karlyn Hixson, Sean Delone, and Dana Trocker, along with so many others on the Atria team!

Also, thanks to Rose Garden Creative, my design team—Kyle and Kelsey Kupecky—whose unmatched talent in the industry is recognized from Los Angeles to New York. Very simply you are the best in the business! My website, social media, video trailers and newsletter—along with so many other aspects of my touring, signature events, and writing—are top of the book business

311

because of you. Thank you for working your own dreams around mine. I love you and I thank God for you every single day.

A huge thanks to my sisters, Tricia and Susan, along with my mom, who give their whole hearts to helping me love my readers. Tricia, as my executive assistant for fifteen years, and Susan for many, many seasons as the president of my Facebook Online Book Club and Team KK. And Mom, thank you for being Queen of the Readers. Anyone who has ever sent me an email and received a response from you is blessed indeed. All three of you are making a tremendous impact in changing this world for the better. I love you and I thank God for each of you!

Thanks also to Tyler for joining me to write screenplays and books like *Best Family Ever, Finding Home, Never Grow Up,* and *Adventure Awaits,* from the Baxter Family Children Book series. You are a gifted writer, Ty. I can't wait to see more of your work on the shelves and on the big screen. One day soon! Love you so much!

In addition, thank you to EJ for singlehandedly running the You Were Seen movement. Your passion for seeing people have a way to love others is breathtaking! Love you always!

Thanks, too, to my son, Austin, for joining my staff as my event director. I couldn't have finished this book without all the work you took on. You are kind and talented, and God has so much ahead for you. I treasure this time, and I thank God for this beautiful season. Love you so!

Thank you to my office assistant Aurora Galvin. You create space for me to write, and my storytelling wouldn't be possible without you.

There is a final stage in writing a book. The galley pages come to me, and I send them to a team of several of my most dedicated reader friends and family. My nieces Shannon Fairley, Melissa Viernes and Kristen Springer. Also Hope Burke, Donna Keene, Renette Steele, Zac Weikal, and Sheila Holman. You are my volunteer test team! It always amazes me the things you catch at the final hour. Thank you for loving my work, and thanks for your availability to read my novels first and fast.

Also, my books only happen with the help of my family, especially my amazing husband, Donald. Honey, thank you for your spiritual wisdom and leadership in our home, and thanks for talking through books like this one from the outline to the editing. The countless ways you help me when I'm on deadline make all the difference. I love you!

And finally, thanks to a man who has believed in my career for two decades, my amazing agent, Rick Christian. From the beginning, Rick, you've told me to dream big, set my sights high. Movies, TV series, worldwide reach. All for God and through Him. You imagined it, believed it, and prayed for it alongside me and my family. You saw it. You still do! While I write, you work behind the scenes on film projects, the Baxter family TV series, and details regarding every book I've ever written. You are brilliant and driven, compassionate and dedicated. I used to dream of having you as my agent. Now Tyler and I are the only authors who do. God is amazing. Thank you, Rick, and thank you for praying for me and my family. That most of all.

Finally, my greatest thanks to God Almighty, who is First and Last and all things in between. I write for You, through You and because of You. Thank You with my whole being.

Dear Reader Friend,

This truly is the book that's been missing from the Baxter family.

With *The Baxters*, we have a new Book One, a starting place for you—if you're finding the Baxters for the first time. From here you can move on to the book *Redemption*, and read straight through the saga while you watch the TV series - coming soon. The complete list of books is at the front of this novel and you can find a printable list of all my titles on my website: KarenKingsbury.com.

Or you can read my latest novels and get a feel for where the Baxters are today.

I cried when I wrote this book and through every stage of editing. It's deep. It holds pieces of my soul. A part of the Baxters' story that had only lived in my heart until now. And now with this book it can live in yours, as well.

As you close the cover on *The Baxters*, do me a favor. Think about who you can share it with. A friend or a sister. Your mother or coworker. The librarian at your child's school. Someone struggling to make sense of a loss? Or just that person who loves to read.

A book dies if it's left on the shelf. So please share it.

At my website, you can sign up for my free weekly newsletter. These contain my encouragement and devotions, event updates and insights. This is where you will first learn of details on *The Baxters* TV Series and many other exciting television and film announcements. All contest winners are also announced on my newsletters, so sign up today! You can also stay encouraged with me on Facebook, Instagram, and Twitter.

If you are seeking a faith like that of the Baxter family, find a Bible-believing church and get connected. God sees you, what you're going through. There is a reason you came across this book. Remember, the Baxter family isn't just my family. It's yours. And with them at the middle of our reading lives, we are all connected. Until next time . . . I'm praying for you.

Thanks for being part of the family.

Love you all!

THE

BAXTERS

DISCUSSION QUESTIONS

1. Historically, how trustworthy are your feelings about a certain day or event? Give an example.

2. Have you ever had a bad feeling about a certain day? What ended up happening? How did you handle this?

3. Do you think God sometimes sends warnings to us? Talk about a time when that happened for you.

4. What was troubling Elizabeth Baxter at the beginning of the story? Who do you talk over your troubles with?

5. Did you come from a big family? Was everyone close? Talk about it.

6. Do you have a big family now? Share about it or share about a big family you're familiar with.

7. What are some of the amazing advantages of having a large family? What are some of the struggles?

8. Elizabeth recalls a time when they would have family meetings, and afterward everything would always be okay. Did you grow up with family meetings? How did they work and were they effective?

9. If this is your first time reading about the Baxter family, do you think Kari is doing the right thing by marrying Tim?

10. Talk about a couple you were concerned about from before their wedding day. How did things work out for them?

11. If you've read about the Baxter family before, what surprised you about Kari and Tim's wedding day?

12. Tragedy marred Ashley Baxter's view of God. Has tragedy ever changed your faith or the faith of someone you know? Explain.

13. What caused Ashley to keep pushing Landon Blake away? Has shame ever caused you to walk away from a good thing? Talk about that.

14. Landon Blake is determined to see the good in Ashley. Who in your life is determined to see the good in you?

15. Jefferson Bennett lost his life helping Ashley save hers. Talk about a situation like this in your life or

the life of someone you know. Read John 15:13 from the Bible. What does it mean that the greatest love is to lay down your life for a friend? Who is an example of this?

16. How important is it to have someone cheering us on? Talk about an example of this in your life or the life of someone you know.

17. Luke is young, but seriously critical and judgmental. Was there a time when you acted this way? Was there a time someone you know acted this way? How did that turn out? How did it make you feel?

18. The averted crisis with baby Cole and the juice cap helped Ashley realize several things about her life. Talk about that moment. How do you relate to it?

19. John and Elizabeth were determined to pray for each of their children, believing that their stories were not fully written. There was more to come. What are you praying is yet to come in your story?

20. Talk about someone you are praying for, and how you've seen God work in his or her life.

ONE CHANCE FOUNDATION

The Kingsbury family is passionate about seeing orphans all over the world brought home to their forever families. As a result, Karen created a charitable group called the One Chance Foundation.

This foundation was inspired by the memory of her father, Ted C. Kingsbury. Ted always said, "Life is not a dress rehearsal. We have one chance to love, one chance to truly live!"

Karen often tells her reader friends, "You have one chance to write the story of your life!"™ Now, with Karen's One Chance Foundation, readers can join her in the belief that all of us have one chance to make a difference in the lives of orphans.

In the Bible, James 1:27 says people with pure and faultless religion look after orphans. The One Chance Foundation was created with that truth in mind.

If you are interested in giving to Karen's One Chance Foundation and having your dedication printed in one of Karen's upcoming novels, visit KarenKingsbury.com.

The following are dedications from Karen's reader friends who have contributed to the One Chance Foundation for this book:

- To My Sis, You were & still are like my 2nd Mom. I love you with all my heart. Thank you for all you do for me. Love, Lil' Sissy

- In memory of my Uncle Ronny Allen who served during Vietnam and my Papa John Cloud who served during WWII.

- For my two blessings, Caleb and AnniJo. Love you!

- Happy Birthday Jael <3 Mom

- To Denise B. Edmond

- Happy 29th Anniversary Niccole. My love for you grows stronger with each passing year. Love, Brett

- Landon, Ethan, and Micah, you boys are the sunshine in my day. Remember to have courage and be kind. All my love my sweet boys, Mama

- Happy Birthday Missy! Love Always and Forever, Daddy and Super-Step Mommy!

- Kylie + Caroline - God has a precious purpose just for you. Keep Him close and be still. Love, Mama

- Maisy Todd, you are our precious treasure. Congrats grad! We love you today and always, Mom & Dad

- God bless the families who open their hearts!

- Luv you always Nana, Col

- Emma Nelson Bedford IN-waiting with open arms to feel your love-Gram DD My son Cody-love & miss you!

- For answered prayer. Diane Ferreter Weimer

- Love you Don Thompson- Dee

- Arlene Harper, Mom, our loving, faithful prayer warrior. Thank you! Love all your kids and grandkids

- In loving memory of Pam George. July 13, 1963-November 10, 2020. I LOVE YOU Sis and MISS YOU every day.

- Happy Sweet 16 Birthday Katherine! Praying you have your own Bailey Flanigan love story! <3 M&D

- In loving memory of Judi Nicholl, an amazing wife, mother, grandmother, daughter, sister, teacher, and faithful servant of our Lord. Her life made a difference, and she will be carried in the hearts of many. We love you!

- My Family Forever ❤ LYMTTCT ❤ Peters-Alexander-Massie-Mendez-Fisher-Perez. Grace Peters Alexander

- Gram, I treasure our relationship! Thank you for the impact you've had on my life. Much love, Cindy

- Our sweet mom, Janet, is a big blessing to our family. We love you! Hannah, Maggie, Andrew, & Thomas

- For Mimi! - Love Aliyah

- To Marcy & Jessica at Rock Solid Teen Center: You two are awesome; so caring and supportive! Thanks, Dave & Jan K-M

- JMW 08/02- Love, me

- To Jennifer Schmid, the most courageous and strong person I know. You're my inspiration. Love, Jeff

- In memory of my precious mother, who left us ten years ago to live with Dad and Jesus. A precious soul. Love, JoAnne Burruss

- For Baylee - We love you! -John & Family

- Betty and June, my forever friends! Love, Karen

- Gina & Staci- The JOY & SPARKLE you bring! Mom

- For Ivey M. Welch, the one who taught me that "the greatest of these is love". I love you mom! -Karen Welch

- Elizabeth & Abigail Abraham, you can do all things through Christ who strengthens you. Love you with all our hearts, Mom and Dad.

- My "Nitro Pam," forever blessed by you! Love you – Sharon

- For Grandma Margaret, Jeremiah 29:11, I love you - Your pretty girl, Audrey

- To the best family ever! In memory of Uncle Danny, Mema, Grandy, and Grandpa. I love you all! ~Katie Beavers

- Honey & Tee, I'm so thankful for our own Baxter family. I love you & thank God for you! Love, Kellie

- To the One Chance Foundation! Love, Kristen Yeatts

- Lori, love seeing your faith grow! - Stotzer family

- Janice Chanaberry my sister my best friend I SURE DO LOVE YOU! You are God's gift to me! Love Linda

- Heather & Paul, your family is now complete! Adoption date 5/23/19. Lots of love! Sandra & Lionel

- Happy Mother's Day! Love you so much! Xoxo -Lois

- Mary Jo, thank you for being the best mom/mawmaw and for loving us so well! We love you and thank you for all you have done for us! Love, Mardee, Ben, Jaxon and Kaia.

- Anna H. You are the best thing that ever happened to me, I couldn't imagine my life without you. Love Mom

- To my dad and his love of books. Love, Marnie

- Thanks to my sister Lila & her husband Jim for always being there for me. During divorce, death, snowstorms, & joyous times you have always been there. You have been rocks my family has always been able to depend on. I praise God for you & pray you are richly blessed forever. Mary Lou

- Marsha Ross, a special Christian lady Love, Mary

- To my Momma who has always been my best friend and points me towards Jesus daily. I love you! Meggie

- Nicki you were taken from us to soon but we are at peace that you are with our Jesus. Not a day goes by that without me thinking & missing you.

- In honor and memory of my mother, Jan Richardson, who loved reading about the Baxter family with me. Love, Meredith

- To my husband, Arturo...I am forever grateful, we have truly been blessed by God's mercy & grace for our Time To Dance ♥ Happy 30th Anniversary! 6/10/2019 ~ All my love, Michelle

- Mom, Thanks for always being our Rock. We love you! Love, Dad, Misty, Ashley, Kayleigh and the Grands!

- To God be the Glory Amen.

- In loving memory of my mother, Linda Piper who gave me wings & taught me to fly! Love Your Daughter, Nan

- Love you mucho Mama Renee! -Nancy

- Dedicated to Lyn and Bob Briscoe who adopted 3 kids, and helps parents with the adoption process.

- For Jess & Alex

- My beautiful daughters and best friends, Stacie & Katie! I love you!! Smile and be happy! Mom

- Lisa, you're inspiring by not giving up! Love Pam

- Family is everything: Jeff, Dusty, Stacie, Shannon, Nicole, Paul, Sarah, Jim, Sami, Spencer, Morgan, Kewen, Joslin, Maxine, Luke, Leo, and Sam. Love you, Grammie Pammie

- To Grandma Donna: Thank you for all of the fun memories of road tripping to Florida and Nashville! Love, Rachel

- To my Mom (Penny): Thank you for your constant love and for always pointing us towards Jesus! Love, Rachel

- Love from, The Rhonda Rodgers Family

- Vanessa Todd, Thank you for being my wife and my best friend!! Love Rodney

- To my special sister Sue! Love, Sandi Nagel

- Elaine R., You are a blessing to so many! Love, Sandra

- Missy- I love you to infinity and beyond! Scott

- Chris Graham

- Brett, I miss you. Mom

- Celebrating the blessing of children being united with their forever families! With joy - Kurt & Sheila Holman

- To my husband, Eric McClanahan, who continually shows me love that I never thought possible! XOXO

- To Dawna Owenby, My Love! Forever yours, Steve Owenby

- I'm so proud of you Megan Marie, and I love that we read books together! Love, Aunt Suz

- Love To My Family KIERS with John-A&A-M&J-M&A+Grandkids - Sylvia

- In loving memory of Janet Elaine Clinkenbeard. I love & miss you. Your daughter & best friend, Tammy

- Mom, Catherine Taylor, thank you for being my prayer warrior partner. I love you so much, Tori Ann

- With loving memories of our parents Thomasena & Walter. Together a lifetime of love with God first. Mom read every KK story as though she knew each Baxter personally and then passed each book on to us to enjoy. "Love is the only thing that we can carry with us when we go, and it makes the end so easy." Until we are reunited with our Lord in eternity. Always in our hearts! Patricia, Sarah, Barbara

YOU WERE SEEN
MOVEMENT

His name was Henry, and I will remember him as long as I live. Henry was our waiter at a fancy restaurant when I was on tour for one of my books. Toward the end of the meal something unusual happened. I started to cry. Slow tears, just trickling down my cheeks. My husband was with me and he looked concerned. "Karen, what's wrong?"

Our waiter," I said. "He needs to know God loves him. But there's no time. We have to get to our event, and he has six other tables to serve."

Henry was an incredibly attentive server. He smiled and got our order right and he worked hard to do it. Everywhere he went on the restaurant floor, he practically sprinted to get his job done. But when he was just off the floor, when he thought no one was looking, Henry's smile faded. He looked discouraged and hopeless. Beaten up.

That very day I began dreaming about the "You Were

331

Seen" movement. Many of you are aware of this organization, but I'll summarize it. Very simply, you get a pack of You Were Seen cards and you hand them out. Where acceptable, tip—generously. From my office in the past few months more than 250,000 You Were Seen cards have gone out. We partner with the Billy Graham Evangelistic Association's plan for salvation and other help links.

And so it is really happening! People like you are truly seeing those in their path each day. You are finding purpose by living your life on mission and not overlooking the delivery person and cashier, the banker and business contact, the server and barista, the police officer and teacher, the doctor and nurse. You are letting strangers see God's love in action. Why?

Because Christians should love better than anyone. We should be more generous. Kinder. More affirming. More patient. The Bible tells us to love God and love others. And to tell others the good news of the gospel— that we have a Father who is for us, not against us. He loves us so much that He made a way for us to get to heaven.

Hand out a pack of You Were Seen cards in the coming weeks and watch how every card given makes you feel a little better. Go to www.YouWereSeen.com to get your cards and start showing gratitude and generosity to everyone you meet.

Always when you leave a You Were Seen card, you will let a stranger know that their hard work was seen in that moment. They were noticed! What better way to spread love? The You Were Seen card will then direct people to the website—www.YouWereSeen.com. At the website, people will be encouraged and reminded that God sees them every day. Always. He knows what they are going through. Every day should be marked by a miraculous encounter.

YouWereSeen.com